T0385144

The MARGARET CODE

The MARGARET CODE

RICHARD HOOTON

SPHERE

First published in Great Britain in 2025 by Sphere

1 3 5 7 9 10 8 6 4 2

Copyright © 2025 by Richard Hooton

The moral right of the author has been asserted.

All characters and events in this publication, other than those clearly in the public domain, are fictitious and any resemblance to real persons, living or dead, is purely coincidental.

All rights reserved.
No part of this publication may be reproduced, stored in a retrieval system, or transmitted, in any form, or by any means, without the prior permission in writing of the publisher, nor be otherwise circulated in any form of binding or cover other than that in which it is published and without a similar condition including this condition being imposed on the subsequent purchaser.

A CIP catalogue record for this book is available from the British Library.

Hardback ISBN 978-1-4087-3104-8
Trade paperback ISBN 978-1-4087-3103-1

Typeset in Sabon by M Rules
Printed and bound in Great Britain by Clays Ltd

Papers used by Sphere are from well-managed forests and other responsible sources.

Sphere
An imprint of
Little, Brown Book Group
Carmelite House
50 Victoria Embankment
London EC4Y 0DZ

The authorised representative
in the EEA is
Hachette Ireland
8 Castlecourt Centre
Dublin 15, D15 XTP3, Ireland
(email: info@hbgi.ie)

An Hachette UK Company
www.hachette.co.uk

www.littlebrown.co.uk

To Nana, Dad and Uncle Barry, with love.

When I was younger I could remember anything,
whether it happened or not; but I am getting old,
and soon I shall remember only the latter.

– Mark Twain

PROLOGUE

Our transistor radio, perched on the kitchen counter, fills the silence. Andy Williams's golden timbre: 'Moon River'.

You enter the room, Albert. Take my hand as if it's a gift.

'May I have the pleasure, Margaret?'

Merriment sparkles in your deep voice. You pull me into an embrace. The woody, citrus fragrance of Floris No. 89.

This could be our first dance: hesitant, a stranger's body close, uncertain where to place feet and hands.

It's a struggle to move creaking joints and aching muscles. Your hands support me, somehow firm and gentle. Steadfast. We find our rhythm, movements mirroring, we're one with the tune. The cold linoleum becomes Blackpool Tower Ballroom's warm, sprung floorboards, and slowly the decades fall away.

One-two-three. Rise and fall.

My summer dress sways, our steps light and loose. You whisper three wonderful words in my ear that I haven't heard for so long.

The radio crackles occasionally. No trouble, the melody's within.

Our shadows stretch across the floor, and suddenly I am

uneasy. This could be our last dance: holding on for dear life. I can't bear for the song to end. I close my eyes, willing us to stay in this moment forever. But the night is already fading, and you're falling from my grip.

CHAPTER 1

A beautiful blue light dances effortlessly across the ceiling. It illuminates our bedroom, helping my eyes adjust to the dark.

Curious noises intrude on night's stillness: car doors shutting, hurried footsteps, urgent voices. The golden bells of our alarm clock, which sits alone on the bedside table, glow eerily. I struggle to make out the tiny hands. It's one o'clock, I think.

I look across to where you lie, Albert, always on my left. That side of the bed is empty. I sit up. You've always favoured sleeping nearest the door.

'So I can leap up to protect you if anyone bursts into the room,' you sometimes say, your bony fists raised in the mock pose of a boxer.

'Would be just my blooming luck if they snuck in through the window,' I'll shoot back.

We both know full well that you sleep nearest the door so as not to disturb me in the night when you go to the loo. Up and down like a fiddler's elbow.

The blue light whirls across our cream ceiling. My head is a little muzzy. I lie back down and close my eyes, waiting for sleep to wash over me. Tyres grumble over gravel. A squeak of brakes. More car doors clanging.

My mind is alert to the sounds. Once the synapses are firing it can be difficult to switch off.

Snippets of conversation drift into earshot like clues to a crossword puzzle: 'secured the scene', 'officers stationed', 'means of entry'.

It's no use. I have to investigate.

Lifting the duvet, I slowly swivel my legs until they're out of the bed's warmth. Lowering them to the ground, I ease myself upright. Cold air nips my ankles. I put on my non-slip slippers, then switch on the light. The click matches the sound of my hip as I turn. I wrap my flannel dressing gown around myself, pulling the cord tight and fastening it into a bow. Opening the curtains, I peer out.

Several police cars are parked at odd angles across the street as if discarded by a tornado. Their blue lights spin towards me. At first, I think the uniformed officers are stationed outside Jean Brampton's house, opposite. Then, with a sharp intake of breath, I realise it's the one next door, it's Barbara's house.

Oh, what on Earth has happened? I've no choice but to get out there to find out. I can't sit around waiting for you to finish in the bathroom. You'll be in there forever.

The floorboards from bedroom to staircase creak louder than my joints. At what point did my body become my enemy? Niggles that once disappeared became aches, aches became pains. My body seems to have forgotten how to repair itself. Unlike that Doctor Who you love to watch on a Saturday night, it's lost the ability to regenerate. Our real doctor's still debating whether I need a hip replacement – 'I'm concerned about an operation at your age, Margaret' – so I have to put up with it and use that blasted stick when it gets too sore. Still, mustn't grumble.

The bathroom door is shut, a sliver of light spilling from beneath. The trickle of a running tap. Nothing wrong with my hearing, as you well know.

'I'm going outside to see what all the fuss is about.'

No answer. Deaf as a doorpost without your hearing aid in.

'Deaf from all your nagging,' you often say. With a smile. Always with a smile.

Something else niggles at my smoggy brain. Never mind. I grip the staircase's wooden rail and focus on the task in hand. Oh, to be able to slide down the banister with the glee of a child! I resist the urge. I'd only end up a crumpled heap in the hallway for you to discover in the morning.

I descend one step at a time. Everyone will have gone by the time I get out there.

Finally reaching the bottom of the stairs, I unlock the front door and haul it open to be greeted by a blast of icy air. Goosebumps crowd my skin. I grit my remaining teeth and venture outside. The night air is stodgy with petrol fumes. So many police officers. Must be serious. Though I'm always reading in the paper about them rushing off to some petty incident while not attending when something disastrous happens.

One officer is standing outside Barbara's gate, staring straight ahead. Behind him, blue and white tape bearing the words POLICE LINE DO NOT CROSS twists in the wind. Another officer is standing with his back to me, next to a panda car at the foot of our drive. I shuffle towards him, the concrete chill permeating my slippers. I've not been out this late in years. Not since we went ballroom dancing, decades ago when we laughed and twirled into the night. I reach our gate. How different the street looks at this hour without daytime's revealing light, the houses and gardens shrouded in darkness and mystery. The stars are pinpricks in the blackness; their radiance still with us, despite some of them burning out long ago.

I reach the policeman. Tap him on the shoulder.

'What's going on?'

He jolts around, then regains his composure. 'Sorry, madam. Didn't see you there.'

He says nothing else, so I stare at him intently.

'Nothing to see out here,' he says, eventually. 'Best you go back inside.'

'But what's happened at Barbara's place?'

'I don't know, but you'll catch your death out here.'

Policemen really are getting younger these days. He can't be much older than our James, who's what, fifteen now? He too has spots and no sign of stubble. The policeman looks downcast. Maybe this isn't what he had in mind when he signed up.

'I can't go back in without knowing how she is.'

He doesn't look at me but round me. I don't have to hear a sigh, it's there in his crestfallen expression. The bitter wind whips around us.

'Honestly, I don't know myself. Now I must insist you go back inside.'

'Don't tell me what to do, young man.' I pull my dressing-gown cord tighter and refasten the bow. 'This is a free country and you're right outside my doorstep.'

A policewoman gets out of the car, alerted by the raised voices no doubt.

'You all right, love?' She smiles insipidly. 'You really shouldn't be out dressed like that on such a cold night.'

'I'm worried about my neighbour.'

Unease is growing in the pit of my stomach. All these officers. That tape. No answers. There was something I needed to remember about Barbara. But what?

'We're still establishing the circumstances.' The police officer's voice is lilting, intended as a balm. 'Once we know more, we'll let you know. For now, you'd be much more comfortable in the warmth of your home.'

The icy wind picks up. Even the policeman's teeth are chattering. They don't make them tough any more. And they're not as good as that nice Bergerac. You never come across one as lovely as that.

It's no good. They're not going to tell me. I let her guide me back inside. The young policeman looks relieved.

We stand in the hallway, the front door ajar.

'What's your name, love?' the policewoman asks.

'It's Mrs Winterbottom.'

In the unforgiving hallway light, I can see her face more clearly. Glossy, auburn hair cascades from beneath her hat, framing her pretty face. My lank, grey locks hang dismally around mine. Her skin is taut and smooth, mine crumpled by wrinkles. Her complexion is so clear that she mustn't have had time yet for the sort of troubles that leave a mark.

Sympathy invades her eyes. I don't want that. I haven't asked for that. I just want to be treated the same as anyone else and given God's honest truth. I know how she sees me. She'll find herself old one day. You can't stop that with crime prevention advice.

'Now, Mrs Winterbottom, there's nothing you can do to help at this time of night, so I think it's best if you head back to bed. We'll be able to tell you more in the morning once things are a little clearer.'

People always think they know what's blooming best for you when you get to our age, Albert.

'I won't be able to sleep thinking that something's happened to Barbara.'

'You mustn't worry yourself. Once you're tucked up in bed, you'll soon drift away.'

She's not telling me that everything will be all right though. It's what they don't tell you that's important. Six decades in our safe haven of Garnon Crescent without a single crime and now something dreadful must have happened. There's been the odd cross word now and again, I grant you, but nothing to attract the attention of the law.

'Can you at least tell me that she's OK?'

She looks past me. 'Are you here on your own, Mrs Winterbottom? Is there anyone I can call for you?'

The words jar something inside me. I stare at her. The crisp fresh air has cleared my mind and a cold knowledge buried within is creeping through me. I glance upstairs, thinking of the shut bathroom door, the trickle of the tap. Then shake my head. Suddenly, I want her to leave.

'Well, just make sure you lock the door,' the policewoman says breezily as she steps outside. 'Though you couldn't be safer with all these strong, handsome policemen guarding your front gate.'

I shut the door behind her with a thud. Lock it as instructed. Trudge back upstairs. I enter the bathroom. It's empty. I turn off the tap. Switch off the light.

Once in our bedroom I gaze out the window. Curtains are twitching in neighbouring houses. Word will soon spread.

I scan Barbara's house. No shattered window or battered door. No blackened frames or trails of smoke. Her garden so neat and tidy, just like her. Not an inkling of disturbance.

I look to our bed, Albert, where you've lain beside me for sixty years. Your pillow remains plumped. The duvet carefully tucked in on your side. That blue light swirls in discordant patterns that make me feel nauseous.

More lights stream through the darkness. An ambulance approaches, parks outside Barbara's house. Its back doors swing wide open. Paramedics wheel a stretcher from within and pass under the tape. I catch my breath. My best friend, my friend of fifty years, one of my few remaining friends. Tears prick my eyes, but I will not cry.

After an age, they bring the stretcher back out, now bearing a weight completely covered with a white sheet.

That memory slaps me, Albert. Of when they took you away and you didn't return. Of that morning when the sun didn't rise. The blue light cold and silent.

I didn't know a heart could break twice, but that agony is burning in my chest once again.

CHAPTER 2

'Must have been there hours that copper, just stood outside the front gate as if he's one of those fancy-dress blokes in town who pretend to be statues.'

James is at our lounge window, Albert, surveying the crime scene. He's been there quite a while himself. Our grandson is upright and alert – like those meerkats on the David Attenborough television programmes we loved to watch together. There's an edge to his voice, a nervous energy. He lowers his head, his long hair tumbling in front of his face. Wish I had a pair of scissors handy to give him a good trim. And a needle and thread as his low-slung jeans are ripped at the knees. I offered to buy him a new pair for his birthday but apparently that's the fashion. I'll get him a belt instead. He's also wearing a black T-shirt with 'My Chemical Romance' scrawled in white across it, whatever that means.

'Police van's pulled up. Men wearing those white boiler suits have got out. Forensics. Must be collecting evidence.'

He was very quiet earlier but seems to have picked up now. It's like having your own personal commentator on the wireless: I don't need to see for myself. All that he's watched on television is real and being played out in front of him, a piece of theatre on his doorstep.

'James, come away from that window, it's not the done thing.' Shirley's more on edge than usual. Understandable really. We all are. James isn't shifting, though, whatever his mum says. Same as she is in the Boxing Day sales queue, he's not giving up his prime position.

'They've trooped right in,' says James.

Doesn't even sound as if they're wiping their feet. Barbara wouldn't like that. She was very house-proud. All those people trampling over her carpets and touching her things. She wouldn't like that at all.

I'm in your armchair, Albert, out the way. I look for today's newspaper, in the pile at my feet. Better make sure I've got the right date. There's the one, 18 February 2012. Heavens, that year was science fiction when we were courting. The years go by so fast, the days so slow.

I have a flick through but there's no mention of what's happened. It's all telephone hacking, record unemployment and quantitative easing, whatever that is. It must be too soon to have reached the printed press.

I'm so tired from the disturbed night, and all the chatter makes it hard for me to concentrate, my thoughts swirling like smoke in a squall. I couldn't get back to sleep, could I. Just lay until dawn on the king-size bed, which seems awfully large with only me on it. Sometimes, love, it's better not to sleep than to wake up without you.

'Didn't sleep a blooming wink,' I say.

'We know, Mum, you keep telling us.' Shirley's prowling the lounge, picking things up, then putting them down elsewhere.

Just as you always pointed out, she's the spit of me – small and demanding. She's had her hair cut into a tight bob, but it's gone more shaggy than sleek with all her rushing around. 'What were you doing going outside so late? It's February. You could have caught pneumonia.'

There she goes, telling me off again. I know she always wanted a second child, and we all wished it could have happened, but I don't want it to become me.

'I didn't know what was going on and the police wouldn't tell me anything.'

'You didn't have to get involved.' Wish she'd just sit down rather than flit in and out of my vision.

I phoned Shirley first thing to tell her something dreadful must have happened. They were over like a shot. Been here for an hour or so now. Our son-in-law's here too, somewhere; Matthew drove them all round. It would have fallen on a Saturday so that the whole family is available. Funny, isn't it? As much as I need their company, I could do with some quiet time to think.

'They won't tell you anything if it's really serious,' says James. 'Gotta be bad if they've got forensics.'

His knowledge of police procedure comes from watching all those crime shows.

'Poor Barbara,' I mutter.

It's you that I really need, Albert. Your quiet presence. A reassuring squeeze of the hand. A strong cup of tea with a spoonful of sugar. Without your grounding, I feel untethered, drifting.

'James! You're upsetting your gran,' barks Shirley. 'Let's not speculate, it's unpleasant and disrespectful.'

'Then they should tell us what's gone on,' James shoots back. 'Wouldn't have to guess if we knew.'

That memory resurfaces of being told what had happened to you, Albert. Being ushered into that small, cold room in the hospital and told to sit down. The doctor in his starched white shirt, the news engraved on his face before he even uttered a word. Mumbling his sorrow, his sympathy, his condolences. Your heart had given way, your beautiful heart. And yes, I know the biology, I know how it works, but I still can't understand how it happened, when there was so much life still inside you, when that heart contained so much goodness. Mine's been left a black hole.

How strange it is that some memories are ingrained, so vivid, as if they've only just happened, when months, years, even decades have passed. And they rise whether you want to recall them or not. Yet sometimes I can't even remember what I was doing five minutes ago. The mysteries of the mind, a sea of unfathomable depths. Who knows what might swim to the surface or sink below.

I try to focus on Barbara's situation, to work out what's gone on. What did I need to remember about Barbara? I try to picture last night's scene again, looking for clues.

My thoughts are swept away by a commotion at the front door; stamping and clapping. Matthew enters the lounge, blowing on, then rubbing, his hands. He's the human equivalent of a penguin that man: will never soar and he waddles around in an ungainly fashion.

'Flipping freezing. Don't know how you managed to be out there at night without catching pneumonia, Margaret.'

'Just what I was telling her,' says Shirley.

'Where on Earth have you been?' I ask.

'Nipped out to see if the police could tell us more.'

Shirley will have sent him, her little errand boy.

'Well?' she asks, hands on hips.

'They're sending someone over.'

'A policewoman's coming up the path now.' A strange foreboding permeates James's tone. He really hasn't seemed himself all morning. I hadn't expected him to be troubled, but I guess it affects everyone. Well, we already know it's bad news, but I have to know what happened.

Shirley rushes to let her in. My house hasn't been this popular since your wake, when it was like Piccadilly Circus, so many family and friends round, some I hadn't seen for years, all telling me how sorry they were, that glisten of sympathy in their eye that I didn't like.

Shirley and the policewoman step into the lounge. I can't tell if it's the same officer I spoke to last night – everything seems different in daylight, doesn't it? – but she smiles in a friendly way when she sees me.

'It's Mrs Winterbottom, isn't it?'

'What's happened to Barbara?'

Shirley groans. 'All in good time, Mum.'

The policewoman declines a drink, then takes a seat on our floral-patterned sofa, the daisies still fresh and vivid after all these years. Proved a bargain that sofa, it really has.

'How are you doing?' she asks me.

'I'm fine. Mustn't grumble.'

'Good.' That smile again. Wide and toothsome. 'My name's Detective Constable Alex Read. As you know, we're investigating an incident across the road.'

An incident! I tell you!

She surveys our faces: James now perched on the windowsill,

his eyes cast downwards; Shirley and Matthew stood either side, gawping a little, and me leaning forward in our armchair.

Her demeanour turns serious. 'I'll try to explain what's happened. Then I've a few questions.'

James should be thrilled at being part of a crime investigation and having something to impress his pals with at school on Monday. But he's got the expression of someone being taken to the dentist.

'Can I first establish who you all are?'

She whips out a notebook and pen from her pocket.

'Margaret Winterbottom,' I announce. 'Age eighty-nine. I live here. Have done for sixty years.'

'And you live here alone?'

'I try to.'

She smiles, then turns to James.

'James Thomas Stone. Aged fifteen. Gran's grandson.'

'Thank you, James. I don't really need your ages though.'

'Shirley and Matthew Stone. I'm Margaret's daughter and this is my husband.'

'Now, I'm afraid I've some bad news, Mrs Winterbottom.' The policewoman cocks her head to one side, as Princess Diana used to do. I smooth the armrest. 'Your neighbour Barbara Jones passed away yesterday.' Even though I knew, it still hits me in the stomach, and my body tenses. 'She'd been due to visit a relative yesterday evening and to stay the night but didn't arrive. A neighbour who called round saw that something was wrong and contacted us to check on her welfare. My colleagues forced their way in and Mrs Jones was found on the kitchen floor.'

Shirley clasps a hand over her mouth. Matthew places an arm

around her shoulder. James is listening intently; I can almost hear the cogs whirring.

'What time was she found?' My voice sounds small, shrill.

'Around eleven-thirty p.m., I think.'

I must have been sound asleep when they first got here. They didn't disturb me until later.

'How did she die?'

'We won't know for sure until tests are carried out by a pathologist. The death is being treated as suspicious.'

A coldness grips me, my tiredness evaporating. 'Murder?'

The policewoman sniffs. 'As I've said, it's being treated as suspicious. We're investigating thoroughly.'

'Was she injured?'

'I can't say anything more at this stage.'

'How long was she there for?'

'We don't know exactly. We believe Mrs Jones passed away the same day.'

She doesn't try to tell me that Barbara wouldn't have suffered, which leads me to think the worst. I picture her prone on the floor, her life ebbing away. I hold my face in my hands and blink away a tear.

'I have a few questions of my own if that's OK, Mrs Winterbottom? If you feel up to answering them?'

Shirley takes a chair from the dining room, positioning it next to me. She sits beside me, taking my hand in hers, her smooth skin warm on the cold, rough ridges of mine. 'Will you be all right, Mum?'

Thoughts spin and clash in my head. Why would someone kill Barbara? Such a gentle, compassionate lady. An uneasy feeling troubles my gut.

'I'm fine. I'll do whatever I can to help.'

'Appreciate that,' says the detective gently. 'Now, how long had you known Mrs Jones?'

'Since she first moved onto this street with her husband Don fifty years ago. She was twenty-nine then as she's seventy-nine now.' I catch myself. 'I mean … was.'

Too many loved ones, friends, acquaintances not with us any more. Another one lost.

'Don had just had a promotion and they'd moved from a terraced house near the town centre. He was a bit of a rum 'un, died five years ago from a stroke.'

That grief was strange for Barbara, wasn't it, Albert? Don's death was more of a release, a freedom for her, but with sadness at the wasted years, at what could have been.

The detective scribbles some notes, seemingly impressed with my memory.

'She was a lovely lady, would do anything for anyone.'

Shirley strokes my hand.

'And when did you last see Mrs Jones?'

I must get it right. Didn't see her yesterday, nor the day before. Always a busy lady with all her voluntary work. But I'm sure I spoke to her this week.

The detective glances up from her notebook. 'Yesterday?'

'Definitely not yesterday.'

'Earlier this week?'

'Yes,' I say, searching for the memory. Was it on Monday or Tuesday? The days get muddled, it's hard to order them. Especially when all I can picture is poor Barbara lying there helpless.

'I think it was Monday.'

'Did she call round? Or did you visit her?'

I didn't go round to hers, but then I don't think she was here either. I can't visualise it. But where else would we meet? I rub the base of my neck with my free hand. There was something odd about our meeting, I just know it.

'I'm not sure.'

'Do you remember how she was?'

And then it's like a bulb, dim and distant, comes on somewhere in my brain. Barbara's face. Usually so calm, so unflappable, creased with distress. *Promise me you'll do it, Margaret.* The thought pierces me like a red-hot poker. I try to grasp the memory. What was she so worried about? But then the light is extinguished.

'Mrs Winterbottom?'

'She was upset.'

'Can you remember what about?' The detective's studying me now, her pen poised, the ink ready to flow.

'I . . . erm . . . I think . . .' My blood seems to have turned to sludge. We met somewhere unusual, she wasn't herself, she was distraught. I'm certain. But all these thoughts are so scattered around my head that I can't collect them, can't piece them together, it's just feelings over facts, sensations instead of specifics. The corners of my lips twitch. 'I don't know.'

'She gets confused,' says Matthew, giving the policewoman a knowing glance. The note of apology in his tone shoots sparks of anger through me. I could do without him making me look worse.

'Something bad had happened,' I insist.

Shirley's strokes quicken their laps of my hand.

I grasp for something from the blackness. 'It was noisy.' An awful racket, Albert. Couldn't hear myself think. A word, a curious word, comes to me from the dark, as if I'm leading a seance. 'Bilkers.' It solidifies and sticks in my mind. 'The Bilkers.'

'An unusual word.' The policewoman holds the pen's tip to her lips.

'She's said stranger stuff,' mutters Matthew.

I glare at him. If he can't be helpful then he could at least keep quiet.

'What does it mean?' My neck is practically polished from all my rubbing.

'It's OK,' says the policewoman, her smile now tight with sympathy. But her pen is no longer continuing its function. 'It might come back to you later. What about yesterday? Did you notice anything untoward?'

All I remember is watching television. 'No. I didn't leave the house.'

'Didn't hear any disturbances outside?'

'Not until I was woken by yourselves.' I heave a wintery sigh. 'I'm sorry. I'm not much use in helping you find out what's happened to Mrs Smith.'

Concern flashes across the policewoman's face. 'You mean Mrs Jones? I think you've got your Smith and Jones mixed up.' She laughs, though it seems forced and fleeting.

'Is that not what I said?'

A slip of the tongue. Shirley frowns at me.

'Any previous problems on the street?'

'Oh, no. This is a very nice neighbourhood.'

The policewoman looks at the others. 'Is there anything you think might help?'

James studies his trainers. Matthew has the look of a man given a tricky starter for ten.

Shirley purses her lips. 'I don't think so. As Mum says, Barbara was lovely, can't think of anyone who'd want to hurt her.'

'That's all for now.' The policewoman snaps her notebook shut. 'I'll return if I have any more questions. Sorry to have to break such news to you.'

James looks relieved. Returns his focus to the scene outside. Shirley sees the policewoman out and I can hear them talking in hushed tones on the way. My body feels stodgy.

'You OK, Gran?' James rests a hand on my shoulder, his touch gentle. He seems more like his usual self, caring about his old gran. I pat the crests of his slim fingers and nod.

'Do you need a rest, Mum?' Shirley asks on her return. I wouldn't be able to sleep but I could do with some peace and quiet to think things over. To let that memory of meeting Barbara ease its way back into my mind.

'I think I'll have a lie down. No need for you lot to stay.'

'It's awful,' she says. 'Sure you'll be all right on your own?'

'You mustn't fuss.'

'We could do with going,' says Matthew. 'We've got to get James to football.'

He still dreams that James is going to become a Premier League player to make him rich, though I don't think there's much hope. I don't know how he can even see the ball with all that hair in his eyes.

I lock the door behind them with a slight tremble. It seems an act of wickedness has struck at the heart of our street. Anger burns through my tiredness.

I have to know who's done this to Barbara and why.

I have to remember what she said to me.

CHAPTER 3

They'll never find it. Doesn't matter how hard they look. They could search all blooming night. I've told them until I'm blue in the face, Albert. Because it's just not there.

'I've looked in every drawer, through your wardrobe and under the bed but it's not in your bedroom, Mum.'

I'd told Shirley it wasn't in there, but she wouldn't listen. You know what she's like.

'I've gone through all the cabinets, drawers and cupboards in the kitchen, Gran, but I can't see it.'

James wouldn't be bothering in this pointless search if his mum hadn't ordered him to. Not while there's still police officers outside for him to stare at, just like yesterday.

'I've checked the bathroom.' Something simmers in the weary sludge of Matthew's tone. 'It's definitely not in there.'

Why on Earth would my blooming purse be in there? I know that man thinks I've completely lost my marbles, but I haven't. It's not in our house.

'I'll look in your spare room, Gran. It's always in the last place you'd expect.'

Now the lad's just being daft. No one's set foot in there for weeks and I've only been missing my purse today. The three of them continue to spend their Sunday clattering around upstairs.

I'm sitting in your armchair again, Albert. This is where you'd read your newspaper, occasionally looking up to see what I was watching on television as I did my knitting. I know I never once sat here in all the years we were together, but it's become a habit since you left. It feels like a fresh experience, a different perspective, seeing things from where you'd always sit, as the world rushes by outside.

'What are they like, Albert?'

You smile down at me from the most recent photograph I have of you, in a polished silver frame on the mantelpiece. Your handsome face: short waves of winter white hair, wisps of salt and pepper eyebrows, strong chin and cheekbones. A twinkle in your eyes, creases of kindness radiating, two perfect dimples giving a mischievous look. You're tucked warmly beneath an open-necked shirt, jumper and tweed jacket; both smart and casual.

My enduring image of you, frozen in time. It's not an old man with liver spots, loose skin around the jowls and timeworn grooves across the forehead that I see, but the shy boy I met seventy years ago, the proud man I married, the stern but fair father and the doting grandfather.

I just see you.

I reach out, then stop. Your photograph's just an imitation of life.

It fills me with happiness to see and speak to you. But there's no reply, no comforting word, no piece of wisdom. I'll never experience your affection, your reassurance, your presence again.

Silence used to be companionable. Now it's lonely.

I sink further into the armchair and stare at the ceiling, listening to the footsteps bounding above. In the corner, a spider is making a web, industrious in its intricate design. It has a plump body, spindly legs. I know how it feels. I've never liked spiders; I'd usually call for you to evict it, Albert. Not that I'm scared of them, I'd just rather not have to deal with them. I'll ask James to remove it while he's here.

My eyelids feel heavy. I let them fall and let my mind drift.

A loud clang jolts me upright. The grandfather clock striking the hour. I take a deep breath and settle back down. You never seemed to notice its noise, being a bit mutton, but its hourly cry still disturbs me, despite having lived alongside it for so long. It's been here as long as we have, the pendulum swinging as it meticulously ticks every passing second.

I can hear the creak of our front door closing. No, I definitely haven't lost my hearing.

The lounge door opens.

My heart skips like a rabbit's. Daft, I know, but I still hope that it's going to be you, stepping back into my life. As if you'd just popped out for a stroll or a pint.

My heart always sinks when I see it's someone else.

Mr Braithwaite enters the room. 'I've had a good look round your garden, Mrs Winterbottom, but it's not there.'

I hadn't asked him to. Hadn't asked any of them to do this stupid search.

You never met Mr Braithwaite, Albert. He moved in next door not long after you left us. It was empty for quite a while after Terry died and poor Mavis moved into sheltered. Their children had difficulty selling it, something to do with the housing market collapsing. Apparently, Mr Braithwaite got it for a bit of a steal. He's a bachelor, living in that spacious house on his own. You know my feelings about bachelors over the age of fifty. Has to be something wrong if they haven't found someone to share their life with by that age. Must say I find him as wet and weak as a twice-used teabag. And he isn't one for a brew and a natter, not like Mavis.

Shirley bustles in, looking flustered, with Matthew in her wake. 'Oh Mum, where have you put it?'

She's all het up because I'm causing a problem that she doesn't have time to deal with. That's twice she's been called round in two days and she'll have washing and ironing to be getting on with. But it's not my fault. I didn't want them to look. I just wanted them to listen.

Matthew walks slowly towards me, as though I'm a wounded animal. He bends forward to bring his face near mine and says loudly: 'You're sure you've checked all your bags and coat pockets, Margaret?'

'Of course,' I snap.

He shakes his head as if it's a fiendish conundrum on *Countdown*. 'It must be here somewhere.'

No, it's not. And that's why they'll never find it. Because, as I've told them, it's been taken.

Matthew crouches down on his haunches, so that his face is lowered to my level, and asks slowly and loudly: 'Can you remember where you were when you last had your purse? If we retrace your steps we might find it.'

'I told you,' I say, just as loudly and right in his ear. 'It was in my shopping bag this morning and now it's gone. It's been stolen.'

'Stolen!' He pauses, letting the magnitude of the word sink

in, before dismissing it with a roll of his eyes. 'What on Earth makes you think that?'

'Because I know it was there and now it isn't, so someone must have taken it.'

He looks incredulous despite the fact it's quite simple.

Matthew wanders over to our solid oak writing bureau. It's stood there proudly for as long as I can remember, the brass handles still glistening against the warm woodgrain, the leaded glass display cabinet showing off our finest china, so delicate within its sturdy surround.

'Have you looked in here?'

'It's locked. It can't have got in there.'

'It's worth checking.'

'No. You mustn't look in there.'

He gives me a quizzical glance, then turns back to the bureau. I take a gasp of breath and hold it. I want to yell at him to step away, but I can't draw attention to what's inside, that's the last thing I should do. I've already checked that it has remained untouched. I exhale slowly.

'Stolen,' I repeat, to distract him.

'Mum, don't be silly. You've just put it somewhere and forgotten.'

'I have not!'

'It's happened a lot recently, Margaret.' Matthew sighs, but his attention is back on me. 'Things getting lost, then turning up later in strange places. Your chequebook we eventually found in the airing cupboard. Took us a day to discover the remote was on top of the bookcase. I don't even know how you got it up there.'

I have had a few senior moments of late. But who doesn't forget things? It's perfectly normal. Who hasn't gone into a room and then completely forgotten what they went in there for? You feel quite silly at the time but it happens to everyone and it'll come back to you later. That conversation with Barbara needles me, I wish that would pop back into my head.

'This is different. This time I know it's gone.'

'I've spent more time searching for your belongings than I have in my own home. And you keep leaving the TV on when you go out.'

Sometimes, I think it might be you, Albert, moving things around and putting the television on. Perhaps it's your way of telling me you're still with me. Or maybe you're trying to get me into trouble. You could be quite mischievous, that knowing, schoolboy glint in your eye, even in your twilight years.

'You have been getting very confused, Mum. You couldn't remember Uncle Harry's name last week.'

Harry. I freeze. The silence hangs heavy. It's been so long. And yet . . .

Shirley blushes. 'Sorry, I shouldn't have brought him up. The point is you're getting very forgetful.'

This little brain can't hold everything. When you get to my age it's obvious that some memories are going to have to make way for new ones. It's just a case of getting rid of the clutter to clear space, like a good old spring clean.

'I'm eighty-nine, Shirley. I can't remember everything.'

I point a finger at Mr Braithwaite to change tack. 'Why is he here anyway?'

His lips purse. Behind gold-framed glasses, he squints down at me as he runs a hand through short greying hair, disturbing a neatly combed side parting. He has bushy eyebrows that move with his expressions as if they're two drowsy caterpillars. He's wearing faded blue jeans and a baggy grey jumper over a striped shirt that makes him look like an accountant on his day off. I can see why he might struggle to attract a suitable lady.

'Mum, don't be rude. Steve very kindly offered to help. I'm sorry about that,' Shirley simpers at him. 'She doesn't mean it. She just says the wrong things sometimes.'

Is the heating on? It's getting cold in here. I shuffle in our chair, trying to feel comfortable again.

'It's quite all right, Shirley. I appreciate your mother's on edge. After everything that's happened and now she can't find her purse as well. It's quite understandable.'

I can't hear the boiler rumbling or the pipes clanging so I guess it's switched off.

'That awful business across the road has upset everyone,' says Shirley.

Awful business? It wasn't some blooming bank bailout. Why won't people be straightforward and call it what it was? Barbara's dead. It's as if avoiding it denies it actually happened. Well, it did happen. And someone needs to get to the bottom of what's gone on.

Again, I see Barbara's face. *Promise me you'll do it, Margaret.* But then it's just her lips moving. Her words are missing.

'Did you see or hear anything, Steve?' asks Matthew. 'The night it happened.'

'No, I was away on business. Told the police I couldn't help them, sadly.'

I can't quite place Mr Braithwaite's accent. He's certainly not from round here. But it's indistinguishable. As if he's not from anywhere, really.

'I was out myself,' says Matthew, scratching the back of his neck. 'At a work do.'

'You must worry about the effect on your mother,' adds Mr Braithwaite to Shirley.

'Of course. She was very close to Barbara.' Shirley shivers. Not from the cold though, she wouldn't notice it. She flits around too much, constantly fussing. A whirlwind. I used to be a whirlwind too, until time caught up with me and pegged me down like a tent.

'I am still here you know.' I do hate how people talk about me as if I'm invisible.

James careers into the room and flops down on the sofa, flicking his hair out of his eyes.

'Spare room all clear,' he says, slouching into the cushions. Terrible posture that lad, he'll regret it in years to come. Not like you, Albert, you'd sit in this chair with your back ramrod straight.

James has shot up in the last year. I've told him to stop getting older but he won't have any of it. Got a bit different in his tastes though. Not only is he growing his hair but his T-shirts are as loud and brash as his music. I've warned him he'll end up as deaf as you are. And always wearing black.

'Where's that nice orange sweater I bought you, James?'

He looks away. 'It's in the wash. Anyway, why d'you reckon your purse has been nicked, Gran?'

I lean across. 'I had Irene Broadbent on the telephone earlier. She said Vera Smith had her purse stolen. That's when I realised mine was missing.'

No crime on this street at all and then a killing and two thefts. Everything's gone wrong since you went, Albert.

James nods in acknowledgement. A strange expression, a mix of sadness and something else. Still, at least he listens to me.

Why don't the rest of the fools listen to me?

Shirley glares. 'You said that out loud, Mum. Who were you talking to? Not to Dad again?' I'm not even allowed to communicate with you these days. 'You know he's no longer with us, don't you?'

You'll never truly leave me.

'You never want to talk about him.'

'It won't bring him back,' Shirley says.

People avoid mentioning you, as they think it'll upset me. But the memories keep you alive.

'Anyway.' Shirley dismisses it with a wave of her hand. 'No one can get in to steal your purse.'

'People were in and out here all yesterday.'

'Was there anything of importance in your purse?' The caterpillar eyebrows crawl up Mr Braithwaite's forehead.

'Everything of importance. My bank card, money – I think a tenner and some change – my house keys, a lottery scratch card – I don't think it was a winner – my emergency telephone numbers list and, well, I can't remember what else but there will have been other stuff.'

A purse is sacred to a woman. A private space, full of my vital things, somewhere I can keep order in the world. And a way of showing a sense of style no matter how awful I look. You'd keep everything in your trouser pockets. The jingle jangle of all those coins and keys used to irritate me, but now I'd give anything to hear that tune again.

'Ooh, I remember, some lipstick as well.' I know I'm

eighty-nine, and you're no longer with us, Albert, but a girl still has to try to look her best.

'Great. Now I'll have to get the locks changed and cancel the card. More hassle and time wasted.' Shirley has a face like a rumbling volcano.

'Let's not be too hasty.' Matthew puts an arm around her. 'It could well turn up.'

'You're right.' Irritation crawls around Shirley's voice. 'Everything else does in this house eventually.'

'I can use my spare key in the meantime,' I say, trying to be of some use.

'Whatever you do, don't lose that one.' Shirley hesitates, her expression softens. 'I just don't want to leave you vulnerable.'

'I'm not vulnerable. If anyone dared get in, I know exactly where Albert's old rifle is. You can shoot burglars now.'

The volcano erupts. 'Mum, you know I got rid of that.'

At what point does the child become the one telling off the parent? When's the moment that the roles reverse? And whatever happened to respect?

James's petrol-blue eyes ignite. 'Was there really a gun in the house, Gran?'

I give James a wink. The mischievous smile that reminds me of you lights up his face.

'Thanks for your help, Steve.' Shirley ushers Mr Braithwaite out of the room. Despite their low voices, I can still hear them in the hallway.

'Mentioning Harry seemed to startle her. Is that her brother?'

'Sore subject. I shouldn't have said anything in front of her, it just causes upset.'

I don't listen to any more. I can't think about Harry now, not on top of everything else. I'm cross with Shirley: talking about me behind my back and making out that I've put my purse somewhere daft.

But I swear I haven't lost the purse, Albert.

And I'm not losing 'it'.

CHAPTER 4

Daylight's fading. I reach to close the lounge curtains, having given up on watching the comings and goings across the road and trying to force that memory of Barbara back into my mind. There's nothing on television. It'll be the London Olympics soon. You'd have that on all the time, Albert, but it fair wears me out just watching them, all that running, jumping and swimming. Even thinking about it is draining.

My hand halts, the curtain suspended. A figure on the other side of the road, his curved back to me, as motionless as my raised arm, staring at Barbara's house. I can't tell who it is from this distance, though there's something familiar about the outline. I make my way outside, but by the time I get there, he's gone. I go back inside, secure the door and close the curtains. After all the unrest, tiredness is dragging me down. Time for an early night.

I head upstairs. All right, I admit it's become a burden climbing them several times a day. I know I refused to move to a bungalow, but I didn't want to lose trusted neighbours. No, this is our home and where I'll stay until I die. And I won't contemplate getting a stairlift. Matthew nearly got a slap when he suggested that.

Halfway up, there's a knock on the front door. I plod back down, unlock, and open it to a stranger. He's wearing a worn black coat, a burgundy tie hanging loose over his grey shirt, the top button unfastened. He looks young but almost as tired as me, bags beginning to show beneath his brown eyes, a few days' worth of stubble. He's much younger than the person I just saw.

Cigarette smoke coils in the air.

'So sorry to disturb you.' His voice is gritty. I try to work out his age but can't really tell. Just young. 'I'm a reporter. From the *Evening News*. Just hoping to have a chat about what's happened . . .', he glances behind him, '. . . across the road.'

I hesitate, a small knot in my stomach. Should I be talking to reporters? It doesn't seem my place to do so, but then it is my street, my neighbour, my friend. 'The police wouldn't tell me much.'

'Maybe you can tell me about the victim.' He looks at a notebook. 'A Mrs Barbara Jones. I've been getting tributes from your neighbours. Maybe I can come inside and have a quick chat about her?'

That knot tightens. I'm not sure I should be letting people in, either. Especially with what's happened.

'Quite cold out here today.' He shuffles his feet.

It's not in my nature to be inhospitable, and he's unlikely to do anything with half of Greater Manchester Police milling around. Why shouldn't I tell him things? I want the truth to be told, for people to know who Barbara was. This wasn't some little old lady reaching the end of her life but someone who continued to give so much to others.

'Yes, yes, come in.'

I put the kettle on while he waits in the lounge. I try not to shake under the strain as I carry a tray laden with the teapot, a little jug of milk, sugar pot and two cups – a Prince Charles one for him and one with Her Majesty on for me – as well as saucers. A small spillage as I lower it onto the coffee table, thankful to have put it down. He doesn't notice, his eyes flitting around the room.

I settle into your armchair, Albert, as he leans back into the sofa. He's the same as that policewoman, wanting to know if I saw or heard anything and, again, I don't have any answers. It's like when we used to watch *Mastermind*, until we gave up when we couldn't get any right. But he also takes a keen interest in Barbara and there I can help, telling him what a wonderful woman she was as I pour out the tea, filling the Queen and Prince to the brim. He makes lots of notes, then asks if I have any photographs of her.

I lumber over to the writing bureau and fish out its little black key from a pot on a shelf, covering my movements with my body so he can't see. I unlock the cupboard at its base. Inside sit two boxes. One is even older and stiffer than me. A small Victorian pine trunk, its varnished lid curving down to a polished brass lock that catches the light, gleaming with all the promise of a treasure chest. Except that what it contains is far from treasure. At least nobody knows what's concealed there, Albert. No one apart from you, and, of course, Barbara, as my best friend. I've learned the hard way to trust nobody else. There is history in a scar.

I pull out the second box, made of flimsy cardboard and full of photograph albums. I choose one and search through the cellophane leaves that cling to each other, until a photograph stops me in my tracks. It's of Barbara from a couple of years ago, taken on your birthday, Albert, when Shirley and Matthew did a barbecue outside. Such a gloriously sunny day. There are others from that occasion. Tanned faces and beaming smiles. Plates full of burgers and hot dogs, caramelised onions and tomato relish. I think Matthew took the pictures, fancying himself as the next David Bailey at the time. I take the photograph of Barbara from its cover. He has captured her contented smile in the sunlight, though, and that genial glint in her eye.

I hand the photograph to the reporter. 'Nice pic,' he says, slipping it under his notebook. 'I'll bring it back once we've scanned it.'

I sit back down and he brings the conversation back to yesterday. Yes, I agree with him, it was a shock, to see all those police, to find out my friend and neighbour had died.

He sips his drink, a lopsided Prince Charles grinning at me. 'The police say it's murder.'

I can feel his eyes on me, gauging my reaction.

I stiffen. 'They would only tell us it's suspicious.'

I tip a spoonful of sugar into my drink, the spoon clinking as I stir. So, someone did murder Barbara. Those questions swirling my mind. Who could do that? Why? That photograph. So small and slight, the bright summer dress baggy over her slender frame. And shaking when I last saw her. Yes, that was it, clearly shaking in front of me. No threat to anyone. A sparrow brought down by a hawk.

I take a mouthful of hot, sweet tea. I suddenly feel wide awake.

The reporter fires questions and I answer with equal speed. No, I'm not frightened of being here on my own, but it is disconcerting to have something like that happen on your doorstep and to such a dear friend. No, there's never been any trouble before.

'The police tell you anything more?' He taps his biro against his lips, a smudge of black ink on his fingertips.

'No.' I swallow more tea, strong and reviving. Time to turn the tables. 'What have they told you?'

The tapping stops. 'She was found in the kitchen. Signs of a struggle.'

I bite my lip. Barbara fought back! Brave to the end.

'Anything else?'

'Seems she was strangled. Certainly no weapon. No major injuries, but bruising, round the neck.'

'Good Lord!' I put down my cup with a clatter, the Queen recoiling. 'Who could do such a thing?' That image of Barbara, prone on the kitchen floor, shifts to one of her being overpowered by some monster.

'No sign of a break-in though.'

I frown. 'None of this makes sense.'

He shrugs, then smiles. 'Anyway, it's my job to ask the questions.'

Something distracts him. He's looking past me. I turn to see he's spotted a picture of James on our mantelpiece, above the coal fire that's kept us cosy all these years and its shiny brass surround.

The reporter gestures at it. 'That your son?'

I roll my eyes. 'Grandson.'

I turn again to look at the framed photograph of James all dapper in his school uniform: smart blue blazer, crisp white shirt and straight tie. Can't help but feel that it's ruined slightly by the hair dangling down to his shoulders and a surly look, defiance in his eyes and on his tightened lips, as if the last thing he wants is a camera pointed at him.

'That's St Damian's School he goes to, right?' He's identified the badge on the blazer pocket.

I nod and pick up my drink, which is now tepid. 'Is there anything else I can help you with?'

'I've everything I need. Thanks for your time and help.' He rises, glances at his watch. 'Deadline's fast approaching.'

I shuffle forward to get to my feet.

'It's OK, Mrs Winterbottom. Don't get up. I'll let myself out.'

The reporter leaves and I sink back into the armchair. I stroke the soft fabric of its arms. Breathe it in. It still has your masculine, musky scent, Albert. Even now. And when there is such evil lurking out there, I need that comfort more than ever.

CHAPTER 5

She's a mine of information that Irene Broadbent. You don't have to dig deep to uncover a rich seam of local knowledge and the occasional nugget of gold. And she's always around; when I pop out it's not often that I won't bump into her in our street.

'You're the third,' she tells me. 'First Vera Smith and just now Dora Singleton was saying her purse has been stolen too.'

To think Shirley was insisting I'd lost mine. Suddenly, crime is rife on this street. It all seems very peculiar. And poor Dora. She's only just recovering from breast cancer. That look on her face when she told me the diagnosis still haunts me. She's been incredibly brave with all the treatment and now this.

'Dora swears she left hers on the kitchen counter. When she went to pick it up to go shopping it was gone. Looked all over the house she did.'

'Same with me. My family hunted high and low, bless them, even though I said they wouldn't find it.'

Irene harrumphs in sympathy, sucking in air like a vacuum cleaner. She towers over our front gate with her stout frame and broad shoulders, her fleshy arms folded. A hurricane couldn't drown this woman out when she's in full flow. Wouldn't even put her off her stride.

Irene's reserves of news have been exhausted. She toys with the zip of her padded gilet. A late winter chill is creeping in after a bright, sunny morning. But today, I have more fuel for the fire than her, thanks to that detective and reporter. A thought snags in my mind though, as she warms to my contribution. That I'm supposed to be doing something else. She listens intently as I tell all, while the thought slowly blossoms.

'I heard,' says Irene, bending closer to my ear and lowering her voice, 'that Barbara was to visit her niece that night but wasn't keen to go.'

Barbara's only remaining relative. My brow acquires some extra creases. 'That's odd. Barbara and Lisa were very close.'

'Something must have happened,' mutters Irene, her nose twitching to delicate airwaves.

That thought reaches full bloom. 'Oh dear, I'd better get inside. I'm meant to be helping James with some schoolwork.'

Despite it being a Monday, Shirley dropped him off on her way to work. A teacher training day apparently, though I would have thought it was best to train them before they started teaching others. I'm sure James would rather be out playing with his friends than stuck indoors with his old gran, but Shirley says he needs my help. He's writing something called a Life Story to help him with his English and History. And it'll also help me remember things, according to Shirley. I'll get a nice book at the end of it about my past. It's good to know I'm now so ancient my life is considered history.

'We'll have to cut down several trees to produce a book that size,' Matthew had quipped. I should be allowed to slap him.

I know it's really just an excuse to have someone keeping an eye on me. They're frightened to leave me alone for one minute. I'm not sure what they're most scared of: a killer on the loose or me making mistakes. Bodyguards surround me at all times. I finally know how the Queen feels.

James is sprawled on the sofa, fingers gambolling his mobile phone's screen. I'd promised to show him old photographs. He thinks they'll not only help him describe my past but might also jog my memory of that conversation with Barbara.

I open the bureau and there are the two boxes. I run my hand over one lid, caressing the smooth contours of the wood. Reassuringly solid. The contents reassuringly safe. I drag out the cardboard box, so fragile in comparison, that I can open in front of him. I take the lid off.

My stomach lurches.

Lying on top of all the photograph albums is my purse. Bold as brass, almost mocking me. How on Earth did it get there? I swear I didn't put it there. My jaw clenches. Someone's playing a trick on me. Who?

I place a hand over my mouth. It was only this morning that I'd phoned that detective to tell her about the purse thefts. Just in case it was connected to the murder. And when she wasn't interested, I'd phoned the *Evening News*. That reporter who called yesterday was much more intrigued.

I glance at James, but he's fixated by his phone. While he's distracted, I click the purse open. Everything seems to be there: keys, bank card, money, bits and bobs. With trembling hands, I stash it in my cardigan pocket. No need to tell James or anyone else, not until I've worked out who put it there.

I spot a distinctive cream folder covered in a pretty lace

trim. Our wedding album. I take it over to James and sit beside him. I'm immediately calmed by the sight of you in your smart grey suit, top hat and tails. So young and dashing. The parish church in the background is majestic, its steeple soaring into the blue sky and colourful stained glass windows sparkling in the sunshine.

'That's sound, Gran.' James holds the photograph around the edges. 'Love the sepia tone. Use that setting on my phone sometimes to make pics look arty.'

Can you believe they try to make new images look old?

'Look at Granddad. Top hat! So posh.'

I glance between the photograph in his hand and the one on the mantelpiece. Time never faded your looks, nor the spirit that shines through in both pictures.

The grandfather clock chimes, interrupting my thoughts. I notice James gazing at me.

'You and Granddad were perfectly synched,' he says, softly.

I nod, an unwelcome tear in my eye.

'Miss him, don't you?'

'More than I could put into words.' My voice cracks around the edges.

James shuffles closer, extends an awkward arm around my shoulders and squeezes me to him, with all the uncertainty of an adolescent. 'It'll get easier over time, Gran.'

I doubt I have enough time left on this Earth for my grief to fade.

After you went, Albert, it was James that stayed over to keep me company. He didn't leave my side, quietly trying his best to do things for me, making breakfast and sandwiches and endless cups of milky tea. I didn't realise at the time how much I needed that.

'I miss him too,' adds James, letting go. 'He was always good to me.'

'He was very proud of you.'

Beneath all that blond hair, James has a long, lean face, with none of the puppy fat you might expect at his age to soften the sharp edges. But he has your eyes, Albert.

James carefully slides the photograph back into place.

We flick through the folder as I name the bridesmaids, best man and a host of relatives. I can recall every aspect of that day, when I felt the luckiest girl in the world, the clarity as crystal as the champagne glasses we're holding. I cannot help but smile.

'Knew it.' James grins. 'Nothing wrong with your memory, Gran, you know every name here and it was, what, seventy years ago. Tell me about Mum growing up. Where's the embarrassing photos?'

I open another album and he's in fits when he sees Shirley as a baby. And at a lovely photograph of her as a tot in her little hat and booties – she was sweeter then and much easier to handle. There's his Uncle Tom as well in short trousers, born ten years before Shirley.

We go through photographs of all the birthdays and other celebrations like christenings. James isn't keen to view his own. He prefers the ones of Shirley marrying Matthew. She looks so beautiful under that veil and at the same church as us, Albert. We were so proud. Despite my comments, Matthew kept that awful moustache. I wish I could erase it. And there's Tom's wedding to Catherine a few years later. We'd begun to fear he would never settle down. He looks so handsome and Catherine so pretty and elegant as well.

James scribbles away making notes, same as that reporter.

And he pays more attention than the detective. Maybe he'll master one of those professions. He's as eager for details about the war as a ration-era boy for a chunk of chocolate. Oh, the stories I could tell him, if only I was allowed to divulge my secrets.

Instead, I show him my favourite games as a child: tiddlywinks and marbles.

'People actually played them!'

He's in hysterics when I demonstrate how. It's marvellous to hear laughter echoing around the house again.

He's fascinated by dates: car seatbelts I remember coming in about the time the Queen took the throne; Hillary and Norgay conquering Everest not soon after; Roger Bannister breaking the four-minute mile in the early 1950s. I was enchanted by America as a young woman and the fashions from across the Atlantic. Oh, the screams as Elvis gyrated on *The Ed Sullivan Show*, the tears when James Dean died in a car crash. I'm quizzed about politics and I remember the Suez crisis in 1956 and Rosa Parks in America bravely refusing to give her seat up on a bus the year before. He loves the history of space travel: Laika, the first animal in space, the Soviets launching the first man into the stars in 1961, I think, and Neil Armstrong the first man on the moon in 1969.

All these events in my lifetime. I'm surprised by how well I remember them. I could be a history teacher.

'You're better than Google, Gran.' I can see James checking the dates on his mobile phone. 'What about the seventies?'

'The 1970s. Let's see.'

The strangest sensation shudders through me. My mind is suddenly blank.

I recall the beginning of the decade and having to get used to decimalisation to work out the price of shopping. After that? Nothing. I grasp in the dark for a memory. We'd be hitting our fifties, with Shirley becoming a teenager and Tom in his early twenties. What did we do? I remember family holidays in Bournemouth when the children were young but not when they were older.

I rack my brain through the topics we've covered. Politics? I remember Margaret Thatcher's swinging handbag but didn't she come to power in 1979? Music? The shock of John Lennon shot dead but that was in 1980, I think. Films? The children liked *Star Wars* and *ET* but they were the end of the decade, possibly afterwards. The Falklands, that was in the eighties too. My love of America. What happened to Elvis or Nixon? My mind is a maze of dead ends. I feel slightly sick.

James's pen is poised, awaiting a stream of dates and facts but the flow is frozen.

'Gran, what's wrong?'

'I'm struggling a bit.' I smile, but it falters. 'All this looking back has exhausted my brain.'

'If you can remember the fifties, the seventies must be simple.'

'It's just . . .' How to make him understand? 'It's as if a chunk of memory has been wiped, as you would a cassette tape.'

'What about the pics? They might jog your memory.'

He opens an album. I scan the photographs, all bell-bottom trousers and floral shirts. That tape can't be restored. I feel breathless.

One photograph catches my eye. A dapper man who, despite the greying hair and creases forming around his eyes, is still very handsome. I'm next to him, but there's something odd about the way we're standing. Something forced. On the other side of him is Barbara, she must be in her late thirties.

James looks at me nervously. 'That's Uncle Harry, isn't it?'

Harry. Of course it's Harry. An iciness in my veins.

I take the album from James and flick through it. There are no photographs of Harry after that.

James sweeps his hair back, clearly keen to change the subject. 'No matter. Looks like a decade best forgotten.'

I slam the album shut and make my way to the window so that James can't see my face. 'I think this project is too much for me.'

'No probs. I've got more than enough.'

Dusk is descending, that unsettling moment when light turns towards darkness. The streetlamps flicker on. 'It's getting dark, James. You'd better get going.'

'Mum's not picking me up for another hour.'

The crime scene tape is still stretched around Barbara's gate but there's no one posted outside. The police must have finished their investigations, they're no longer buzzing around like bees outside a hive.

'Have you remembered anything else about Barbara?' asks James as tentatively as a dentist probing a rotten tooth.

Promise me you'll do it, Margaret.

I close my eyes and try to concentrate on that image of Barbara's face. I will my mind to shine a torch into the darkness that surrounds it. Where were we? What had happened? I clench a fist and hold it against my lips.

'There's nothing there.' My eyes sting when I finally reopen them.

'Don't stress it. It'll come back to you.'

I give him a weak smile but it feels as if something vital has been lost.

'You heard anything else?' he asks.

'Not a thing. Not sure the police know what they're doing.'

'Maybe we can help.' A note of optimism chimes.

'What on Earth can we do?' I can't even recall the one thing that could be useful.

'Nobody knows this area better than you. We could use your local knowledge and my knowledge of detectives.'

The young have always been prone to flights of fancy. I know what you'd say, Albert. You'd say to remember what I'm capable of and what we did. Oh, but that was all so long ago. I don't think there's much of that left in me.

'We owe it to Barbara. Somebody has to find out who did that to her.' He sounds a tad desperate, but he's right. The only thing worse than what's happened is the idea of someone getting away with it.

'And it's not like we haven't got time on our hands.'

'Suppose it wouldn't hurt to make some enquiries.' We do all have a duty to do what we can. Something stirs inside me. A sensation I haven't felt for so long. A tremor of excitement? A sense of purpose? I'm not quite sure.

'Any suspects?' James flicks his notebook to a blank page. He can move on so quickly. 'Who would want to hurt Barbara?'

'There's the rub. I can't think of anyone who'd do that.'

'We should think of a motive then. Was she rich?'

I sit down next to him. 'Barbara was never interested in money. She was quite frugal, shopped at Aldi and bought her clothes from charity shops.'

She wasn't one for luxuries, was she, Albert. I prefer

Sainsbury's and the odd treat, along with my garments, from Marks & Spencer.

'Her husband never let her spend money on herself.'

'Tight as my dad, was he?'

'Even worse! I can't see her having much money in the house.'

We're not getting very far. James's hair flops across his eyes and he sweeps it to one side. Then his face lights up.

'At school, we did some philosophy, the teacher talked about some French guy called Descartes and how he wanted to find out truth. So, he put aside everything he thought he knew and started from scratch to work out what had to be true. We should do the same. Start with what we know and build our case around it.' He looks at me searchingly. 'So what do we know, Gran?'

'We know the day she was killed. That a weapon wasn't used. Family wise she only has a niece left, that's the relative the police said she was due to visit. She lives a good hour's drive away so Barbara would have to catch a couple of buses.'

The facts course their way back to me as easily as his pen flows. I don't know whether to feel pleased or frustrated that I can remember some things so easily, when other important things slip like smoke from my grasp.

'But we need some evidence, James. It's following a trail that leads you to a killer.'

'You're right, it's forensics that solve these cases. There's always some DNA left at the scene.'

'I was thinking of more old-fashioned methods. We should question people carefully and methodically, that will lead us to the truth.'

'Nah, forensic science is best. Nails them every time.'

'I was thinking more along the lines of Miss Marple.'

'You're so old school, Gran. It should be more *CSI*.'

I guess we have very different tastes in crime programmes.

'It'll be *CSI Garnon Crescent*,' laughs James.

'As the Bard might say, "Something is rotten in the state of Garnon Crescent."'

He looks at me blankly. What do they teach children in school these days?

'What next?' he asks.

'We should utilise our differing skills. I'll talk to people who knew Barbara. And you see what you can find out through technology.'

'It's a deal, Gran.'

We shake hands.

He shuts his notebook.

Another morsel drifts back to me. 'Someone said there was no sign of forced entry. Barbara was very meticulous about security so it's unlikely she left a window open or door unlocked. What does that mean, James?'

'Dunno.'

'It means it's likely she let the killer in.'

His eyes widen. 'It's someone that knocked on her door?'

'I would go even further. Barbara would never let someone in that she didn't know. So, by logic, it must have been someone she knew.'

Now we're getting somewhere.

'It wasn't a random attack.'

'No.'

James looks at his notebook. 'I need you to list everyone that knew Barbara and their connection to her.'

I get a writing pad of my own from the bureau and begin to fill in a sheet with names. 'It'll take me a while.'

'That's fine. Just keep adding to it whenever you remember someone.'

Headlights shine into the lounge. The low rumble of an engine. I turn to the window. Now it really is getting dark. I can just make out Shirley walking up the garden path.

'I think it actually is time for you to go now, James.'

We both grimace. Our crime-fighting is over for today. I feel a pang of regret. Wouldn't it be nice to have grandchildren without having children first? With grandchildren you don't have to worry as much about nurturing, teaching, discipline. You can relax, spoil them and enjoy seeing them grow and blossom.

We traipse to the hallway and I unlock and open the door before Shirley can rap it with her knuckles. She breezes in.

'Behaving yourselves?'

We glance at each other. Then we both nod.

'We've had a splendid time,' I say. Behind Shirley's back I raise a finger to my lips. I don't want his mum to worry about our crime-solving plans or my memory lapse. James smiles back.

Shirley looks into the lounge and sees the photo albums.

'You found out all about your gran's past?'

James holds up his notebook. 'Oh yes, there's gold in here,' he says, with a sly grin.

CHAPTER 6

My trusty shopping trolley rattles behind me. Despite the uneven paving slabs jolting it about, it's just as good as when you bought it for me, Albert, over ten years ago. Hardly any sign of wear and tear. Not like me.

The sky is bright blue and I breathe in crisp fresh air. A good night's sleep has invigorated me, which is handy as it's 'shopping day', a chance to make the most of my energy and get what I need. My hip's not too bad so no need for my stick. It's not far into town, though it takes me a little longer these days. Shops begin to appear as I reach the outskirts, encouraging me onwards.

At a litter-strewn bus shelter, a group of youths cluster like gulls around rubbish. Six of them, restless and rowdy. They have their own uniform: all in black; heads down, hoods up; and those bubble-type coats that the young favour that make them resemble a dark Michelin Man. I'm not scared – we've faced far worse foes in our lifetime and I doubt they intend me any harm – but there's still something a little unsettling, intimidating, about their presence. When I near, their chatter stops. One turns his face away. Familiar strands of blond hair poking from beneath his hood. My shopping trolley's wheels squeak to a halt.

'James?'

He freezes, mumbles something, then turns towards me and nods.

'Are you OK, James?'

A snigger from one of them perched on a plastic seat. 'This your bird, Jay?'

I'm about to give him a piece of my mind when I glimpse James's reddening face, his eyes cast downwards. I keep my mouth shut.

Silence and a sickly sweet smell hang in the air. The youths stare at me with casual indifference. They seem older than James.

'Well, I'm off to do my shopping,' I say, finally. 'You boys behave yourselves.'

I trundle away, their muttering resuming, the odd squawk of laughter. I put it behind me. What teenager would want to be embarrassed in front of their friends?

Instead, I concentrate on my shopping. Shirley's always offering to get things for me, but I insist on my Wednesday shop in town, so long as my hip isn't playing up. Shirley buys all her groceries from the supermarket, but I like to do some of my shopping elsewhere so that I can chat to the butcher as I get my cuts of meat and pop into the little bakery for fresh bread, pastries and pleasantries and the pharmacy for toiletries, prescriptions and to pass the time of day. I know you saw shopping as a chore, but it's one of the things I look forward to, getting out and about and seeing different people and products. We loved our countryside walks together though, didn't we?

Alongside the canal's still waters and through woodland tracks, hand in hand, drinking nature in.

I've soon ticked off everything on my list and set off home. The usual route, I'll be back in ten minutes.

Something's not right. I look around, an uneasy feeling in the pit of my stomach. I recognise the sequence of semi-detached properties lining one side of the street. And on the other, the huge house that was converted from the old train station. And the trees of Ashfall Park that tremble in the distance. But I don't know where I am. I can't think how it all fits in relation to where I live, like a jigsaw puzzle missing key pieces.

This is silly, I've walked these streets for decades. I'm so close to home. But I could be in Shanghai or Sydney or San Francisco for all I know how to orient myself. That feeling in my stomach intensifies.

There's the corner shop where the kids sometimes bought sweets. It's now a house, the large window display someone's lounge.

This is Durham Street, I'm sure of it. But where do I go from here? I walk to the former shop, shopping trolley dragging behind me like a reluctant dog, then survey the scene from a different viewpoint. No better. Familiar but amiss. Should I go left? Right? Straight on?

The most peculiar memory comes to me, of when I was a young girl and got separated from Mother on a shopping trip. I'd stood there bewildered and alone as the menacing world I'd been warned not to interact with bustled around me. I'm that small and helpless child again. Tears sting my eyes. I mustn't panic or get upset, that won't help. Just stay calm, Margaret, and work it out. This is what happens when you get older. If buildings are going to change then you're bound to lose your bearings.

I will my brain to expand the buildings and roads out into a map in my mind. But searching for the memory is the same as glimpsing something out of the corner of your eye, only to turn and find there's nothing there.

Walking to a crossroads, I check the street signs. Durham Street continues straight on, while Union Street crosses from left to right. I'll have to go one way and see what happens. Which way, Albert? Come on, help me out.

I plump for left. Walk a few yards. Beads of sweat rise on my neck like dewdrops. This isn't right, it's just sending me back into town. There's no one around to ask. I can't go all the way to town for help and I'm not sure I'd remember anyone's directions anyway. I head back, cross the road, go the opposite way. Each disorientating step takes me further into the maze, the buildings looming higher, the street stretching further. I plough on. The sweat slips down my spine in a cold trickle.

I look to the heavens, praying for inspiration. A flock of birds soar, wings arching up and down in unison as if controlled as one. A united team, they have an innate sense of direction, know exactly where they're going.

After several minutes I reach a T-junction. There's the Crown and Anchor across the road where you'd nip for a pint and a game of dominoes. I could do with a stiff whisky now. I push and pull the doors and they jangle against a heavy lock. Perhaps it's too early. Then I see a sign saying that it's closed for good. When did that happen?

Something taps on my brain but can't get through. Those

words again, *The Bilkers*, springs to mind but I've no idea why. I take a few deep breaths.

I keep going. Turn left. The trolley feels heavy, as do my legs. Another choice of roads. Nothing is familiar; a bland parade of identical houses. All roads are a dead end. I can't go on. My hip aches, my legs are too stiff and I'm feeling dizzy.

I sit on a low wall by the pavement, the wind rushing past. The stone's coldness penetrates my dress, the sweat has turned icy. Shivering, I look in my purse and take out the slip of paper Shirley gave me of emergency telephone contacts. But there are no telephone boxes any more and I don't own a mobile phone.

I can't sit here forever. Must soldier on. I haul myself up to cross over. A couple of steps into the road, my shopping trolley sways precariously as it drops from the kerb. I battle to keep it balanced.

A horrid blaring. Louder and louder. I look up to see a car heading straight for me. I'm a statue, no energy or time to move.

I close my eyes, hold my breath, wrap my arms around myself.

Air hurricanes around me, the bottom of my dress billowing, a swirl of dust and dirt making me splutter.

The car swerves around me. Another blast of the horn.

'Get out the road, you stupid woman.'

The driver's words trail as he screeches away.

Legs wobbly, I stumble to the wall of a house and lean on it, the rough brickwork reassuringly solid against my fingers. I try to control my rapid breathing, try to calm the ringing in my ears.

A rumble of tyres. Is it the same driver returning to hurl more abuse? Maybe it's someone else who I should wave down to help? But I'm as concrete as the wall. Wheels roll to a halt. The electric whirr of a window winding down. A handbrake clicks.

'Margaret?' A recognisable voice, hesitant. 'Margaret.' More certain.

I manage to break free and turn, peering through the window of a familiar Ford Fiesta. Matthew stares back.

'What are you doing here?' Exasperation in his voice. 'I've been looking all over for you.'

For once, I feel pleased to see him. Relief flows through me, turning my legs back to jelly.

'Well get in then. I'll drive you home.'

I hobble to the car. Matthew leans across from the driver's seat to open the door and I haul myself inside. In my effort to shut the door properly it slams, making the whole car shudder.

'Is that your shopping bag?' Matthew looks at the trolley in the road in front of us. He shakes his head. 'It's OK, I'll put it in the boot. You stay there.'

He manages it in seconds and we're soon away. He glances at my trembling hands and puts the car's heater on.

'You all right, Margaret?'

'I'm better now.' A quiver in my voice.

'I've been searching for you for ages.'

The warm air brings feeling back to my limbs. 'I hadn't been gone long.'

'Where've you been?'

'I got lost.'

'Lost?'

'It's a Wednesday. Shopping day. I walked into town but wasn't sure of the way back. I'd stopped to rest.'

Matthew frowns. 'It's Tuesday, Margaret.'

'Oh.' Is it? The days blur into one.

'Shirley's got a day off work and called round to take you to lunch as planned.' I can't remember us arranging that. 'It's another inset day for James, he's with his friends somewhere.'

The words needle a memory of cold stares, that sickly sweet stench and squawking laughter. 'I'm not sure about his friends.'

Matthew glances across, his eyebrows knitting together. 'No. I'm not either.'

He turns the steering wheel nonchalantly, the car gliding round a corner, the ride smooth under his control.

'Why aren't you at work?' It sounds more accusatory than I'd intended.

'I bloody well should be. Shirley called me. She found your front door unlocked, the back door wide open. You nowhere.'

Doors were always open when I was a child. We've driven back round to where I was, outside the Crown and Anchor. There's something not right about that pub.

'And the TV was still on. She checked with the neighbours. Steve said he saw you walking towards the town centre with your shopping trolley. I've nipped out of work to help look.'

I didn't mean to be such a nuisance. I focus on the route Matthew takes. Straight on, further down Durham Street, a right into Rochester Street. Then across a roundabout onto the main Manchester Road. It's all coming back to me now, the map re-forming in my head, the jigsaw pieces slotting into place. Of course that's the way I should have gone. It's the way I always go.

We take a left into Garnon Crescent before pulling up outside our house. Shirley's in the doorway, her face a hotchpotch of anger and relief.

'Thank you,' I say.

Matthew mutters something under his breath.

I get out of the car, thinking that I might have been safer left on the streets.

'Where the hell have you been?' Shirley marches out and gives me a right look. 'I was worried sick.' Then she swamps me in a tight hug. 'Come on, get inside.'

Matthew follows with my shopping trolley. 'She thought it was Wednesday. Went into town but got lost.'

'Lost? You know your way.'

'I don't want a fuss.'

I settle back into our armchair, Albert. My legs are dead weights. I let the cushions bolster me. Squeeze the padding of the armrests.

'Found her propping up a wall in Dale Crescent.'

'Oh, Mum.' Shirley clutches her head.

'Everything's all right now.' I've no wish to dwell on this afternoon, it's best forgotten.

'We can't go on like this.'

I stay quiet, listening to the clock tick and breathing in your scent that still clings to the armchair.

'I'll make an appointment with your doctor.'

My body tenses. 'I don't need to trouble the doctor.'

'Well, you're troubling me.'

A headache's coming on. I could do with a cup of tea, but I don't want to bother them further. 'You need to relax more, Shirley. Trust me, you'll live longer.'

'Relax! Chance would be a fine thing.'

'You should stop still every now and again. And spend time on yourself.'

She gives me a stern look.

'And there's this.' Matthew grimaces as he passes Shirley a copy of the *Evening News*. I can see the word **murder** in bold, black letters in the front-page headline. And that photograph of Barbara that I gave the reporter. Has he returned it? There's one of her house as well, with all those police officers outside.

'Several paragraphs down,' says Matthew. 'A familiar name.'

'Oh, Mum. You're on the front page.'

She holds it up as if it's a filthy rag, her nose wrinkling. 'Neighbour Margaret Winterbottom, eighty-nine, said: "I've known Barbara Jones for more than fifty years, since she first moved to Garnon Crescent. She was such a kind and generous neighbour and friend. She wouldn't hurt a fly. It's terrible to think there's someone out there that would do something like that to her."'

Sounds just as I told the reporter.

'Look.' Matthew points at a paragraph. 'What she said here.'

I could do without him landing me in it. He's always making me look bad in front of Shirley, turning her against me.

Shirley goes on: '"There's been a spate of thefts around here in the last few weeks," Mrs Winterbottom adds. "I've had my purse stolen from my house and a neighbour has reported the same thing happening to them. The police haven't been interested at all."'

Shirley shakes her head. 'We're back obsessing about the purse again, are we?' She glares at me as though I'm a naughty child. 'You can't tell the newspaper all that stuff about the police. We didn't even report it to them. It wasn't even stolen.'

I'm not getting dragged into that argument again. Shirley

wafts the paper about, as if to create a cleansing breeze. I snatch it from her. Haven't seen my name in print since your death notice went in, Albert. I ignore Shirley to focus on the story. It's all there. Claims the murder happened some time between five p.m. and eight p.m. on Friday, a few hours before poor Barbara's body was found. The only item the police know for sure is missing from Barbara's house is her purse. Nothing else was taken. The paper is suggesting it could be connected to Dora's missing purse, which was thought to have been stolen exactly a week before.

'See, they're linking it to the purse thefts.' I shake the paper at Shirley triumphantly. That headache bites into my forehead as I realise that I found my purse and I haven't told her.

'It's just speculation.' She sounds weary. 'Don't get involved in things that don't concern you.'

'Course it concerns me. It's my friend that's been murdered.'

'I'm off back to work, love,' says Matthew. 'I'll leave you to it.'

He kisses Shirley on the cheek, then makes his escape. There's no quick exit for me.

'I've a good mind to call the editor and complain,' says Shirley. 'They shouldn't be interviewing vulnerable old ladies like that.'

'I'm not vulnerable. And I was happy to speak to them.'

'Well, I'm definitely taking you to the doctor's.'

She's moving around the room so quickly that my eyes can't keep up. My head's starting to pound. I need to think straight. If the thefts and murder are connected then was it an opportunist thief caught red-handed, who lashed out?

'These crossword puzzles are littering the house, Mum. Can't you just bin them?' She's picking up newspapers and magazines, bundling them together. 'I'll put them in here out the way.'

She's heading for the bureau, its key still in the lock. I don't want her touching the wooden box.

'Leave my things alone.'

I drag myself out of our armchair, my legs sore, my hip aching. I grab her arm, stopping her opening the bureau. She can't go rooting through my things; she can't see what's in that box. She shakes free of my weak grasp.

'Mum, don't be silly.'

Her fingers are on the key. Blood pulses in my temples. The headache throbs. I smack her arm as I would when she was an infant, the sharp echo of skin slapping skin. She recoils from me.

'Mum!' Her voice shrill. She touches her arm as if trying to work out why it's stinging. I didn't mean to strike her so hard, Albert. I just had to make her stop.

The room plunges into silence, punctuated by the ticking of the grandfather clock. Shirley drops the bundle of papers to the floor with a thud. 'What's got into you?'

Her eyes moisten. I don't know what to say, so I stoop to pick up the newspapers scattered at my aching feet and feel twinges pinch all over.

I hear Shirley cross the room and, soon after, the slam of the front door.

I've too many secrets, Albert. I can't contain them.

It's been a rotten day.

Best forgotten.

CHAPTER 7

'Condition in which a name's muddled, I assumed.'

It's one down, seven letters, with the third letter an N. I just can't get it, Albert. I've been stuck on this one for several minutes now. I'll try another clue.

'Boastful talk makes the balloon go up.'

It's twenty-three down, two words, three letters in each. It sounds easier but I can't think of the answer. It used to take me minutes to do these crosswords. Takes hours now. I hate seeing those empty white spaces incomplete and forlorn. I enjoy the challenge, however. It reminds me of back in the day, combing through *The Times* for coded messages. The intense concentration, blanking out the rest of the room as I scanned the page, determined not to miss anything. My eye would be drawn to words that had something about them, like iron filings to magnets. A pattern slowly emerging. That buzz of adrenaline as jumbled letters re-formed into clear words. From chaos came communication.

Now I can't even get these simple clues. To be boastful would be to brag but I can't think of any synonyms that would make a balloon fly. My brain's foggy today. I feel like a bear waking from hibernation, struggling to place myself in a world that has moved on.

I could try another puzzle but I don't do these new-fangled sudoku ones. 'They'll help keep your brain sharp,' James says, but I've never been interested in numbers. Words are much more my thing.

I might have to accept that my crossword-solving days are over. But if I can't answer a simple crossword clue then how can I expect to unravel a murder? A week on, there haven't been any developments from the police. I've watched all the news programmes and been through the newspapers but it's barely warranted a mention.

I sit back in our armchair. Outside, the window cleaner's tuneful whistle fades. He'll have finished his round. Almost forgot that I'd paid him earlier, to save him having to call back. He seemed a little subdued.

That spider's returned, crawling across the ceiling. It freezes as if aware it's being watched, then suddenly scurries to a dark corner.

A sharp knock on the front door.

'It's open,' I shout.

James pokes his head around the lounge door. 'All right, Gran?'

'What are you doing here?'

'Great to see you as well.' He laughs. His tie is dangling loose while his crumpled white shirt hangs out. 'Just calling on my way home from school. Told Mum I needed more time on this Life Story.'

'Life Story' is now our code for 'Murder Investigation'. He's carrying a large sheet of white paper rolled up under his arm.

'Are you planning on redecorating?'

'Don't be daft. Saw something on telly I thought might help.'

He puts the rolled-up sheet on the floor. 'First, though, I've read some tips for recalling memories. To help bring back that conversation with Barbara. We should try relaxation.'

I'm all for that!

'Are you sitting comfortably, Gran?'

I shuffle in my seat, then lean back. 'It's the most comfortable chair in the house, James.'

'Good.' He lowers and softens his voice as if narrating a perfume commercial. 'Now take a moment to calm yourself. Close your eyes. Take three deep breaths.'

I enter darkness. Breathe in and out. I'm feeling sleepy.

'When you're chilled, think back to that conversation.'

Barbara's anguished face appears. *Promise me you'll do it, Margaret.* A stab of guilt so sharp my eyelids snap open like blinds.

'I can't do it.'

'Try again. Make sure you're relaxed.'

I rest my head right back. Close my eyes. Breathe deeply.

Barbara's staring straight at me, her bottom lip trembling, her voice equally shaky. I think she's going to say something else and then a mist around her thickens and she's lost in the fog.

'I'm sorry, James, it's no good.'

'Oh well.' Disappointment clouds his face and voice. 'Worth a shot.'

James picks up and unfurls the sheet. 'Let's try this, instead.'

He stands on the sofa. I grimace but bite my tongue in case he's unveiling something important. He takes blobs of Blu-Tack from his trouser pocket and sticks the sheet across the wall, then pulls out a thick black marker pen.

'When the police investigate a murder, they make a chart of everyone who could be involved. Like a family tree but including friends and enemies. Thought it might help us, you know, narrow the field. On the internet it says most murders are committed by someone the victim knows, nearly always a relative or partner or whatever, hardly ever a stranger. Let's play the odds and look at those closest to Barbara.'

'I'm not sure this should be like gambling; it should be very matter-of-fact.'

'That's why I asked you to collect the names of everyone she knew and a bit about them.'

I wrote them all down so I didn't forget. And something came back to me: that falling out between Barbara and Jean Brampton. Do you recall, Albert? It got quite nasty. Was it a new fence that divided them in every sense of the word? I'm not sure why that should have bothered Jean so much. What does she have to hide? I've made a note, now where did I put that writing pad? I had it before doing the crossword and after lunch so it could be on the dining table. Ah, yes there it is. You can find these things quite logically if you trace your steps back.

I hand it to James. My handwriting used to be so neat, now it's spidery and slants down the page.

James begins to write on the large sheet of paper now stuck to my lounge wall. I do hope that pen's not going through otherwise we're going to have a permanent reminder of Barbara's connections on my wallpaper. And then he really will be doing some redecorating. Thankfully, the paper seems thick enough.

James starts with Barbara's niece. *Lisa Wardle*, it says in jet black. *Last relative. Single. In regular contact.*

'She's the closest,' says James.

'Isn't she the person who most cared for Barbara?'

'No room in crime-solving for sentiment, Gran. We need to pay her a visit.'

'I'm not sure of her exact address. We'll need to find out.'

James moves on to Barbara's friends. *Irene Broadbent.* 'She's big and terrifying enough!'

'James! She's a good friend!'

'She's a suspect now.' *Retired pub landlady*, he writes, *married, long-time friend, knows all the goss, strong, scary.* 'She knows everything that goes off, controls the flow of info. She's like the Mafia, telling people what she wants them to hear. Can you really trust her?'

He's seeding my head with doubts. 'She's just interested in people and current affairs.'

'Likes spreading fires and watching the impact you mean, like an arsonist.' James wriggles his fingers. 'Those big, meaty hands.'

Irene does have a strong grip in every respect. Heavens, those seeds are sprouting!

Dora Singleton is next on the sheet of shame. *Former dinner lady, divorced, friend of forty years, quiet.*

'Dora only lives round the corner,' I say. 'So she's a neighbour too. She's recovering from breast cancer and wouldn't hurt a fly.'

'She's on the list.'

Rev. Brown, parish church vicar of twenty years, married with three children.

'We can't suspect a man of the cloth!'

'You put him down here, Gran.'

'They were good friends and Barbara was a church regular. It feels wrong to doubt him.'

'We all know how sinful vicars can be. He's staying on.'

It's the neighbours next.

Vera Smith. Former hairdresser, stylish, sensible, married. Lives a few doors down from Barbara.

'I'm not aware of any problems between them,' I say. 'Vera also had her purse stolen.'

'Is your purse still missing?'

I hadn't thought any more about it. Suddenly, there's a lead weight in my cardigan pocket.

'Must be.' I know I should tell the truth, Albert, but I'm in enough trouble as it is and I don't want him to think less of me. It's just a little white lie.

James moves on to his next suspect: *Jean Brampton, Barbara's next-door neighbour, single, former cleaner, has a temper, feud.*

'What's this?' James points to the four-letter 'f' word.

'I didn't really think about it when the police came round, but Barbara and Jean had a falling out a while back.'

'What about?'

'I can't quite remember the details. Something to do with their border, a fence, I think. It was all so petty but there were some quite fierce rows. Things were tense between them even before that.'

'This is great.'

'It wasn't. It was blooming awful.'

James underlines the 'f' word. 'A motive. A past.'

Thinking about those rows, something else comes to me. 'A few nights before Barbara died, Jean was hammering on her front door; something had gone on between them. I didn't think much about it at the time. Jean can fly off the handle over trivial things, and it never occurred to me to mention it to the police.'

'Really?' James looks thoughtful. 'Feels important. You don't remember what it was about?'

I shake my head. 'I didn't ask. It wasn't unusual, they were always snapping at each other over something or other.'

'All right, see what else you can get on her.'

He moves on: *Steven Braithwaite, my next-door neighbour, businessman, single.*

'I'm not sure a businessman would be robbing old ladies,' I say. Something about Mr Braithwaite comes back to me. 'He told your dad he was away on business that night.' I'm quite pleased that I've remembered. I try to picture the scene outside when the police came. 'And his car certainly wasn't there. Emergency vehicles everywhere, but his wasn't in its usual spot on the drive.'

A lovely looking luxury car, Albert. You'd quite like it. Raises the tone of the neighbourhood.

'He's on the list anyway. Let's keep an eye on him.' James peers at my scribblings. 'What's these?'

I take a look. 'Ahh, that young family that's moved in three doors down, the Martins. They only arrived a few months ago and would barely have met Barbara. Their two children are very young. I don't think they're married. Who is these days? There's another couple at number twelve, but they're only just in the process of moving in, if this hasn't put them off.'

Lots of new people moving into the street now. Everything's changing. There's going to be very few of us older ones left.

James writes: *The Martins*, then, *New Couple.*

'Anyone else? You sure there's no other relatives?'

'Absolutely. Barbara never had children and her siblings are all deceased. Just the one niece.'

'Maybe I should put your name down. You're a friend and neighbour.'

'I wouldn't hurt anyone.'

'I know you wouldn't, Gran.' That smile and a cheeky wink. 'It was only bants.'

I gather myself. 'Well, what about your name then?'

'Don't even go there.' He writes both our names on anyway.

James jumps off the sofa and stands next to me. We gaze up at his handiwork. All these connected names.

'Much easier when it's laid out in front of you,' he says.

'What do we do with it now?'

'These are our suspects. We need to investigate each one, starting with the key ones.' James stares at the list. 'Anyone else . . .'

He lets the words drift into a silence punctuated by him patting the pen against his forehead, like the soft tapping of Morse code. 'Someone she knew and trusted.' His voice almost a whisper. 'Could it have been a delivery or a workman she let in?' The pen freezes. 'Did she have her shopping delivered, Gran?'

'No, she'd use the bus. She hadn't had any work done on the house either.'

'I've remembered another clue.' He hops around. 'Can't believe I'd forgotten.' See, it's not just me that forgets things, even the young aren't immune. 'In the paper, the detective said the murder happened between five and eight p.m. It happened exactly a week ago today. Is there anyone who calls round on a Friday?'

'Only the window cleaner. He did his round earlier and I paid him then. He normally returns late afternoon to collect.'

'Late afternoon!' James has the look of someone struck dumb by the sight of gold. 'Do you know what time exactly?'

'I don't keep a record. It varies, depending on how long it's taken him to do his round, who he's stopped to chat to, the weather if—'

'But roughly, can you remember when he came last week?'

'I'm not sure, would have been, I don't know, about five-thirty p.m., maybe a bit earlier. Or later.'

'That puts him in the frame.'

'I hardly think the window cleaner will have attacked her. His prices are very reasonable and he puts a lot of effort in. The windows are spotless.'

He still writes *window cleaner* on his chart. Then looks at my face. 'I could put the postman and milkman on as well if it makes you feel any better.'

'We don't have a milkman any more.' Something else that's stopped since you've been gone, Albert. Not enough customers to make it profitable. I have to buy a large plastic container to last the week but it soon goes off. 'And the postman only delivers in the morning.'

'See. The process of elimination.'

'I suppose Barbara trusted the window cleaner enough to let him in if she needed to get change. I can't imagine him being capable of hurting anyone. He's very friendly.'

'How well do you really know him?' James's eyes narrow. 'Could all be appearance. Deep down he could have some pretty dark secrets.'

I'm a little worried about the boy's imagination.

'We need a profile on him. Everything you know about him. How long's he had this round?'

'Oh, a good few years.'

'What's he look like?'

'Tall and slim. Gets lots of exercise up and down that ladder all day. A very healthy complexion from all that fresh air as well.'

'Anything to make you doubt him?'

'He does have rather unruly, long hair that he often covers with a sort of tea cosy.' I look at James's mane. Where are my scissors?

'That's a beanie hat. I'm not sure it's incriminating.'

'With a nice haircut he could be rather dashing. If I was forty years younger.'

'Gran, gross.'

Only joking, Albert. You're the only man for me.

'Anything else?' asks James.

Something chugs into my brain like a late train. 'I've got it.'

'What?' Eagerness animates his face.

'Hot air.'

'What you talking about?'

'The crossword clue. About talking and a balloon going up. Just wouldn't come to me but now I know it as clear as day. The answer's hot air.'

James sinks down on to the sofa and groans. Where's that newspaper to fill in the answer?

'The window cleaner, Gran. Anything come to you about him?'

'Sorry, where were we? Well, I guess I don't really know him at all. We mostly talk about the weather and football.'

'See, you don't know what he's capable of. And those timings really fit so there's a window of opportunity.' He laughs. 'Get it, Gran.' I shake my head. 'Might need to work on a motive though.'

'What next?'

'Any idea where he lives?'

'Not a clue. Can't be far.'

James shrugs. 'We'll have to question him when he returns next week then.'

A week feels a lifetime away.

We look up together at the sheet hanging from our lounge wall. Underneath the names in black are some big, blank spaces.

'In the meantime,' says James, with a steely-eyed seriousness, 'we've got work to do.'

CHAPTER 8

If you fall off a horse the best thing to do is get straight back in the saddle. That's what you'd tell me to do, Albert, so I'm out proving I can find my way around. I can't stay indoors forever! Not too far, though, just to the post office to collect my pension and send a parcel. Ten-minute walk to a little shopping oasis of a precinct.

The slate sky, concrete and traffic fumes don't matter; at least I'm out. The hip doesn't feel too bad. It's quiet, a chill and apprehension in the air. I've heard some folk are too frightened to step outside knowing there's a killer on the loose. Well, I've lived through a world war, nuclear bomb threats and more worldwide flu epidemics than I care to remember. I'm not hiding away. Justice is all I'm worried about.

I find the post office easily. See, nothing to fear. Heat hits me as soon as I step through the swishing doors, like stepping off a plane into a tropical climate. It's changed since you last stepped inside, Albert. There was talk of it closing but it's been modernised instead. No queuing in straight lines formed by a rope that weaves you out the door and into the street any more. Now you sit on a plush red sofa with a ticket and wait for a computer to call your number out, same as the Co-op's deli counter. It means I don't have to stand for ages.

I press a screen for my ticket. I use a card to collect my pension, they don't send it by cheque any more. Times have changed so much, and you've not even been gone a year. The cost of a blooming stamp is outrageous these days. Not to mention our gas bill. Matthew's always trying to wind me up about my pension, saying the elderly are living far too long and a burden on the state. After all we've done for this country, we deserve what little we get. I told Shirley my card hadn't been in my purse after all so we don't need to replace it. Don't think badly of me. I didn't want her thinking she was having to do yet another thing for me.

While I'm here I'll post a birthday present to Tom. I don't see much of our son. I've got a book on the history of the British Isles that I know he'll love. He shares a birthday with Harry, but it's a long time since I've given my brother a gift. I recall that photo of us with Barbara. It makes me as overcast as the sky, a spark of something else skulking in the clouds.

Two familiar figures are hunched over on a sofa. Well, well, if it isn't Jean Brampton! And Vera Smith, who'll know all the gossip as a former hairdresser. This should help with the 'Life Story'. Just a few other people in, so despite only two cashiers being on I don't think we'll be waiting long. I haven't a second to lose.

I can hear Jean before I even reach them.

'Could snow tomorrow.' Her puffy face puckers as if she's sucking a lemon. 'Could be a bad 'un. Won't be able to get out.'

Never stops moaning that one. When she joins you in heaven she'll pick fault with the place. She's supposed to have a bit of money tucked away, though you wouldn't know it to look at her and she's as tight as my slimmest dress. A fleece jacket zipped up to the chin makes it look as though her head is balanced on top, and she's wearing thick grey jogging bottoms. She's long given up fashion for comfort. Her hair has greyed to almost white and is cut flat to a practical, rather than stylish, short length. What was it that James called her once? Oh yes, 'a chav'. When he said it, Shirley gave that look of disapproval that she does so well, but when she explained to me what it meant it seemed quite accurate.

'Ooh look, it's the celebrity,' Jean says as I sit down next to them. What have I done now? 'Saw your name in the paper.'

'You really think it's connected to the purse thefts?' Vera leans over, her voice low. She always looks glamorous, even if it's just a trip to the post office. She's wearing a lovely purple hat over thick curls that are dyed a russet brown, and a smart, matching jacket over a floral-patterned blouse and black ankle-length skirt. Her handbag is perched on her lap, both hands clutching the handles. She had her purse taken, of course. Here's my opportunity to do a bit of subtle detective work. I won't be able to make notes, I'll just have to remember what they say.

'What happened to yours?' I ask, gently.

'Mine was before Dora's.' Vera gazes into the distance. 'I know I left it in the hallway but couldn't find it. No sign of a break-in so the police weren't interested. My daughter thinks someone snuck in while the door was unlocked.' She shudders. 'After what happened with Barbara, I'm just glad I wasn't in their way. Maureen Stapleton refuses to leave the house until they've caught them.'

'It's awful,' I say.

'I visited Barbara's niece,' adds Vera, her hat wobbling. 'To pay my respects. She was shattered, the poor love. And very anxious that this whole thing is sorted quickly, she doesn't want it dragging on.'

Jean snorts a bellow of hot air like a dragon.

'Do you have her address, dear?'

Vera fumbles in her bag and hands me a scrap of neatly torn, lined paper that I secrete in my coat pocket.

'Have the police spoken to you, Jean?' I ask, politely.

'Course they have.' Her face screws further, the temperature dropping as if the doors have swished open. She's always been brusque. Something not right about that woman.

'Were you able to help them?'

Vera grips her handbag a touch tighter. Jean glares. I've seen that look before.

'It's not something I wish to discuss.'

Jean purses her lips like a petulant child. The atmosphere is so cold I actually glance to see if the shut doors are open.

'Did you mention you and Barbara falling out?'

Jean's eyes burn with indignation. Vera gulps like a fish out of water.

'That's got nothing to do with it.' It feels as frosty in here as outside. I remember being caught in the middle of their feud. I was supporting Barbara and Jean was on my doorstep, eyes blazing, tongue sharp. Such language. I wouldn't let her intimidate me though. Gave her a few choice words back, didn't I, Albert.

'Was it about a new fence?' Jean's a good few years younger than me. Would easily have the strength to overpower the slight figure of Barbara. A cat pinning the sparrow. A shiver runs through me.

'A fence?' Jean chews on the thought as if it's a piece of gristle. 'That was nothing. It didn't start over a fence.'

Jean stares at me in a peculiar way, as though I've missed something obvious.

Vera's eyes dart between us.

'There were some quite fierce rows between you,' I say.

One memory leads to another. Of comforting a trembling Barbara, more bone than flesh to hug. Two neighbours divided so unpleasantly.

It bursts into my head. *Promise me you'll do it, Margaret.* The look of anguish on Barbara's face is the same.

I compose myself. 'So the police don't know about it? I remember you banging on Barbara's door a few nights before the murder as well.'

'I had every right to be upset.'

I don't need to ask why though; I can tell Jean's going to justify herself.

'She'd started a fire in her back garden and left it roaring, the smoke ruining my washing, sparks practically igniting the fence, she could have burnt our houses down.' Jean's face recaptures that moment of acrid fumes striking her nostrils.

'A fire?' It's my turn to be alarmed. 'That's not like Barbara. She was very proud of her garden, she wouldn't have a bonfire blazing away and certainly wouldn't leave it burning.'

'I had to grab the hose and put it out.' Jean recreates the action. 'Who knows how bad it could have been if I hadn't managed.'

What on Earth caused Barbara to do such a thing, Albert?

The frostiness is heavy. Vera becomes preoccupied with her handbag. Wouldn't say boo to a goose that one.

'So what did the police ask you?'

'If you must know it was me what found her.' A haunted look in Jean's fierce eyes. Wouldn't James say the one who finds the body is prime suspect? 'I still hadn't had a chance to have it out with her over that fire. She wasn't in when I knocked when you saw me, or the next day. I admit it was quite late when I went round but I'd been stewing and I thought she'd be more likely to be in. No answer, so I went round the back.' Jean looks into the middle distance. 'I took a peek through the kitchen window.' A crack in her steely expression and a softening of her gravelly voice. 'Saw her lying there. Knew straight away . . .' She shakes her head as if trying to rid herself of fleas. 'I rushed home to call the police. Could hardly breathe. Couldn't get the words out when they arrived. That's when they forced their way in.'

Her shoulders shudder. Grief or guilt? How do detectives tell? She has a grudge, a temper, was the one who found the body. Did this falling out escalate? Was Barbara turning to me to be comforted from Jean's spite yet again?

Vera pats Jean's knee, a trace of disapproval in her frown.

'Always have to stick your nose into other people's business don't you.' Jean stands up. 'You'd do well to keep out.' Plunging her hands into her fleece pockets, she marches off.

I pull myself upright. Investigating isn't going to make me popular. What did James say? No room for sentiment.

A robotic voice breaks the awkward silence, calling out a number. There's only one other customer left, who's ambling to the counter. I look at my ticket. My number's two less than the one called. Must have missed it while we were talking. It's happened before, getting so engrossed in conversation that the queue skips right past me and I've had to get another ticket. It wouldn't surprise me if on occasion I've been gabbing so long the numbers have gone full circle and come round to my turn again.

'I'd better be off too.' Vera has the whiff of a woman who can't wait to leave. 'My husband will be wondering where I've got to. I left him in the car outside.'

The other customer has finished anyway, so I go to the counter and explain why I didn't take my turn. Once I have my money and the package is paid for and handed over, I retrace my steps home. Even with everything rattling around my head, it's a doddle, and I wonder how I went so wrong the other day.

Reaching our street, I see a youth loitering. He looks like one of those lads that was with James, his hood pulled up, dark tracksuit bottoms and trainers. I feel him watching my every step. I've no choice but to walk by him.

He steps across my path and looks me up and down, which shouldn't take him long. 'You Jay's granny?'

I nod and steel myself. 'What are you up to?'

'His dad at yours?' He glances at our house.

'I wouldn't have thought so.'

'When you see him, tell him Liam's looking for him.'

I stare into his vacant eyes. What the devil would he want with Matthew?

'I'll be sure to pass on the message.' I push past him; there's no use me querying it further, I've more chance of getting sense out of a waxwork.

I scurry like an arthritic beetle through our front gate and see Shirley at the window with the look of a prison warden awaiting a convict's return after they've skipped parole. If she keeps that frown up much longer she'll soon have more lines in her forehead than me.

'Not sure you should be out alone again, Mum. Not after last time.'

I've barely closed the door and not had a chance to mention that strange encounter. 'Just nipped to the post office.'

'If you need anything just call me.'

'I'd go stir crazy cooped up all day, Shirley.' I shuffle off my winter coat and hang it on the wooden stand. 'Why are you round, anyway?'

'To let you know that as soon as I have a free moment, I'm booking an appointment with the doctor. I'll come round to pick you up.'

I don't want to see the doctor – there's no cure for old age – but I know I'm not going to win.

'And I've been thinking about your missing purse.'

That lead weight is now burning a hole in my cardigan pocket.

'I was hoping it'd have turned up by now but we'll have to accept it's lost. With what's gone on I don't want to take any chances so I'll get the locks changed. I'd rather have the inconvenience and expense than more worry.'

My stomach lurches. I could tell her, I know I could, Albert. But it would become another misdeed on my crime sheet. I'd rather carry the guilt that's growing in my gut than suffer the look she'd give me.

'I wish Tom was here sometimes to share the load rather than me doing everything,' Shirley adds. 'There's a street party soon as well in preparation for the Queen's Jubilee. To bring everyone together, improve community relations. I'll have to bake something for that.'

Please stop thinking badly of me, Albert.

'Oh, and James is here. Needs to check a few things on the Life Story. Turning into a proper little Michael Aspel.'

I head for the lounge, focusing on what I need to tell James, pushing everything else out of my mind.

'I'm just going to thank Steve for his help the other day.'

A chance to speak to James in private. He's stretched out across the sofa, fiddling with his phone. I should tell him to sit upright, but time is of the essence.

'Gran, please take a seat.' As if he's a psychiatrist ushering in a patient.

'It is my house, James.' I settle into our armchair, taking the weight off my feet.

'Soz.' James swings his legs off the sofa.

'Your mum says you've got some more questions.'

'That's just a cover. Wanted to tell you what I'd found from my investigations. I heard they were having a press conference this morning. Should be on the news later. As it's a Saturday I went along.'

'They let you in?'

'Well, I sneaked in. It was at the Civic Centre. Loads of big TV vans there with camera crews and photographers. So busy they didn't check who was who.'

'You're a little young to be passing as a television presenter.' Though they do all look the same age as him.

'I hung around the cameramen. Figured people would think I was helping them carry things or on work experience or something.'

I can't decide if it's enterprising or deceptive.

'Did they reveal anything important?'

'The conference was boring. Just repeated the appeals for info, answered some questions, going over and over how they're determined to catch the killer, doing everything possible, blah, blah, blah. They were hoping Barbara's niece would make an appeal for the TV cameras but she wasn't feeling up to it.'

'Poor girl. What must she be going through?'

'Then there was a bit they said was off-record. The police chief clarifying a few things. Definitely no break-in, tests showed she was strangled after a struggle, only her purse was taken. They think the killer fled in a panic.'

James looks down at his trainers, his hair masking his face. Is he more sensitive than I thought? Youngsters aren't as resilient these days. They haven't had to go through what we did.

'I overheard one of the reporters talking to the top cop.' His voice quiet. 'Trying to keep it between themselves, not realising I was behind the pillar next to them.'

I lean in, all ears.

'Lee Spade, I think the reporter said his name was. From the *Evening News*. Reckoned he'd heard a key witness had come forward. Top cop just fobbed him off, saying he couldn't comment on investigative procedures.'

'Great work, James.' Nothing wrong with a touch of espionage for the greater good.

Something catches my eye. A splash of colour on his shoulder blade, peeking from underneath his black, crew-neck T-shirt.

'What's that?' I point to it.

James looks down, his eyes widen like footballs being inflated and he mutters something under his breath as he yanks up the T-shirt to cover it.

'What have you done, James?'

He reluctantly pulls down the sleeve to expose his shoulder, a lion's head inked on it in red, white and blue. 'Just a small tattoo. A lion's brave and fierce. And patriotic.'

'The only lions in Britain are caged in zoos.' I don't understand the fashion for tattoos. People are covered in them these days. Once you're marked, it's permanent. 'Are you old enough? Did your mum give permission?'

'Friend of a friend did it.' He looks more worried than ever. 'Part of a dare.'

'I don't think they're allowed to do that without parental consent. Your mum will go spare.'

'I know.' He crashes back against the sofa and groans. I can't help but feel sympathetic. 'I thought it'd be easy to cover up, but it's too high.'

'You'd better get a turtleneck.' I laugh, but he seems more confused than amused. 'I suppose it's another secret.'

I feel the need to cheer him up. 'I've got news as well.'

I tell him about Jean.

'Really think she could have done it?' he asks.

'I think she's capable.'

'A neighbour with a vendetta reacting in the heat of another row.' He rubs his hairless chin. 'I like the angle. How could we prove it's her?'

'Why would she take the purse though? Did she panic and try to make it look like a theft?'

Before James can say anything, I hear the front door opening.

'James, you finished?' Shirley's voice is loud and clear. 'Time we got going.'

James jumps to his feet, pulling the neck of his T-shirt to his chin. 'Yep. Got what I wanted. The project's coming on well.'

I don't think James has any intention of doing the Life Story, Albert. I think he has a more pressing engagement in mind.

CHAPTER 9

I recline in our old, striped deckchair. The sky's a little overcast, but I don't want to be stuck indoors on my own. I've taken to sitting in the garden, Albert, chatting to passers-by. I remember how you got into fishing as a way to relax. I'd love the tranquil scenery but not the solitude. I see myself as a sort of social fisherman these days as I sit in our deckchair and read the novels and poetry I loved to study when I was younger. I cast a look to those walking by, a friendly smile, a pleasant greeting, and, if they take the bait, reel them in for a natter before releasing them back into the urban stream.

Getting absorbed in those conversations is a welcome distraction. It seems to take me longer and longer to finish the books. I often lose the thread and find myself having to go back several pages or begin again a poem I once knew off by heart. On my worst days the words float around like slippery fish until I have to give up and let them swim away. I do love words: how they look and sound, their depth and many meanings. I love them even while they're becoming more difficult to understand. Like teabags and patience, I only hope I never run out of them.

I spy two people up the road, chatting. It's Irene, I'd recognise that shot-putter frame from a mile off, but I can't tell who she's with. It's a middle-aged man, smart looking. Something familiar about his stance, though he's too far away for any detail. I stand up and move to our fence. Is it the man from the other night, who was staring at Barbara's house? The same height, slim build and posture.

Their conversation seems to have finished. The man starts to walk away in the opposite direction. I shout out 'Helloooo ...' and wave my arms as if I'm drowning. A shiver down my spine makes me stop. He fades into the distance.

I catch Irene's eye and she bounds over. 'You all right, Margaret?' Her voice reaches me first.

I point at the disappearing figure. 'Who was that man?' I'm breathless even though I haven't been moving.

'Oh, that was nothing.'

Irene's dismissive flap of a hand startles me. She's usually so forthcoming, will tell you everything and anything.

'I just thought—'

'Are you going to the community meeting tonight?' Irene zips her gilet as far as it will go.

A sudden suspicion creeps through me. I want to enquire further, the need for any kind of confirmation is overwhelming, but her question makes my brain stutter. 'Community meeting?'

'Police are holding a public meeting about the *murder*.' Irene breathes the last word as if it's a profanity. 'Say they'll provide an update and some reassurance.'

'Not sure if I knew.' My head is in too much of a spin to pin down any knowledge.

'It's at the community centre. Been two weeks now with no sign of an arrest.' Irene moves closer, leaning onto my fence so much that I'm not sure it will take the weight. '*There's a lot of anger.*'

James has been busy at school so we've not had a chance to make any progress either. The window cleaner didn't call round today, which was a setback.

Irene straightens. 'I'm looking forward to it.'

A million questions battle for dominance in my brain. I pluck one out. 'Did Barbara ever confide in you, Irene?'

'No, no, she was a very private person. She wouldn't have disclosed anything to me.' Irene gives a knowing look. 'You were much closer to her, Margaret. I'd have thought she was more likely to divulge things to you.'

Guilt's red heat prickles my skin at my failure to recall Barbara's words. 'Who would want to hurt her?' I glance across at the modest house. 'It's not like she had a fortune tucked away.'

'She was wealthier than she looked.' Irene gives a throaty grunt. 'That husband of hers made a fair amount of money but was too miserly to spend it. He left her a tidy nest egg, but I think Barbara got so used to her way of living that she never splashed out.' Irene takes in the bricks and mortar of what was once a warm home. 'Sometimes I even thought she was punishing herself, as if she wouldn't allow herself an indulgence, as if she didn't deserve more.'

I'm not sure about that, Albert. Barbara was just content with her lifestyle, she had no need or desire for expensive things, she just wouldn't have seen the point.

The fence bears Irene's weight again. '*I know she left a will.*'

I immediately think of Lisa as the only surviving relative. Then ponder how Irene knows. 'That poor niece of hers.'

Irene's nose convulses. 'Apparently, they had a falling out. That's why Barbara wasn't keen on visiting her, she didn't want the aggro.'

That's such a shame, Albert. Barbara talked about Lisa a lot, being the last of her family, and I thought they'd always got on well. I've been racking my brain to recall if there was any animosity. Obviously, there were some criticisms but I just put it down to the sort of disagreements and irritations that every family has.

'What was it about?'

'I don't know . . .' Irene folds her arms into a corpulent cross, a glint of steel in her eye. '. . . Yet.'

That determined look reminds me of when Irene was a tough, no-nonsense landlady. Those stories about her, Albert. How she dealt with the drunkards, turfed out the troublemakers. Upturned tables and smashed glasses. She wasn't one to get on the wrong side of.

Another question plucked like an eyelash. 'I've been trying to remember those rows between Jean and Barbara. Do you know what went on between them?'

Irene and Jean have never had time for each other; Jean's not one to share in the gossip. But Irene might have heard something.

'There were squabbles going years back.' Irene tinkers with the gilet zip again, a rapid up-and-down readjustment. 'Sorry, I must get going, I've left a shepherd's pie in the oven. Let's see what the police have to say tonight, they might have more to reveal.'

She starts to walk off.

'The man you were talking to before . . .' I try again, but she carries on away from me, her long strides quickly stretching the distance between us.

I stare down the street as if that man will magically reappear. A thought makes my throat tighten. It looked like him all right, but it couldn't be.

CHAPTER 10

'I can assure you that we are doing everything in our power to solve this case. I have a team of twenty detectives working around the clock on numerous lines of enquiry.'

The policeman looks very smart in his uniform, all crisp and neat, stiff collar, shiny buttons. I forget his name but he said he was a detective inspector so that's quite high up.

'Why's no one been arrested?'

'We're confident that the leads we have will result in an arrest in due course.'

His voice has the jaded monotone of a reluctant robot. He looks in his early fifties, with a trim moustache. Despite his self-assured appearance there's a weariness in his eyes. He would need to be high ranking to hold his nerve standing in front of this baying mob, with questions fired from all directions like bullets at the Somme.

'They'll have killed again by the time you lot have got anywhere,' shouts a woman.

'We have increased the number of officers on patrol, particularly in the evening, and set up a mobile station in the ward to act as a deterrent and a reassurance. We ask that the public remain vigilant and report any suspicious activity.'

It's packed in the community hall. I've spotted several neighbours, or *suspects* as James calls them. Irene managed to get a seat right near the front. Vera's a couple of seats back and wearing a lovely hat for the occasion, and there's Mr Braithwaite alongside Dora, who's looking well, which is good to see. The vicar's here too. We managed to get a good seat, but there are people stood at the back who weren't so lucky. Must be more than a hundred people here, such is the anger and fear spreading like a virus.

'That won't stop them killing someone else.'

'We ask you to stay calm while we investigate fully to bring the perpetrator to justice.'

I hand James a humbug. I'd felt young again when he'd taken my arm to guide me through the crowd. For a moment I'd thought it was you, Albert, leading me onto the dance floor. But these rows of plastic chairs jarred; I wanted to kick them to the corners for the wallflowers. Such a strange sensation, the memories of a place where we'd danced decades ago clashing with seeing it in a different context. No musicians on the stage, just the solemn faces of this police inspector, his two colleagues and three borough councillors.

'Jean Brampton's on the far side,' James whispers. 'Even the window cleaner's here.'

I suppose he did know Barbara, and nothing attracts a crowd like a crowd. In the corner is a press table with that reporter sat there, scribbling away.

'Wasting our time,' shouts one man. No need for a microphone with this lot, Albert, you'll be able to hear them up in high heaven.

Now that I'm settled it feels good to be out the house and doing something different, being part of the community again. And it's more entertaining than what's on television these days. Matthew hadn't wanted to drive us all here, grumbling on the way about how he didn't have the time and didn't see the point, but I'd insisted. He's still got a face like a heartbroken haddock. Shirley's been a bit off with me since that slap, but she agreed to come.

The inspector gives the panicked expression of a comedian dying on stage. He'd said there'd been a lot of unhelpful speculation, and he'd wanted to give the facts and an opportunity to ask questions. He might be regretting that now.

'I can provide some details about the crime scene.' Throwing crumbs to the pigeons, the pecking muted as instantly as pressing a button on a remote control.

'We know the murder was committed between the hours of five p.m., when the victim was last seen alive, and eight p.m., when she failed to answer several phone calls.'

'Who saw her at five p.m.?' mutters James. He looks across at the window cleaner.

'We know the victim put up a struggle in the kitchen where she was killed. The post-mortem shows the victim was strangled. We believe the offender was wearing gloves, which from the marks left we suspect were made of leather. There were no fingerprints left on the victim or at the scene.'

The inspector holds up a large photograph of a shiny, silver button. 'This was found at the crime scene and is of particular interest.' Eyes focus in. 'It's a button we believe to be from a jacket that does not belong to the victim. We strongly suspect it belongs to the offender. We're currently working to identify the type of jacket it came from. If anyone has more information on this item, please let us know.'

He pauses for a moment, letting everyone absorb the information.

'I'd like to appeal, again, for anyone who saw anything that evening, no matter how seemingly insignificant, to come forward and tell us. Even the smallest detail could help. And if someone that you know was acting strangely or out of character that evening, please report your suspicions.'

Jean's red face flashes into my mind. I need some evidence before I'd be confident enough to tell the police. Grumbling builds again, the crowd unsatisfied by the meagre morsels tossed their way.

'Couldn't catch a cold never mind a murderer,' bellows a woman from the back.

'They should bring someone in who knows what they're doing,' shoots a sniper from the safety of cover.

I have a touch more sympathy for the police. This case is not straightforward and I don't like people being disparaged in their jobs, not if they're doing their best. It's time someone stood up for this policeman as his colleagues don't seem willing to. Hauling myself to my feet, I cough loudly to clear my throat.

Shirley glances up. 'Mum, what you doing?'

People nudge each other. A few sniggers.

'We need to pull together.' I put on my best public-speaking voice as a frisson runs through me. 'All this bickering is not what Barbara would have wanted and isn't going to help anyone. We should be conducting ourselves in a much more civilised manner. Give the police a chance.'

A respectful hush. There are some advantages to growing old: nobody is going to argue with me. My family shuffle in their seats.

'I was telling my grandson, James, the other day about people in times gone by being there for one another.'

'Christ, don't bring me into this,' James mutters under his breath, but loud enough for me to hear. 'I don't need any bloody attention.'

He stares at his feet, face flushing. His mother quietly admonishes him for his language and I'll be having a word later too for his blasphemy.

'Where was I? Yes, as I was telling James, we need to recapture that community spirit. We all have a duty to do what we can. I'm certain that Barbara told me something important—'

'Not that sodding memory of meeting Barbara,' hisses Matthew. 'It's not important.'

I glare down at him. '. . . that there's more to her death than some random burglary.'

The whole room seems to pause, my words echoing from the wood-clad walls.

'So it might not have been a break-in gone wrong?' someone says.

'Let her speak,' says another.

All eyes are on me. I feel like a diva expected to burst into song.

'I just can't remember what it was, but I know it will come back to me.'

Murmurs simmer from the audience, unsettled, curious.

'Margaret, just sit down.' Matthew leans across James to tug on my sleeve. 'You're making a scene.'

'No, I will not sit down and shut up, Matthew.' I say it louder than intended, which causes Matthew to flap about as if he's been thrown into a fryer. 'We shouldn't be criticising and complaining, but helping. Let's show people what this neighbourhood's all about and how we can work together to catch whoever did this.'

'She's right,' says one man near me. 'Most important thing is to lock the bastard up who did this, pardon my French.'

'We've all got a responsibility to help,' says another.

Applause ripples around the room like the adrenaline surging through my tired body.

The inspector looks happier if a little bemused. He sits down, probably not knowing what more to say. I sit down too.

One of those councillor fellows, who had kept very quiet while all the flack was flying, stands up.

'Hear hear.' He looks pleased with himself. 'Very well said. We're all on the same side and should use this terrible situation to show this community at its best. Now, are there any issues that the council can help with?'

A lot of talk follows about the need for more street lighting to make people feel safer, securing alleyways to stop undesirables prowling around the backs of houses, and repairing fences to protect and smarten up certain streets. My interest wanes.

Matthew turns to me. 'You satisfied? Can we go home now?'

'Yes, I thoroughly enjoyed that.'

'It wasn't a stage show!'

'I found it quite interesting. It's good to see our community leaders engaging with the public.'

James is quiet and keeps looking around. People begin to disperse as quickly as they arrived. We head for the exit too. Wish I'd brought my stick with me because my hip has seized up from sitting for so long in that uncomfortable chair. I don't really like using it when I'm out in public. Shirley and Matthew are already ahead of us. I lean on James to help me walk as I try to loosen my hip into steady movement. We pass the reporter, who's questioning the detective inspector. We stop.

'Where exactly was that button found?'

The policeman shrugs. 'On the victim.'

'A source told me it was in her hand, that she'd pulled it from the murderer during the struggle. That right?'

The inspector stiffens. 'I can't tell you more than I've already said.'

'I was told the pathologist had to unclaw her hand to prise the button free.'

The inspector grimaces. 'I wouldn't write something as horrible as that if I were you.'

Suddenly, they seem to have realised we're eavesdropping. James pulls me away. Maybe he's worried about being recognised from that press conference.

Going outside is like stepping from a sauna to an igloo. Shirley and Matthew are waiting by the car, coats zipped up, hands tucked into pockets.

'Wondering where you'd got to,' says Shirley, as we all climb inside the vehicle.

'We might make it home not too late,' adds Matthew, gloomily.

The car pulls away. I gaze at the night sky, thinking of Barbara on her kitchen floor, the picture changing. She's clutching that button in her fist, a last-gasp clue snatched from the killer. I watch buildings whizz past, grateful for the silence that's engulfed us. There'll be no opportunity for me and James to discuss it tonight. That image will stay with me until the early hours.

Promise me you'll do it, Margaret.

I'm so sorry, Barbara. I'd do whatever you wanted, if only I could remember what it was.

CHAPTER 11

The bus judders along Manchester Road, bumping in and out of potholes. I grip the seat in front, the blue and yellow fabric coarse against my skin. No, the council still haven't got round to fixing this road, Albert. I don't know where all that Council Tax goes. And I don't think this bus has any suspension. My hip and back will be as ruined as Hadrian's Wall by the end of this journey.

The Sunday service isn't great; we had to wait a while. The other passengers are pensioners or teenagers too, at either end of the age spectrum, travelling for free or at a reduced rate. A toxic mix of diesel fumes, body odour and the rubbish scattered on the floor, on top of all this jolting, is making me a little nauseous. Using my coat sleeve, I clear the condensation fogging the window to focus on the view and take my mind off of it. James had the window seat on the first bus we caught and then we swapped over for this one. He's been quiet since an initial burst of conversation, like a firework that's fizzled out. Perhaps he shares my apprehension about how this is going to go. It's not far now.

We turn a corner and I have to cling on. The bus straightens up and finds a smooth strip of asphalt. An old building lures my eye. It's that pub again, the Crown and Anchor. Its honey-coloured stones are chipped and weathered into a dull brown. A large 'for sale' sign juts from one wall, planks of plywood are nailed firmly across the front door and metal sheets cover the windows, acting as blindfolds to a condemned man. The once cosy, hospitable place for people to gather and make merry now has the air of an old prison. Something about it causes my stomach to tighten. I almost reach across to press the little red button to make the bus screech to a halt so that I can step off and stare. Then we've trundled past and I'm left looking back until it recedes into the distance.

James sees my face. 'Takes forever don't it? Wish I could drive.'

I pat his knee, which pokes through a frayed tear in his black jeans. 'You've a few years yet before you can get behind a wheel.'

I can't help but think of him as a toddler in his red toy car, his little legs pushing it along, his palm blasting excited honks of the horn. A mixture of pride and sadness swathes me at how he's grown and is ready to go through the rites of passage into the real world. Nothing stays the same.

'I can apply for my provisional driving licence when I'm fifteen and nine months. I looked it up.' Wanderlust glints in James's eye. 'I'd have to wait until I'm seventeen for lessons but Dad says he'll teach me. He doesn't want to fork out for an instructor.'

My nose scrunches. 'I think you're better off with a professional. I'll book your first lessons for your seventeenth birthday.' I'd better make a note on the kitchen calendar, Albert, now that I've promised.

The bus meanders around a few more corners, a couple of roundabouts and then into a housing estate.

James leans across. 'Think this is our stop.'

Thank goodness he's alert. I don't know this area. I'd have gone straight past.

James is on his feet in no time. It takes me a little longer to grab my stick, bottom-shuffle my way across the seat, then haul myself upright using the metal frame for balance. James holds my stick and takes my arm as I stand up, guiding me along then down the steps onto the pavement. We say 'thank you' and 'cheerio' to the driver, who's patiently waiting in his starched white shirt and navy tie, the engine trembling as if it's anxious to be on its way.

We walk slowly; after sitting for so long it takes a while for my joints to ease into movement. James spots a street sign. 'This is where she lives.'

It's a humble road of red-brick terraced houses that front the pavement. James looks for the numbers as we pass each home, the white-framed windows giving a glimpse into the lives of others.

'Number twenty-seven, this one.' James halts outside a brown door as I catch up. He sniffs. 'Looks a bit rough round here.'

'Don't be judgemental, James.' I reach his side. 'Lives shouldn't by valued by material things.'

'Just thinking about our investigation,' he whispers. 'She might be in need of cash.'

I reach out to hold a brass door knocker shaped like the face of a lion. I glance across and notice the edge of a dark mane on James's shoulder, peeking above his jumper. What's the appeal?

My hand hovers. I straighten my coat and smooth my skirt with my free hand. 'Ready?'

James brushes back his hair, then nods. I give the knocker a few short raps. Within seconds a key clinks followed by the rattle of a chain being let loose. The door swings open.

I could count on one hand the number of times I've met Lisa over the decades. At a few parties when Barbara had a significant birthday and when we've bumped into each other when she's paid Barbara a visit. It's been a while. I've seen her at different stages of her life and marvelled at the change: the altering of features that you don't appreciate when you see someone every day, though the overall structure's still there, still familiar. So, it's not instant recognition, but neither is she a stranger.

Lisa smiles, a tight-lipped gesture. 'Come in.' She beckons us inside. We step straight into the lounge.

'Take a seat.' Lisa waves her hand towards a plain, three-seater sofa. A furry, beige rug and a glass-topped coffee table are between it and a comfortable-looking armchair. The smell of freshly baked bread wafts pleasantly. 'Can I get you a brew?'

I beam. 'A cup of tea would be lovely.'

James hoists an arm. 'Can I grab a Coke?'

'We're not in a café, James,' I scold.

'It's OK. I've a bottle in the fridge.'

Lisa disappears into the kitchen. I look around. A clean and tidy place, she certainly takes after Barbara in that respect. I notice a carved wooden sign on one wall: *home is where the heart is*. Cards adorn the windowsill and the mantelpiece; a collection of condolences. A vase of flowers brightens the room.

Lisa returns with a tray bearing two mugs, a glass of cola and a plate of home-made biscuits. She places it on the coffee table and we help ourselves to our drinks. She's wearing a long, floral dress, a bit summery for this time of year. It flows from neck to toe, unrevealing. Buttoned-up sleeves. Looks the sort of woman whose hands you expect to be covered in flour. She's put on weight since I last saw her. Her mousy hair is the same wave of curls, but she has a fringe now that covers her forehead. I search for a glimmer of Barbara in her. Maybe in the shape of her button nose or her lips? No, it's in the eyes, I think, the brown, hooded eyes.

Lisa sinks into the armchair. 'So, you're James. You were knee-high last time I saw you.'

James blushes, running a hand the full length of his hair.

'I'm so sorry for your loss,' I say. 'Your aunty was a dear friend.'

'She was always supportive, a good listener.' Lisa stares at the cards and their heavenly images. 'Like a mother to me, really.' Her eyes glaze with a watery grief, dark pools beneath them. 'And I was very protective of her.'

The sorrow seems genuine. I squirm. These suspicions, these questions that saddle us. How could she have done anything to her beloved aunt? Are we to accuse every grieving person who knew Barbara?

'When did you last see Barbara?' His eyes fixed on Lisa, James glugs his fizzy drink.

I wince, but if Lisa is offended, she doesn't show it. 'I remember it well. A few weeks before she passed away.' She turns to me. 'You just never know do you ... that it'll be ...' Silence swallows the end of her sentence. 'I was looking forward to her coming over that night.'

'You didn't meet regularly?' James's eyes flit, taking in everything in the room.

'We spoke on the phone a lot but didn't meet that often, just when we could.'

'She always come here?'

'I'd normally visit her.'

'So why not this time?'

'I was treating her. I'd cooked a lovely meal. And baked a cake.'

'Shame.' James's gaze switches back to Lisa. 'Was it her birthday or something?'

'No.'

'But you decided to make it a special occasion?'

Lisa looks again at the cards, seeming to take each one in. 'I was treating her,' she repeats.

'Barbara couldn't drive. Not easy getting here, took two buses. Why didn't you just go to hers like normal?'

Lisa holds her cup to her lips. 'She sometimes fancied a change of scene.'

'Seems strange to let an old woman struggle to come to you when you could easily drive to her and take her wherever she wanted to go.'

Lisa takes a long sip. 'I was originally going to visit, but my car had been playing up as well.'

'Oh. Had it.'

'It just seemed simpler all round.'

James leans forward. I think he's enjoying this a bit too much. 'What time was she due?'

'Around five o'clock.'

'Five p.m.? She hadn't even left the house then and it took us, what, over an hour to get here. She wasn't . . . it didn't happen until after then.'

A discernible grimace troubles Lisa's features. 'Sorry, silly me, I got confused. That was our original plan. No, I realised it was going to take me a lot longer than I thought to get everything ready so we changed it to eight.'

I can't really criticise someone for getting confused. And it's easily done when you're being interrogated.

James scowls. 'Bit late for tea.'

'I was putting everything into getting it ready.'

'And you heard nothing from her the day she was ... due?'

'I was so worried when she didn't turn up.' Something strange lurks in Lisa's watery eyes. 'I keep thinking, if only I'd arranged to see her earlier maybe she'd still be with us.'

James straightens. 'You think it could have been prevented?'

I interrupt: 'There are always what-ifs. Things we think we could have done, but it's not in our control, dear.'

I've wondered if there were signs I missed before your heart attack, Albert, or whether I'd done something to cause you stress. But I know that's just the mind leading me astray.

'Do you work?' James takes another slurp.

'I was a teaching assistant at a primary school.' That mournful look returns to Lisa's face. 'Sadly, I lost my job a few months ago, after budget cuts.'

'I'm sorry to hear that,' I say, softly.

'And you're Barbara's only surviving relative?' James ploughs straight back into his questioning.

Those cards draw Lisa's eyes once more, a long, hard stare. 'That I know.'

'So you're her sole heir?' He seems to have inherited his father's lack of tact. And I can see he's been doing his homework on the lingo. Probably on his phone on the way here.

Lisa folds her arms so quickly that I half expect to see flour fly from her fingers. 'I understand Aunty Barbara has left everything to me, apart from some donations to charities.'

'Know how much?'

I cough loudly. I'd give him a kick but I can't quite reach.

Lisa's arms tighten further. 'Aunty Barbara rarely spent money on herself, so she'll have left me a generous sum. Can't say it's not needed. I'm very fortunate. But I'd give it all back in an instant just to have her here.'

Lisa's glower is the temperature of James's drink. I gulp my tea and appreciate its warmth.

'Any news on the funeral arrangements?' I say, to change the subject.

'It'll be at the parish church.' Lisa's arms loosen their loop. 'St Michael's,' she adds.

I know full well which one the parish church is. I wonder whether the clarification is for my benefit, in case I've somehow forgotten, or if I'm just being sensitive.

'I've not been able to fix a date yet, what with the, you know, circumstances, the investigation and everything.'

'A horrible thing to have hanging over you,' I say. 'When you just want to pay your respects and let her rest in peace.'

'I'm trying not to think too much about it. My focus is on giving Aunty Barbara the send-off she deserves.'

'Absolutely.' Though remembering that last conversation with Barbara and helping bring the perpetrator to justice is all I can think about.

'How are you, anyway, Margaret? You seem well. Everything *OK*?'

An emphasis on the last word makes me question if she's

heard something about me. 'I'm fine. Mustn't grumble.' I take a swallow of strong tea and put on my most soothing voice. 'I must ask, was everything all right between you and Barbara?'

'Of course, why wouldn't it be?'

'How was she?' James is quick to step in, then crunches into a biscuit. At least he's catching the crumbs in a cupped palm. 'The last time you spoke,' he adds, through a mouthful.

Lisa opens her mouth, then hesitates. She takes another slow sip. 'I did get the impression something was troubling her.'

I immediately picture Barbara's anxious face. 'Any idea what?'

Lisa bites into a biscuit herself, gives a thoughtful chew. 'Aunty Barbara was a very private lady. She was more interested in helping others than talking about herself. I was hoping to broach it when she visited but of course ...' She pops the rest of the biscuit in her mouth and munches. 'Did she say anything to you, Margaret?'

I feel the glare of a spotlight shift onto me. How much should I share? I take a slurp of tea and glance at James. A subtle shake of his head suggests keeping my cards close to my chest. 'Not that I recall.'

Lisa gives me a peculiar look, as if she's trying to read my mind. 'I know you confided in each other. If something was wrong, I'd have thought you were the first person she'd turn to.'

Promise me you'll do it, Margaret.

That image of Barbara suddenly jolts me with guilt. She absolutely did reach out to me and I've let her down.

'You're her family,' says James. 'Wouldn't she turn to you first?'

Lisa rests back into her chair with a satisfied expression. 'As I said, she was a private lady. And as you said, Margaret, let's leave her to rest in peace. It was probably nothing.'

A silence descends, then Lisa sighs and adds: 'I guess our past and our worries get buried with us.'

James jerks upright. His frown is of someone itching to dig deeper.

Lisa bites her lip, then stares at James with raised eyebrows. 'Do you have any more questions for me?'

James downs his drink, disguises a small burp with the back of his hand, then shakes his head.

'Well let's hope the police's investigation ends soon too.'

I finish my tea. 'We'd better be going. Leave you in peace.'

Lisa shows us to the door. 'I'm glad you called.' She glances at James.

We head silently back to the bus stop. Once we're away from the house, James tugs on my sleeve. 'What you reckon?'

'I think you were a little insensitive with how you phrased your questions.'

'You think I'd have got more from her if I'd said them different?'

'No, I think you have to be mindful of people's feelings and not be as blunt.'

He shrugs. 'You got to crack a few eggs to make something stick.'

'I just don't think she's capable of harming her aunt.'

'Anyone's capable, Gran. She's lost her job, needs the money, and she'll get loads from the inheritance. Who's to say this story about Barbara being due to visit her isn't some kind of alibi and that she actually paid Barbara a visit. Must have been someone

Barbara knew for her to let them in. Lisa knows way more than what she's saying.'

The idea of it all brings back my queasiness. 'But we weren't being honest either. Shouldn't I have mentioned that Barbara shared something with me?'

'Nah, let's keep that to ourselves until we've worked out what it was. I'll find some ways to jog your memory.'

He's able to breeze off any chastisements, any qualms, so easily that I wonder if the young are more robust than I supposed. Perhaps we grow more sensitive, more delicate with age. We reach the bus stop and take refuge in its Perspex shelter, the bright plastic seat providing inadequate comfort for my generous backside. I can't contemplate Lisa hurting her aunt, but maybe James is right. You never know what someone could do. After all, who would have guessed that I'm capable of the things I've done?

CHAPTER 12

I give the knives and forks another polish with a napkin until they sparkle. Sunday's the best day of the week when all the family gather round. I'm glad we got back from Lisa's in time to make a roast dinner, even if it's a bit later than usual. Even Tom and Catherine have made it up from London. It's a fair distance to Manchester, so I don't see our only son and his wife that much. Still, we talk more on the phone than when he lived here.

It's lovely to have everyone together; doesn't happen often. Sunday dinners used to be sacrosanct when I was a girl. I'm using the best cutlery, you know, the silver set in the wooden presentation box we were given as a wedding anniversary gift and only bring out on special occasions. The aroma of roast beef spreading through the house makes my mouth water. I think of the thick slices of succulent meat smothered in rich gravy and it reminds me of being at the heart of the family.

I can still cook a good roast, Albert, something you always praised me for. I loved the delight you'd take in eating what I made for you. Shirley has helped with things today. It doesn't come as easy; I need a bit of help with the preparation and timings.

James is watching me, a frown disturbing his smooth forehead. 'How many you laying the table for, Gran?'

'I can still count, James. Myself, your mum and dad, Tom and Catherine and you if you behave. That makes six of us.'

Neatly folded red napkins rest on shiny white plates sitting on flower-patterned placemats, surrounded by gleaming glasses and cutlery. Good enough for the Queen.

'Uncle Tom and Aunty Cath aren't here.'

Footsteps pound the hallway. Shirley must have overheard. She doesn't get her sharp hearing from you, Albert.

'You know Tom's not coming, Mum.' She scoops up the cutlery. Pushes the placemats around. Rearranges the carefully placed settings. 'That's better.'

They're not even straight. My shoulders tighten. I'm certain I was asking Tom about his job earlier. Very career minded, isn't he. He's done very well for himself, though no matter how much he explains I can never understand exactly what it is he does.

'When was the last time you even saw Tom?' That accusatory look flares in Shirley's eye. I'm about to say this morning but keep my mouth shut. 'Wish you wouldn't say he's here when he's not. You know how annoying it is that he's never around to help.'

That ten-year age difference between Tom and Shirley is quite a gap. My mind drifts to the little mites that we lost in between, when we thought that second child, that sibling, the one to complete our family, would never come. I instantly move my mind to something else.

'At least you didn't lay a place for Uncle Harry, that's something to . . .' James's voice trails off and I see the glare that Shirley shoots him, her lips tight shut. James mutters something and before I have chance to say anything, Shirley's scuttled back to the kitchen.

I try not to think about it, I don't want to create an atmosphere. I focus on repositioning the settings so they're perfect. A deep exhale, then I follow Shirley so we can get the food out. Matthew's stirring the gravy in a lacklustre fashion. I snatch the wooden spoon from him and show him how it's done. He whinnies like a carthorse. He's as wet and lumpy as this gravy. I know you've always argued that he's a good man. Steady, reliable and willing to provide for his family. I've just always felt that Shirley could have done better.

'Everything's ready.' Shirley dashes between pots, pans and plates. 'Let's dish up.'

'I'll carry things to the table,' says Matthew, lumbering around. I fear that's all he's good for.

The joint of meat, roast potatoes, Yorkshire puddings and veg – carrots, cabbage, peas and cherry tomatoes – are scooped from the oven and escorted into the dining room. The gravy's now perfectly thick and smooth. I decant it from pan to jug and turn off the oven and hob. Lasted us well this oven, nigh on two decades. British made. There's more gravy than will fit in the small serving jug so I leave the pan on a low heat to keep the surplus warm for when we need it and take the jug through – they don't want their food getting cold while they wait for the gravy.

They're already sat around the dining table. Matthew levers the cork out of a bottle of wine with a pop.

'Don't you dare spill that on the carpet,' I warn. 'You'll never get red wine out.'

He pulls a face. The table's piled high with food, steam rising from the dishes, misting the window. I don't know what happened to Tom and Catherine. It's a shame they're missing this. I take my seat.

'Tuck in,' says James, attacking the food like a spitfire. Spoons and forks clatter. Peas fly everywhere and tomatoes tumble onto the tablecloth.

'How's school?' I ask.

James mumbles a vague response between mouthfuls.

'He needs to knuckle down for his GCSEs,' Shirley says.

'What are you going to do when you leave school?'

'If he doesn't make it as a footballer or rock star,' says Matthew. His long, thin arms reach across to scoop a crisp roast potato from a bowl. I notice he's developing a bit of a paunch.

'Dunno. Maybe police or army.'

'Anything where he can tackle the bad guys,' chuckles Matthew.

'You'll have to buck up your ideas to get the required results,' says Shirley. James scowls and gets a sharp reprimand.

'Aren't any problems at school are there, James?' I ask. 'I hear a lot about schools being rife with bullies.'

'Everything's fine, Gran.' He sinks a little in his seat.

'Any trouble you come straight to me. I'll sort them.'

'OK, Gran.' He slumps further until I'm worried he might slink straight under the table.

If there's one thing I can't stand, Albert, it's bullies. Don't worry, I'll help the lad. A good tongue lashing is as effective as any physical threat.

James pulls his mobile contraption out of his pocket. Starts fiddling with it.

'You gotta get one, Gran. I can get everything on here.' He shows me the little screen, his fingers flicking over it. Record album covers whizz past, photographs pop up then disappear and pages of words grow large then small with a pinch of his thumb and finger.

'It's like a computer.'

'Exactly, Gran. Anything on our computer I can get on here.'

It's so tiny, how do they fit it all inside? And so fast. How frustratingly slow were computers when we used them, Albert?

'I remember the first ever computer, James, back in 1944.'

Colossus was aptly named, wasn't it, Albert? Hidden away in a dark and dusty place, the stench of oil and grease, a metallic taste in the air, and all that clanging and whirring from the tubes and cogs. The assault on the senses felt as if you were in a train station. Then you saw it, this futuristic machine, fair took my breath away, so out of place amid the creaking wood and flagstone floor. Took up an entire wall. I was both frightened and dazzled.

'It was so clever and powerful.'

The hairs on my arms tingle. I look down at all the food on my plate. Colossus was like some hungry, Ancient Greek monster that we had to constantly feed our work into for it to digest and make meaningful. It'll be a heap of rusting metal now. As would the Bombe, those big electromechanical devices that speeded up important work.

'If you saw it today, you'd think it a piece of junk.'

James's wide eyes are fixed on me. 'Did you really use the first ever computer, Gran?'

'She's pulling your leg,' says Matthew. 'The first computer was an Amstrad, I think.'

He knows nothing. I glare at him but delve no further.

'Wish my mind was like a computer. Then I could retrieve that conversation with Barbara within seconds.'

Shirley groans.

Matthew's face curdles. 'Not that again. You've got to get over it.'

'You don't know how frustrating it is, not being able to recall something so important.'

'It won't be important. You probably imagined it.' Matthew slices through a piece of tender beef. 'You've got to stop obsessing about it, Margaret. Let it go.'

I'm about to snap back when I see the alarmed look on James's face. I chew some cabbage instead.

James goes back to prodding his mobile, hunched over it like that fellow from Notre Dame. Isn't it amazing how quickly things advance, that such a small contraption can now outpower the awesome Colossus.

'James, how many times? Not at the dinner table.' Shirley flails a hand. 'Put it away.'

'Just wanted to show Gran how I can get Twitter and Facebook to stay in touch with mates.' He reluctantly returns the device to his pocket.

'Can't you just ring them?'

'Nah. I read their updates and tweets. No matter where they are they can post stuff.'

A telephone that you don't call people on to find out how they are! I'd much prefer a conversation, though these messages sound intriguing. 'You can read them as soon as they're sent?'

'Instantly.'

'Are they secure and private?'

'You can direct message or use privacy settings. It's a community, Gran, you're always in touch.'

'I already have a community around me. I've lived here sixty years. I know everyone on this street and some who've lived here all their lives. We all keep an eye out for each other and help whoever's in need.' I chew on a tough bit of beef. 'I do wonder if you young people aren't too remote. There's not the same neighbourliness any more. No sharing a brew over the garden fence. No real sense of community. Perhaps you're too plugged into your gadgets finding out what people are up to on the other side of the globe and not connected to what's immediately around you.'

James shakes his head, hair swaying. 'The world's much more connected now. Everyone's in reach. Anyone can be your friend.'

'But here, we're always close by. Your friends are miles away.' I stretch my arms to signify the vast distance. 'Not much good if you're in trouble.'

James's mouth opens and closes again. Satisfaction warms me. I might be long in the tooth but I can still win a debate. I stick my tongue out at James and he does the same. We laugh. I'd better stop yakking and finish my dinner before it gets cold. I'm parched as well. Good job, I'd already brewed a fresh pot of tea, kept hot by our knitted tea cosy. I reach over to lift it. It's quite heavy. I'm a bit unsteady as I begin to pour some in my mug.

Matthew stifles a giggle. Not sure what's amusing him. Shirley looks aghast.

'Mum, stop. You're pouring tea into the sugar bowl.'

I look down. The tea's soaking into a full bowl of sugar

lumps, muddying their glistening whiteness. Did one of them switch my mug as a joke?

'Want tea with your sugar, Margaret?' Matthew quips.

'It's not funny.' All the tension returns to my shoulders and my cheeks burn hotter than the tea. The sugar crumbles like a sandcastle hit by a brown tide.

Matthew's laughter rings in my ears.

'Leave it, Dad, you don't have to make fun of her.' James touches my arm. 'No harm done, Gran.'

A forceful knock rattles the front door.

'Come in,' I shout, welcoming any distraction.

Mr Braithwaite enters the room. 'Sorry to interrupt. Didn't realise you were eating.'

'No need to apologise.' Shirley smiles brightly as she uses her napkin to mop up tea spilling over the bowl's edge.

'Saw your car outside. Just returning that drill you lent me, Matthew.' Mr Braithwaite's nose twitches like a startled rabbit. His brow furrows. 'Can anyone smell gas?'

Shirley and Matthew look at each other with horror flooding their faces. They scramble from table to kitchen as if it's a race. A foul odour clings to the back of my throat. I follow them.

'Mum,' shouts Shirley, turning the hob off. 'You left the gas on.'

She opens the kitchen window. Starts flapping around with a tea towel. The stench is quite overpowering.

'I didn't put it on.' I cough and splutter as I speak.

'If someone had flicked a switch you could have blown the kitchen up.'

Such a drama queen.

'Thank goodness you called round, Steve.' Shirley wafts the

tea towel like she's fanning a fire. 'Could have been a disaster if you hadn't shown up.'

Matthew flaps around with a hand towel. He's not making much difference.

'Don't worry, it'll soon disperse.' Mr Braithwaite's the only calm one, his hands nestled in his pockets. 'Better get back to your meal before your dinner's ruined.'

'What are we going to do with you, Mum?'

'It wasn't me.' I can't do anything right today. I don't know if it's the fumes or the distress but I feel light-headed.

'Well, no one else was in here.' The tea towel cracks as she whips, like a head teacher with a cane. 'I can't relax knowing you're here on your own doing things like this.'

'Oh, do stop flapping around.' I grab the towel off Matthew and fling it onto the granite worktop.

'I'm serious, Mum.' Shirley does go on. 'You shouldn't be living on your own any more.'

'I can always call round any time to check on your mother and make sure she's all right,' says Mr Braithwaite. 'It's no bother.'

'That's very kind of you, Steve.' She's all sweetness and light with him. 'But you can't be here twenty-four seven.'

I do wish they wouldn't talk about me while I'm stood in front of them. It makes me feel like a ghost.

James strolls in. Gravy's splodged around his mouth so at least someone's enjoyed finishing their dinner. 'What's up?'

'Your gran left the gas on.' The tea towel's now hanging limp in Shirley's hand. 'Could have blown us sky high.'

James shrugs. 'Sure she didn't mean to.' He bites into a Yorkshire pudding that I hadn't noticed was in his hand. He eats whatever he wants and never puts on an ounce. Where does it go? He moves a lot less than his mother and she puts on a stone just looking at a cupcake.

'James, we eat at the table. You'll get crumbs everywhere.' Good. She's found someone else to pick on. 'I know it wasn't done on purpose but it's dangerous.' No, she's back at me. 'I'm making that doctor's appointment first thing tomorrow.'

Mr Braithwaite makes his excuses to leave and we shuffle back into the dining room. The food's cold now, the air even colder. The grandfather clock tick-tocks the silence, a brief scrape of knives and forks on plates. A rotten end to the week. I pick up my plate shakily and trudge into the kitchen where a toxic whiff lingers. James follows.

'Cheer up, Gran. We've got more important things to focus on.'

I'm Colossus: a once admired and clever machine that's now a useless, decrepit relic.

I look into James's eyes. 'You believe me about having had that conversation with Barbara?'

'Course.' Trust shines in them, Albert, the same as when I looked into your eyes and saw someone to confide in, someone who'd always support me.

'We've got to work out who did it, Gran.' And a glimmer of adventure. 'The sooner the better.'

On that point I agree with him. Wholeheartedly.

CHAPTER 13

I close the curtains and shuffle towards the bed. What a day! I'm fair worn out, what with visiting Lisa, the Sunday dinner and all that kerfuffle, and with these suspects spinning through my head like the reels on a one-armed bandit. And while the meal was delicious, all that stodge is weighing me down, it was an effort just to get up the stairs. After a tot of whisky in my hot milk, my eyelids are heavy. I peel back the duvet. It won't take long for sleep to wash over me and things will be clearer in the morning.

The house seems a different beast at night, Albert, particularly with you not here. Every shadow is more sinister, every sound amplified. I could relax in your presence. Now I go to bed as quickly as possible. See, what was that noise there? Sounded like a clink of metal downstairs. I listen intently. All's quiet now, it must have been nothing.

You get used to the noises a house makes over the years: water whirling in the boiler, pipes clanging, the odd creak of a floorboard. Alone in the silence, they start to sound monstrous. Often, I leave the television on to drown them out and make it feel as if I have company.

I reach to turn off the light. That noise again halts my arm mid-air. This time it's discernible: metal scraping against metal, a whoosh of air, wood dragging against carpet. I think someone's opened our front door. I swallow and tiptoe to the bedroom door, push it quietly ajar and listen again.

Silence.

Then the distinctive squeak our unoiled front door handle makes as it turns. The click of the door closing.

I step onto the landing.

Wait.

Nothing.

Perhaps my imagination is getting the better of me, my exhausted brain getting carried away. Just go to bed, Margaret.

The soft tread of shoes on wooden floorboards, another door opening, something being moved.

I'm frozen to the spot. I picture Barbara's desperate struggle: arms flailing, helpless hands trying to push her assailant away, her face warped by fear. She's lying alone on the kitchen floor, her life ebbing away.

What should I do, Albert? Stay quiet and hope they leave or make my presence known and hope they flee? What are they after?

A reverberating thud makes me jump. Someone mumbles. Have they dropped something or knocked something over? My heart thumps. If only you were here, Albert, you'd deal with them. I crumple the middle of my nightdress into a ball. Pull yourself together, Margaret. Be brave. You can't just stand here. You must face them.

I lean over the banister. 'Who's there?'

No reply.

'I know you're downstairs. I'm calling the police.'

The only telephone is in the hallway.

Silence hangs in the air. I click the landing light on, wishing you still did have your shotgun. Two slow steps. I reach the top of the stairs.

More noise but with the blood pounding in my ears I can't tell what it is. I peer down into a well of darkness. A deep breath. A quick prayer. I steel my legs.

I stop after every step of the staircase to listen keenly. Reaching a gloomy hallway, I scrabble for the light.

Brightness erupts. I twist around. The hallway's empty.

I step into the lounge and click the light switch. No one's there.

Air streams from my lungs and my hands are shaking. I scan the room to make sure no one's lurking in the shadows. Our coffee table is lying on its side like a stricken animal. Feeling cold air on the back of my neck, I spin around. No one's behind me. All this twisting and turning has made me dizzy. Stooping, hands resting on my thighs, I take deep breaths.

What if it's him? I instinctively look over to the bureau. It seems untouched but there's only one way to know. It's as if the world has stopped spinning: time has slowed, everything's weightless. Concentrating hard so as not to fumble, I take the key from its hiding place and struggle through the density of matter to unlock and open up the bureau. The wooden box is still there, secreted like a child playing hide and seek. I lift the lid. Everything seems to be in place. I rummage through until I find the most precious thing in it. The world begins to turn again, the grandfather clock ticking every solid second. I put everything back where it belongs, including the coffee table, then pull myself upright. What if someone's still in the house? What if they're in the kitchen?

The telephone's just yards away. I rush to it, grab the receiver and stab in familiar numbers. I have to redial after getting them wrong in my haste. An urgent ringing tone. I glance around. The hallway darkens towards the shrouded kitchen. Still ringing. Come on. Pick up. Please.

'Hello.' The voice groggy, hesitant.

'Shirley?' I whisper.

'Mum, is that you?'

'Shirley.' I raise my voice one notch.

'Mum, what is it? What's wrong? What time is it?' A pause. 'It's late, are you OK?'

'Someone's in the house,' I hiss, as loud as I dare.

'Someone's broken in?' An alertness to her tone now, a sharpness.

'I heard something,' I grip the receiver tightly, holding it close to my lips. 'Downstairs.'

'But you've not seen anyone?'

'I . . . No. But . . . Someone's been in here.'

A strained silence followed by a cough. No urgency.

'Is there any sign of anyone?' Her voice is clear and cold.

'I think they're still here, Shirley.'

'But you don't know anyone's actually there?'

'I heard someone.'

A long sigh. 'It might have been a dream, Mum.'

'I hadn't even got into bed.'

'Then it might just have been a noise, someone outside or the wind or something. Go to bed and everything will be all right in the morning.'

Why does that girl never listen to me? 'I heard someone open the front door.'

'Is it locked?'

'I don't know, it's closed.'

'Try turning the handle.' Exasperation infuses her voice. But not concern. I look at the front door. What if someone's waiting on the other side? 'Just try opening it. I'll stay on the line.'

I place the receiver on the table and edge towards the door. I gently push the handle down, the door sliding ajar with a metallic squeal. I shut it quickly and return to the telephone.

'It's not locked, Shirley. Anyone could have been in.'

'Sure you remembered to lock it?'

'I always check before I go to bed.' I fear I'll have to be brutally murdered too, before she takes me seriously.

'You might have forgotten.'

'Shirley, I'm certain I locked the door and the table in the lounge has been knocked over. Someone's been inside.'

I glare into the black mouth of the kitchen.

'Settle down, Mum. Don't work yourself up. Look, I'll give Steve a call and get him to check on you.'

'Who?'

'Mr Braithwaite. He's only next door.'

I don't want *him* here, I want her. 'Can't you come round?'

'It'll take me a while and he can be over in a second. He won't mind.'

I swallow. 'I need you.'

I can hear the intake of breath down the line. 'I'll come round as well but if someone's really there then you need Steve straight away.'

The line goes dead, an irritating buzz. I'm left staring at the front door, looping the receiver's coil around my forefinger. I eventually place the receiver on the handset in case she calls back.

I stand in the hallway, uncertain as to what to do, for what feels like an age.

A rap of knuckles on the door startles me. Before I can say anything, it opens and Mr Braithwaite steps inside, shrugging off the cold night air that's following him.

'You all right, Mrs Winterbottom?'

'I'm fine, thank you.'

His face is slightly flushed but I don't detect any annoyance at being disturbed. He's dressed casually: blue jeans and navy jumper, slip-on shoes.

'Your daughter phoned and said you were worried there'd been an intruder.' He studies me.

'I heard someone downstairs.' A quiver remains in my voice.

'I'll take a look around.'

I don't want strangers snooping around my house but what choice do I have?

Mr Braithwaite enters the lounge.

'I've checked in there.'

He looks anyway, inspecting behind the sofa and curtains. Suddenly, it all feels so silly, like a ghost hunt.

I trudge behind him into the dining room, then the kitchen. As light illuminates each room it becomes increasingly obvious that the house is empty. He has a good search anyway, even trying the back door.

'This one's locked. No bolt or anything to secure it further?'

I didn't know I'd hired a security consultant. 'It's just one lock and key.'

Mr Braithwaite walks past me, heading for the stairs.

'No one's been up there so no need to go up.'

He hesitates, one hand on the balustrade, one foot on the bottom step. 'Are you sure?'

'Quite certain.'

My cheeks begin to burn. Pottering around the house in my nightie with a virtual stranger looking for the bogeyman. It's humiliating.

Mr Braithwaite turns around. 'No one else is here then. Sure you didn't imagine it?'

He sounds so superior. Could I have? The noises were so real and the door was unlocked. I don't answer. Just as I think he's going, he heads into the lounge instead and sits down on the sofa.

'I'll wait with you until your daughter arrives.'

'I don't want to take up any more of your time.'

'It's no problem.' He smiles like a psychiatrist to an anxious patient. It shouldn't take Shirley this long. With no traffic it should be minutes.

I sit down in our chair, Albert, and stroke the soft armrests, trying to find your scent in the cold air. The silence is heavy. The grandfather clock chimes, making me jump, but Mr Braithwaite doesn't flinch. What's taking Shirley so long?

I hear a car pull up, then the slam of a door and hurried footsteps. Shirley bustles inside. 'Everything OK?'

Without the aid of make-up she looks even more drawn than usual.

'There's no one here.' Mr Braithwaite stands up. 'Your mother's perfectly safe.'

Under the harsh spotlight the fear feels foolish.

Shirley sees him out, full of platitudes. I stay seated, ruminating.

Shirley's biting her bottom lip when she returns. 'You must have just heard something and forgotten to lock the door.'

'Someone was here.' I stare at the ceiling. That damn spider's still there, crouching in the corner. 'How did they get the door open?'

Shirley rakes a hand through her hair, while looking at me as if I'm attention-seeking. 'With everything that's gone on I suppose it was best to check.'

I spot a coaster on the floor that had been on the table. 'See.' I bend down to pick it up. 'That wasn't there when I went to bed.'

'Let me get that, Mum.' She reaches out.

'I can manage perfectly well, Shirley, I'm not an invalid.' I place it on the table.

'Just trying to help.' Weariness cramps her voice. 'It's not easy when I have so much to do.'

'I'd rather you hadn't come round if it was such an inconvenience.'

'I'm just tired.' She sinks into the sofa, looking like she might fall straight asleep. 'I really don't need this right now.'

Shirley has been very uptight this last year. She's always complaining about how difficult it is bringing up a child, being a housewife and holding down a job, on top of keeping up with family and friends. I don't know about all that. We never had a washing machine, dishwasher, vacuum cleaner, steam iron, fancy oven or a computer, but all the time-consuming and tiring chores still got done. Heaven knows why she has to work if her husband has a decent, full-time job. And James can look after himself if she'd let him. She says that to pay the mortgage and bills you need two wages coming in. We got by, though, didn't we? Maybe we didn't expect as much as they do now. We didn't need fancy contraptions and trips abroad. Shirley was complaining the other day that they'll have to have a staycation this year. In our day, a week in Bournemouth was called a holiday. We were satisfied with what we had and just got on with it. All this modern technology just brings its own problems of having to work out how to use things and repair them when they inevitably go wrong.

'You need to relax more, Shirley.'

She gives me a withering look. 'You don't have umpteen things to stress about, Mum.'

I get up and head for the stairs. I'll leave her to lock the door.

'I'll see you in the morning,' she adds.

'If I'm still alive then.'

'Well, if you're not make sure you give us a call to let us know.'

She has a lovely sense of humour, our daughter.

She thinks I have no worries, but I brought her into this world, paved the way for her family, and fret about every aspect of their lives: their health, finances, employment, relationships.

And now I have to try and get to sleep knowing, *knowing*, that an intruder got into my house.

CHAPTER 14

Our kitchen's duvet-cosy. I close my eyes as the gramophone's warm crackle eases me into a song. A gentle sway of orchestral music builds until Perry Como's voice emerges, as relaxed and effortless as flowers unfurling in spring sunshine.

You put your arm around my waist, Albert, hold my left hand in your right hand, then pull me in, clasp me close. The voice soft, mesmerising. The song a slow-burn favourite. The way we used to dance returning.

A noise from outside tries to disturb us. We cling to each other, struggling to stay in the moment.

Another voice intrudes, breaking through like a stone smashing glass.

'Mum, what you doing shuffling around the kitchen?'

I open my eyes. The music has gone and there's nothing in my arms.

'You in la-la land again?' Suspicion blends with bemusement in Shirley's tone. She looks at me as if I'm from another planet and then fusses with a packet and pan. She puts porridge on the hob, then clicks on the kettle. 'I'll get your breakfast.'

'I'm doing no harm,' I mutter, my throat bone dry.

The kettle reaches its crescendo with a shuddering hiss. I stutter to the sink, which is full of dirty pots, the smell of yesterday's stale leftovers lingering. Through the clouded window, I can make out the garden's tangled mass of frosted weeds and brambles.

'Didn't know you were here.' I lean against the worktop.

'I did knock.' Shirley stands beside me, holds my hand as if it's fractured. 'You're not even dressed, Mum.' She puts a hot hand against my forehead. 'You feeling OK?'

She doesn't wait for an answer, instead heading off down the hall, then twiddling with the thermostat. She's back within seconds.

'It's stifling in here.' Shirley opens a window, letting in a blast of cold air. 'You don't need the heating on full whack.'

I gaze outside, remembering when the garden was beautifully kept with vivid colours dancing.

The tinkling of a waterfall. A soft splash. Clinking.

Shirley hands me my tea in a Camilla mug; it's not my favourite. I blow, rippling the surface, then take a steady sip, the hot liquid soothing my throat. A chiffchaff lands on the dormant grass and begins its song of spring, even though winter's glaze hasn't left. The mug warms my hands into movement.

One-two-three. Fall and rise.

'Is James here?'

'He's at school, Mum. It's a Monday.'

'Oh.'

Shirley flits around the kitchen like a bluebottle. She moves an empty glass onto the draining board, places a packet of tea in a cupboard, returns a milk bottle to the fridge, then stirs the porridge, which huffs and puffs.

'The doctor's appointment.' Shirley gives the pan a final swirl, then gloops its contents into a large bowl. 'Just wanted to make sure you were up and ready.'

She plops in a silver spoon and places the bowl on the worktop next to me. I put the mug down next to it, Camilla's glum face staring back.

'I'll be back in a couple of hours to pick you up.' Shirley gives my papery cheek a dry peck. 'Get dressed once you've had your breakfast so we're not late.'

Her voice trails off as she vanishes down the hallway. I shut the window then follow her. I find her in the lounge, opening curtains, plumping cushions, rearranging newspapers into neat piles.

She fixes me with a stern look. 'The doctor. It's important. Remember?' She nods slowly until I mimic her. Now she's in the hall again. 'See you shortly.' Then she's gone.

I sink into our armchair, Albert, listening to the grandfather clock's metronomic tick. I'm not hungry. I wonder whether I'm supposed to lock the door behind her or just leave it for her return? I suppose I'm not allowed out now and I'm not allowed to let people in who I don't know. I'm a prisoner in my own home. There'll be nothing on the television at this time, just people sitting on sofas chatting about God knows what or restoring houses or flogging antiques. Books are becoming more of a struggle than a delight and the crossword puzzle's little white boxes remain frustratingly blank. How funny that now I finally have more time than ever I've nothing meaningful with which to fill it.

That spider's still there, in the corner where wall meets ceiling, its web complete. I swear it's grown fatter in the last few days. I sit and watch as it patiently waits on the edge of its creation for a strand's tremor. It's quite unnerving, but what am I to do about it?

The telephone rings.

I haul myself up and plod over to the hallway, feeling the size of an elephant, every movement a huge effort. I lift the handset. 'Hello.'

'It's me.' The voice is quiet, muffled. I can barely hear it.

'You'll have to speak up.'

'I can't talk too loud.' A familiarity in the hushed tone that I can't quite place. I think of that man in the street, the one I saw talking to Irene. My stomach tenses. Is it *him*? It can't be.

'You still there?' he asks.

The receiver feels ice cold. He knows where I live, that we never moved from this house. 'You're still alive,' I say.

'What?' Wait, the voice is young. 'It's me, Gran.'

'Oh, thank goodness! James!' Air streams from my lungs, my shoulders loosening into a slump. 'I thought you were—'

'Never mind, Gran. I'm at school so I can't be loud.'

'They let you have phones in the classroom?' So much has changed since our day.

'Nah, it's break. Mum's not there is she?'

'You've just missed her.'

'Good. You remembered anything else about that conversation with Barbara?'

'No.' I feel as useful as a blank piece of paper with no pen.

'I was just chatting to a teacher who said sometimes things come back to you when you're not thinking about them, and doing other stuff.' I don't have anything else *to* think about. 'So, maybe, like, do something to distract yourself.'

I guess I could put the television on and listen to the inanities, or try another crossword, but I'm not sure that would help. 'Have you any suggestions?'

'Dunno. Maybe go for a walk, supposed to be good, ain't it? Fresh air and exercise and all that. People work things out after a walk.' James's voice loses a couple of notches in volume. 'Someone's coming over, soz, gotta go.'

The dull buzz of a flatline. I put the telephone down and take a minute to steady my breathing after that initial shock. These days, it takes me a while to work out who's on the other end of the line. I much prefer talking face-to-face so I can see who people are and read their body language. The telephone used to be the world's best invention to me, as I'm sure you'd acknowledge, Albert! How I worshiped Alexander Graham Bell! I could chat for hours catching up with friends while you'd point at your watch and grumble about the cost. Now, recognising voices has become harder than faces. Sometimes I have to bluff my way through the conversation for a few minutes until it dawns on me who it is.

A walk might be nice. I open the door. It feels warmer now, blueness returning to the sky, the bitter wind gone. I can hear laughter from somewhere up the road that makes me feel lighter, more mobile. How tempting, to fly the coop and head off on one of our walks in the sunshine. I step outside. I could go anywhere I want, I'm free to roam and blow those cobwebs away and then everything will come back to me.

I'm no further than the driveway when I see Irene staring at Barbara's house. She turns, her mouth a tight zero, her eyes blinking at the sight of me. She strides over.

'Is everything OK, Margaret?' Irene looks me up and down. 'Only, you're not really dressed for the outdoors.'

I glance down at the thin cotton of my white nightdress with the sinking sensation of a balloon being tethered. 'I just needed some fresh air.'

Irene accepts my answer with a broad-shouldered shrug. She sidles closer. 'That row,' she whispers, 'between Barbara and her niece.'

I nod my head with the solemnity of the co-conspirator. I feel naked and foolish, but I crave the company, the distraction, the chance to find out more.

'It was over money.' A jet stream rattles from Irene's lips. 'I should have known, Lisa was always pestering Barbara for cash. What was it Barbara once told me?' Irene stares at the blue yonder. 'Ah, yes, it was how Lisa's always needing something, but Barbara just wanted her to be able to stand on her own two feet. You know, Barbara even said that sometimes she felt that Lisa was only staying in touch to use her as a charity and that she'd often had to be firm and say no.'

Those criticisms from Barbara that I mentioned, Albert. I do recollect disgruntlement over money, but I never took it seriously. I stay quiet and let Irene vent.

'Mind you, maybe I'm the last person who should be slating the financial decisions of others.' For a moment, I think that Irene is about to share something personal with me, but she shakes her head and adds: 'Apparently, Barbara was so annoyed this time that she said Lisa wouldn't be getting a single penny more from her.'

It doesn't sound like Barbara to be so curt and final. Another row bothers me. 'Is there nothing more you know about Jean and Barbara? You must have heard something.'

Irene consults the sky again. 'There was some big fall out

between them, but I hate to admit I don't know the cause. Barbara's marriage was always troubled but Jean did something to cause a bigger issue that resulted in all those squabbles. I never did find out the full story. It was decades ago, at the start of the seventies. It's old news, water under the bridge.' She looks behind her, at Jean's house. 'Whatever that woman did is hidden deep inside her.'

The far-off trill of my telephone disturbs the background. Coldness seeps through my nightie, sending me into a shiver. 'I'd better get in. I didn't mean to be out so long.'

Irene watches me with a hawk's gaze as I stumble back inside. I swing the door closed and grab the receiver before it rings off.

'Margaret?' A female voice. 'It's Lisa . . . Lisa Wardle.'

Speak of the devil! Today is proving busier than I thought. For the briefest of seconds, I want the investigation to go on forever. 'How are you, dear?'

'Fine. Look, about my aunt. Yesterday. I just wanted to say, it was a silly mistake, the timings, I wasn't expecting all those questions and—'

'That's fine, dear. Don't worry yourself.' I can hear James's voice in my head. *Don't just let her off the hook, ask her more questions.* 'Though there did seem quite a difference in the timings.'

'It was just preparing all that food, rushing round at the end of a busy day. It seemed easier if we made it later.'

'I see.' Something occurs to me. 'Why didn't you call me when Barbara didn't turn up? You've got my number, obviously. I could have checked on her.'

'I didn't want to disturb you late at night, not when you're . . . I thought it was probably nothing.'

'But you didn't call anyone.'

'I didn't want to alarm people. It was only when the police turned up the next morning that I thought the worst.'

'Oh. By the way, did Barbara ever tell you about the difficulties she had with Jean Brampton?'

'Aunty Barbara was always complaining about her. It was just petty rows.'

'And you're sure there were no problems between you and . . .'

An elongated sigh rattles down the telephone. 'All these questions still! And yesterday, it seemed James was digging for something.'

'He's just showing an interest. He's a teenage boy, gets a bit carried away.' We don't want people getting onto us and scuppering our investigation.

'You know Aunty Barbara, she wouldn't want people prying into her affairs.'

I think of Barbara reaching out to me. Something she desperately needed me to know. 'But if something was troubling her.'

Lisa speaks over me: 'She'd hate all this questioning and meddling in her business.'

'She did seem very—'

'Did she say something to you?' An urgency spikes Lisa's tone. 'I thought you said she hadn't told you anything.'

I'm not good at being dishonest. 'She might have mentioned something to me but I can't recall what it was exactly.'

The pause on the other end of the line is so long that for a moment I think she's hung up. 'If you remember anything then you give me a call, Margaret. Do you hear? As soon as anything comes to you, I want to know.'

'Yes, dear.' She's become a bossy little madam. What is it that she's worried I might recall?

'And have a word with your grandson. Don't let him make mischief.'

'James wouldn't cause any harm.'

'Leave it to the authorities, that's all I'm saying.' Well, they're getting nowhere. 'I've got to go. Call me the minute anything comes to you.'

The flatline again, without even a goodbye. I'm left holding the handle, staring at the voiceless piece of plastic. I put it back in its place.

I go back into the lounge and drop into our armchair, drained from that flurry of interaction. These rows that Barbara had, so unlike her, are they connected, Albert? What's at the root of them?

Those few minutes of stimulation are soon replaced by silence and a smog instead of answers.

I'll just sit here and ponder until someone comes to collect me.

CHAPTER 15

You remember Dr Harrington don't you, Albert? Course you do, he was our doctor for thirty years. A lovely man, very patient, with a gentle way about him, always willing to listen and always spot on with his diagnosis. He was very good with my hip problem and very understanding about your arthritis.

Well, he's retired now and this new doctor is the complete opposite.

Shirley and I sit in his small room, all clinical and white, not a drop of welcoming colour. It's so sterile. Guess it has to be with all the germs and bugs hanging around. I've no time for this, I should be focusing on the investigation.

This young doctor sits on the other side of the desk in an ill-fitting, grey suit. He should have a white coat on and he can't be much older than thirty so he won't have any experience. He's just a smart alec. I don't see how any of this is going to help me.

Shirley's already spouted an embarrassing flow of my misdemeanours: leaving the gas on, getting lost, forgetting names. Put all those together, out of context, and it's going to make anyone seem unwell. Mother Teresa would come across as unstable with Shirley's blabbing. She keeps going on about how worried everyone is, but I can't do anything about that, I didn't ask them to worry.

This doctor, he says his name is Dr Jackson, stares at his monitor as if he's about to play a computer game. He claims to be browsing my medical notes. They collect every scrap of information to use against you in situations like this.

'You're in remarkably good health for your age, Mrs Winterbottom. Very few GP visits. If only all our patients looked after themselves so well.'

Well, he's got something right. I told Shirley you shouldn't trouble a doctor over something minor. They're very busy. There are no ointments for a few memory problems.

He clicks his pen and turns from the screen to face me. 'How have you been coping since your husband passed away?'

That's not something to discuss with a stranger. 'Absolutely fine. Mustn't grumble.'

Shirley shuffles in her seat. I stare at the doctor for several seconds but he just stares back. He looks a little fed up himself, creases forming beneath bloodshot eyes, though mine must look as large as 'bags for life' compared to his. These days if I see a doctor who's smiling, I know he's retired.

'I'd like you to humour me and do a test. Just a few simple questions, nothing to worry about.'

I've been humouring him for the last ten minutes! I don't think I've got any choice but to continue. What a time to be doing this, when my head is full of distractions. And the questions are ridiculous, plain ridiculous. He asks me my age, despite the fact he should be able to work it out himself from my date of birth, which will be on his screen. On a good day I feel twenty-one, on a bad day ninety-nine.

Then he asks me today's date. I'm not very good on dates without checking the newspaper so I have to guess at that. He also asks me where we are. Heavens, he should know where his own doctor's surgery is, he must get here somehow every day! I really don't think this young man is up to being a doctor. He even points to the pen in his hand and asks me what it is.

'Who's the prime minister?'

'It's that Blair fellow.' I think for a moment. 'Or is it David Cameron? No, no, it's that tall one, Clegg. Nick Clegg. Oh, I don't know, they're all the blooming same.'

He then asks me to repeat some words back to him and that's when he starts getting me in a muddle. He pauses so long between each word that I forget the order. My head gets as knotted as my stomach, seeds of irritation scratching inside me.

He makes me touch my left leg with my right hand and point to a chair. It's like being back in nursery school. Those seeds sprout rapidly. And he gives me a piece of card with instructions like 'close your eyes'. I'm about to protest when Shirley gives me one of her looks, somehow seeming stern and pleading at the same time.

The final straw comes when he wants me to draw some strange pentagon shapes on a piece of paper as if I'm joining a pagan cult. What on Earth would that prove? The irritation fully blooms into anger, my hand trembling as I scrawl. Only my impeccable manners stop me from walking out.

'Thank you, Mrs Winterbottom.' He's as calm as a canal when I hand my scrawled effort back to him, though he must be laughing inside after making me look so silly. 'We'll book you in for blood and urine samples as well.' How can he possibly check my mind from that? 'But there do seem to be issues with your memory.'

I could have just told him that and saved us all this farce. Wait until he's my age. No, I really don't like this new doctor, this impostor in Dr Harrington's place. He wouldn't have put me through all this, he'd have listened for a few minutes, smiled warmly and then sent me on my way with some reassuring words.

'You may need to see a consultant.' Dr Jackson's smile is plastered on. Hope I don't have to go through all this again. I fear these new quacks may get more barking the higher up they go.

He wants a quick word with Shirley while I wait outside. I'm just happy to get out of the stuffy little room. A receptionist guides me back to the waiting area.

I don't like these modern surgeries either. You don't even get to speak to the receptionist any more. Everything's run by computers these days. To think how extraordinary and futuristic they seemed when we were young. Now they're taking over the world and will make everyone redundant. We had to press this little screen when we came in, to register our arrival. I don't know why we couldn't just tell the receptionist, that is her job. Then you have to wait until your name flashes up on an electronic board like you'd have at the football to tell you the scores. I kept expecting the pools panel results to come up. Is heaven automated as well now, Albert? Does St Peter hold up a big digital sign with your number on it?

Sighing, I try to balance myself on a curved wooden chair. I don't know what's taking Shirley so long. Hope he's not doing silly tests on her as well. I don't like being surrounded by sick people; I could catch something dreadful. One grey and clammy gentleman is coughing and spluttering, and there's a woman who looks paler than a ghost. The doctor should be helping them not wasting time with me.

A familiar face on the other side of the room catches my eye and makes my heart skip a beat. She turns away, but I know it's Jean. Honestly, she's wearing a tracksuit at the doctor's of all places. Perhaps I should leave her be, but I'm itchy with questions.

As I get up, she takes a sudden interest in a poster on fertility. I park myself on a chair next to her. Her face, craggy from all the scowling, stiffens.

'Hope you've come over to apologise.' A cigarette-coarsened voice.

'I've nothing to apologise for.' I rest my handbag on my lap.

'You bringing the murder up brought everything back and I'm struggling to sleep now.' She spits out the words, shaking her head as if trying to dislodge something. 'I need better pills.'

Guilt or trauma? 'Who else fell out with Barbara?'

Jean's face goes a troubling purple. That image returns, her shouting at me, spittle flecking my cheeks, foul words ringing in my ears. I take a handkerchief from my handbag and wipe my face, but it's dry.

Promise me you'll do it, Margaret. Barbara's anguished face. I shudder.

'Nobody's perfect.' Jean's voice is quiet, mournful. 'I'd known Barbara a long time as well. I know of things about her past.'

A tingle down my spine. 'What does that mean?'

'I'm not saying anything more about someone else's private life. Least of all to you.'

I stare at Jean but she's turned away. Does she really have some insight or is she just casting aspersions?

I return my handkerchief to my handbag and clasp it shut. 'If you knew something important, you'd just say it.'

Jean faces me, a redness in her eye, her top lip curling. 'All these questions and snooping.'

I hold my handbag to my chest. 'Just trying to jog your memory.'

'Not my memory we've got to worry about, is it Margaret?' She breaks into a bitter laugh. 'Nearly blew your house up, so I heard, on top of everything else. Bet that's why you're here.'

I drop my handbag into my lap. Who's spreading gossip? 'That's completely exaggerated. Nothing wrong with me.'

Heads turn towards us and I feel my face flush.

'Concentrate on your own problems.' Her gruff voice loud. She's trying to distract me, throw me off the scent. I can see why Barbara fell out with her; she's as calculated as a sky-high gas bill. 'Leave the rest to the professionals.'

'Least I'm trying to help. If someone was drowning you wouldn't even get your feet wet.'

Jean stands up, towering over me. 'You're just an interfering, old busybody.'

She's a nasty sort. There's real aggression in her eyes now.

'What if it was you that attacked Barbara?'

The rest of the room stare at us, the atmosphere thicker than a pea-souper. I've done it again: said out loud what I meant to say in my head.

'You've lost the bloody plot, Margaret.' She stoops towards me, finger jabbing, another speckle of saliva. 'You accuse me again and I'll—'

I grip both armrests, my heart racing. 'You'll what?'

A gasp from our audience. Jean's mouth opens. But before

she can complete her threat, Shirley marches into the waiting room. We freeze, a portrait of hostility. Shirley looks in a world of her own, though, she just smiles weakly at Jean, doesn't even register the rage contorting her face.

'Better get you home, Mum.' Her voice is so quiet I can barely hear the words.

Yes, it really is time to get going. As I rise, Jean slowly sits back down. I smooth my skirt and hoist my handbag over my shoulder. Eyes return to pamphlets, magazines and mobile phones. I feel a pang of regret at snapping.

Shirley has her head down as she pushes through the main door. I imagine that daft doctor has said something tactless, but I won't ask what's wrong. You mustn't pry into other people's problems; they'll tell you when they're good and ready.

Jean gives me a last glare as we leave, her face as scrunched up and dried out as a raisin. A reservoir of anger dwells in that woman. I must speak to James about her.

CHAPTER 16

The marbles clink as they ricochet around the carpet.

'Great shot, Gran.'

James spreads himself low, taking careful aim with a colourful glass sphere held between thumb and forefinger. He's a sniper in his precision, chin close to the floor, eyes narrowed in focus, a deep breath held and then released as he rolls the marble. It hurtles past, missing everything before crashing into the skirting board.

James howls with laughter. 'Dammit.'

'Language, James.'

I don't mind really. I'm just glad he wants to spend time with me. I didn't think tiddlywinks and marbles would match the latest computer games but James wanted to play them and seems enraptured. It's infectious, the house reverberating with laughter. It takes me back years, that childhood sense of play returning, as if it was only dormant.

I'm going to make us a Friday fish supper later, just like we used to have, Albert. I've got some fresh cod from the market that I'll fillet and batter myself and I've cut some chunky chips ready for the fryer. I'm salivating at the thought of the smell and taste of the seaside. I need to concentrate on my game. I take aim.

There's a knock at the door. Just as I'm winning.

'It'll be him.' James jumps to his feet. He'll have to be more subtle if he plans to go undercover. 'Action stations.'

'Shouldn't I invite him in for a cup of tea?'

'No, nothing out of the ordinary, Gran. He's just collecting on his rounds not coming over for a party. We don't want to make him suspicious.'

'It'll probably come across as the Spanish Inquisition.'

'You'll be fine. Just remember, when you cough up the cash, slip in some questions, see how he answers. You know, lull him into a false sense of security then, bam, catch him off guard.'

James mimics a boxer giving a right hook. I'm not sure that's appropriate.

'Don't think I can do that.'

'Course you can, you're good at keeping people talking. I'll hide in the hallway and make notes.'

You did always say I had the gift of the gab, Albert.

I shuffle to the door, gripping three golden pound coins. James crouches on the hallway stairs, clutching his pen and notepad, out of sight of the doorway.

'Hello.' I try to sound as breezy as I can. Wish I'd taken the trouble to learn his name but it would seem a bit strange to ask now. 'How are you?'

The window cleaner looks the same as always. A black bag, tied around his waist to store his takings, sits over camouflage trousers, though why men who aren't in the army wear them I've no idea. He has a thick blue pullover on, no coat, and his perennial woollen hat.

'Good, ta.' He's rooting through the bag, checking his change. 'And you?'

'Still coming to terms with what happened.' I nod towards the house opposite, all its curtains shut, immersed in darkness. 'Three weeks ago today. Somehow seems like yesterday *and* such a long time ago.'

Though everything feels like that to me.

'I know. Couldn't believe it. Barbara was lovely.'

A moment's silence.

'You must have called round that day.' My voice gently inquisitive. 'Did you notice anything wrong?'

'Nothing.' He shakes his head. 'Collected from her late on and she seemed fine, if a bit subdued.'

I remember James's instructions: *ask him what time he called at Barbara's*. 'And what time was that exactly?'

'Ooh, I reckon around five p.m. or so. I'd nearly finished for the day.'

I hear a noise from the hallway, a kind of strangulated coughing. 'Definitely five p.m. was it? Not later on?'

'I'm pretty sure it was five p.m. That's what I told the police. It will have been just after I'd collected from you.'

'And what did she say?' I smile encouragingly.

'She mentioned she was seeing her niece that evening.'

A dull thud makes me turn towards the stairs. James is nodding at me. 'Niece,' he mouths a few times.

Ahhh. I turn back to the window cleaner who has a bemused expression.

'Was Barbara going to her niece's place?' I ask. 'Or was her niece visiting her?'

'Don't think she said.'

Darn it.

A flash of lightning strikes my brain. 'What about Jean Brampton, did you see her lurking around when you left Barbara's?'

I know what James said, Albert, when I told him all about seeing Jean at the doctor's and how vile she can be: how we need to keep an open mind while we're testing our suspects. But it doesn't hurt to ask.

'Who?'

'Barbara's next-door neighbour.' I point to Jean's house. 'She'll have probably been wearing a tracksuit.'

'She doesn't have her windows cleaned, so I don't really know her. But no, there was no one else around.'

'So, you didn't see anything untoward?' I can't keep the disappointment from my voice.

He scratches the back of his neck. 'Not that I noticed. Whatever happened must have been soon after. Soon as I heard I went straight down the police station.'

'Must have been an unpleasant experience.'

I scrutinise him. Wiry. Agile. Familiar and allowed unguarded access, while possessing knowledge of our properties and movements. Able to sneak in and get around unnoticed. Quick, strong hands.

'They had a lot of questions.' He pauses. 'A bit like now.'

He smiles uneasily, clearly baffled by my interrogation, and I feel suddenly guilty. Will I see a culprit in everyone now?

'Did they give you any idea what happened?'

'Didn't tell me much so I only know the same as everyone else.'

'I see.' I'm not getting anywhere. 'How much do I owe you?'

'Four quid, as usual.'

I look at the three coins in my palm. 'Oh, I'll just have to get some more money. Won't be a moment.'

I creep over to James. 'Anything else I should ask?' I whisper.

He's still writing things down. 'Can't think of anything,' he murmurs back.

'Everything all right, Margaret?' shouts the window cleaner.

'Just looking for my purse.' I can't get my purse out in front of James now. 'I'm not sure where my change is.'

James hands me a pound coin from his pocket, he's such a godsend. 'We'll settle up later, Gran.'

I return to the door. 'Here you are,' I say cheerily, handing over the coins.

I study his face again as he thanks me and leaves but he doesn't seem unnerved. It's much easier to tell when you see killers on television, they're always so sinister.

Closing the door, I turn to James.

'How did he look?' he asks.

'Same as ever. He's always been laid-back. Another benefit from all that fresh air.'

'He says he called at Barbara's not long after he collected from you. What time was that, Gran?'

'I don't remember, James. If he says it was five p.m. then it probably was.'

'But it can't have been then.' Suddenly, James looks as if he's a toddler again, about to stamp his foot.

'Whether it's five p.m. or a bit later it doesn't make much difference.'

James's mouth freezes half-open, then closes.

He traipses back towards the lounge. 'It's just that a couple of weeks ago you said he called at five-thirty p.m. The later it is, I reckon the more chance it was him.'

CHAPTER 17

It's a terrible view, Albert. The opposite of the landscapes that took our breath away on our walks: the deep blue of tranquil lakes, the lush green mountains disappearing into clouds, the emerald sea of treetops rippling below as we climbed higher and higher. But at least it's fresh air and a bit of sunshine. The garden is not what it once was, I'm afraid. You were a wonderful gardener, but I'm unable to tend it as you did. The neat displays of contrasting colours have withered brown and dreary. Nature's delicate, soothing fragrances – the sweet scent of pale pink roses, the subtle spice of carnations – have rotted into a fusty earthiness. The grass is overgrown and knotted with weeds, brambles clogging the borders where the sunlight can't get through. Thick, thorny stalks creep towards the barren grass, entangling. Nature has been allowed to grow rampant. I'm so sorry, my love, I have let your beautiful garden go to seed.

I gaze at the sky instead, where greying clouds crawl across the sun.

What a pair James and I must look, lolling on our blue and white striped deckchairs in the front garden on a lazy Sunday as if it's a beach on the Riviera in summer, not a housing estate stuck in winter. Perhaps I should knot a hanky on my head.

I've sunk so far into my seat that my backside almost scrapes the ground. I'm not sure how I'll ever get back up. Shirley is roaming the house, hunting for some important letters I've supposedly lost. Only bills, I assume. I'm better out here, out of her way. I close my eyes and imagine myself on the south coast, basking in the sun's rays, sand beneath my toes, waves lapping in the near distance. Those bird cries are gulls, not crows, and it's sea air I'm breathing in, not traffic fumes.

My mind drifts like the clouds above. I don't have the energy today and I'm full of ache. I think everything's caught up with me.

A burst of horrific noise jolts me from my slumber, my eyelids springing open. Someone's wailing as if they're in pain. I look across to James. He'd fiddling with his phone, that sound is presumably music exploding out of it.

'Sorry, Gran.' He turns it down, then switches it off. 'I'll listen to it later.'

He's wearing a long-sleeved, black T-shirt that says 'Thank you for the venom'. I'm grateful for the silence, to let my mind rest. I'm drifting again, feeling light as the clouds, the birds squawking far off just background noise.

Footsteps clatter the pavement, echoing in my head. They stop. I open my eyes.

Jean's face, eyes so narrow they're almost hyphens, looks down at us, blocking out a brief glimpse of the sun. She places her arms on top of our fence, it's just the right height for her, and rests her chins on them.

'Look at you pair.' Her voice drips with contempt. 'Want me to fetch you ice creams?'

I sigh, the air leaving my body in a slow heave. I haven't the sharpness to respond.

'You got that apology for me?' Jean jabs a crooked finger in my direction, the heavy lines on her face twisting with indignation. She's a cantankerous old so-and-so.

'I've nothing to apologise for. Nothing's changed.'

'You not heard the latest?' She must see the confusion on my face as she feels the need to carry on. 'Thought you knew everything, Margaret.'

I don't have the stamina for a row. 'What is it, Jean?'

She laughs scornfully. 'Police have found some major evidence and the word is they're questioning someone.'

James lifts bolt upright. We stare at each other.

'You really didn't know?' Jean cackles to herself. It's the first time I've seen her looking so happy.

'What have they found?' I ask.

'Could be a breakthrough.'

She dangles the hook and I bite the bait. 'Just tell us, Jean.'

Her face lights up with the power of knowledge. 'Barbara's purse, in woodland nearby, just chucked, might have evidence of the killer on it.'

Jean says it so dramatically that I sense even James shrink back a little, like meat in a frying pan.

'And who are they questioning?'

'Everyone's talking about him.' That woman could provoke a rapid response from a sloth. 'It's Michael Cavanagh.'

My mind is blank. Is it someone I don't know or is it my brain failing me today? Oh, the look on her face! Pure amusement at my floundering, a cat with a fish. I take a deep breath.

'You don't even know who that is, do you?' The pleasure in her dark eyes. 'Well, I'm not telling you.'

'You really enjoy other people's discomfort, don't you, Jean?'

That seems to sting; she steps back, disgruntlement worming its way onto her face. She takes a moment to consider it, I can almost see her mind whirling back through years of memories.

'There are things that I regret.' She looks behind her at Barbara's empty house. 'But you can't turn back the clock.'

I gaze at that property too, trying to imagine the flames in the back garden on the night that Jean described to me when we were in the post office. Would I have been able to see the smoke billowing over her house?

'What was Barbara doing starting a fire?' I ask.

'Who knows. She'd never done it before.'

A thought occurs to me. 'She had a gas fire, not a coal fire like me. Was she trying to burn something to get rid of it?'

'How should I know?' Jean dismisses the suggestion with a wave of her hand. 'You'd be surprised at some of the things that woman did. Don't go digging, Margaret, you'll just end up covered in mud.'

She marches off.

'What was that about?' James has a strange mixture of concern and hope about him, like someone who's lost something but has a hunch where it might be.

'I've no idea,' I sigh.

'You know this Cavanagh guy, Gran?'

I shake my head. 'I don't recognise the name.'

'You reckon it could be the window cleaner? What's he called?'

I'm good for nothing today. 'I don't think I know.'

The countless times we chatted and really he's nothing more than a stranger. How thoughtless of me to never find out what he was called. It hadn't occurred to us that we'd be accusing someone who we couldn't even name.

'Maybe they've something on him.' James springs up out of his deckchair. 'Let's see what we can find out.'

I'm not going to get any rest now, so I might as well join him. I wriggle around in my seat, limbs flailing like a tortoise turned on its back.

'Do me a favour, James.'

'What's that, Gran?'

I hold out an arm. 'Give me a hand getting out of this deckchair.'

CHAPTER 18

My name's in print again, Albert. I'll soon be a celebrity at this rate. I recline in our chair to take in a newspaper article on the murder 'that has rocked the community'. It's all about that public meeting, complete with me telling everyone to pull together. And it mentions what Jean said about police speaking to a key witness, though nothing about Michael Cavanagh. James and I haven't been able to find anything more about him over the last couple of days. That community meeting was more than a week ago so this must be an old edition, but I can't recall reading it. Hopefully, Shirley hasn't seen it. I don't think she'd welcome the focus being on us again.

I appreciate these things take time but I want this dark cloud lifted. In the basement of my heart, I know it will drag on. There's a story here about that *Costa Concordia* capsizing, the one where that cowardly captain fled the sinking cruise ship leaving all those poor people to drown. More than two months on and another five bodies have been found, seemingly no end to the suffering. The largest shipwreck in history, it says, twice the size of the *Titanic*. Bit before my time that one. And no, Albert, don't say only just!

I turn the page. An advert for broadband catches my eye, in particular its slogan: 'Our most reliable wireless connection ever.'

Those words whisk me back some seventy years to our work. Didn't the enemy think those wireless connections were secure as their messages flitted the airwaves like hummingbirds? But we were the ones making the real connections and trusted to always deliver. I chuckle as my mind is filled with scrambled words and how we achieved the impossible in restoring them into solid sense. That was real pressure: time ticking down with lives at risk. Though it added to the exhilaration when you cracked it. All that adrenaline surging through my veins combined with deep concentration kept my mind alert for hours. I haven't experienced that intensity since, that feeling of importance, of being so alive.

I get up, throw the newspaper onto the chair, and wander to the window. There's no one to share these memories with. I spend an age staring out, the view dominated by Barbara's detached house.

I spot Irene carrying several bags of shopping. She's no need for a trolley! I rush to the door as quickly as I'm able and make it to the driveway before she's out of earshot.

'Irene, dear, do you need a hand?' I wouldn't be able to carry much, what with my hip, but it's the thought that counts.

Irene turns, smiles, and heads over. She places the plastic carrier bags at her feet, though I think she'd be able to carry them for hours.

'It's OK, I'm almost home.' She's not even out of breath; I stifle my wheezing. 'But I'll have a short rest.' She inspects me. 'You look well today, Margaret.'

Something catches my eye in the house next to Barbara's; the twitch of a net curtain in the front window. Is that Jean peeking at us? She's alone in her house too, I doubt anyone calls round. Too many fallings out.

I gesture towards the neighbouring properties. 'If only I knew what went on between Jean and Barbara.'

Irene bears an expression I've not seen on her before: the puckered lips of someone uncertain of whether to reveal all. It doesn't last long. 'I did hear *one* whisper.' She props a sagging bag upright. 'Of an *affair*.'

That word, said so delicately, startles me. I have vague memories, like candyfloss in a windy fairground, of Jean and Don being friendly but then having little to do with each other, though never suspected anything.

'But nothing more,' says Irene. 'Jean would have been in her twenties then, Don much older.'

I think of Jean when she was younger. I suppose she was attractive once, and Don was such a cad.

'Everything changed between them after that period,' adds Irene. 'You could always feel this tension.'

No wonder the marriage deteriorated so rapidly. Poor Barbara. And she never let on. Maybe it tormented her all along. Maybe that's what's bothering Jean. Maybe that's what's at the heart of this.

'Did you hear about the arrest?' Irene's mind sprints ahead of mine. I nod, enthusiastically.

'I know someone in the police.' She says it as if she's friends with the Queen. 'They say Lisa keeps banging on at them about their investigation taking too long. She was straight on to them as soon as she heard. Wants whoever has been arrested to be charged. She'd have them locked up without even a trial.'

She's certainly impatient, but isn't that understandable?

Irene picks up her bags. 'Anyhow, I'd better get these in the fridge. My milk will be going off.'

There must be seven bags of groceries there, Albert, and she carries them away so lightly.

I'm no sooner back inside than there's a knock on the door so hesitant it's almost apologetic for disturbing me. It's not the noise that Irene or Shirley would make. I open it. A pair of anxious eyes on a tanned face peer at me from beneath a tea-cosy hat. I'm about to greet him when an alarm sounds inside my head. I stumble back a step and grip the door frame for support. Should he be here? It suddenly feels as though the only thing I know about him is his name.

'Michael Cavanagh,' I breathe.

He holds up his hands as if in surrender.

'Please, Mrs Winterbottom.' He grimaces. 'I'm not here to cause any bother.'

'Why *are* you here?' I step forward and look around to see if anyone's about, in case I need help. But Irene's gone and the street's deserted.

'I just want to talk.' His shoulders slump, head leaning down, the voice quiet with despondency. He glances around the street as well, at the shut doors and curtained windows. 'People have made it pretty clear I'm not welcome round here.'

I'm frozen by uncertainty. He sees the dilemma on my face, his own creasing at the slight. 'No need to be frightened of me.'

I'm on my own. I shouldn't let him in. 'Why do you need

to speak to me?' I keep my voice polite and composed, as if a Victorian lady to a servant.

'I swear I've never hurt anyone.' A desperation to his tone now, a hint of anger. 'You've been a loyal customer for years. I thought you'd believe me.' He shifts on his feet. 'I just came to tell you I'm having to finish my round.'

His lost and lonely look reminds me of a schoolboy being evacuated during the war. Staring into his eyes, I can't detect any sign of malice, nothing to make me feel afraid. It's hard to know who to trust. Nowadays, my foundations are built on sand and all I can do is go with my gut instinct.

'Come in.' I hold the door wide open.

He gives a wry smile, then takes off his woollen hat, shoving it inside the back pocket of his blue jeans, and wipes his feet carefully on the doormat, before following me inside. I leave the door unlocked so that I'm not completely trapped. I go to make us a cup of tea.

Sunlight through the kitchen window reveals motes swimming in its stream. The dust has settled on the lampshade and furniture, gathering like a layer of fine snow. This place has started to resemble a fairground's haunted house, full of cobwebs and grime, with that damn spider running riot. A cupboard door is even hanging off a broken hinge that I haven't got round to getting repaired. But I don't need any help. As soon as I've got a bit of energy, I'll have a good spring clean – once spring is actually here! It's embarrassing though, having someone round when it's in this state.

I take the tea, in a Princess Diana cup, to Mr Cavanagh. He wipes his hands on his jeans before taking Lady Di from me with fingers that tremble slightly.

'You've already been a lot kinder to me than everyone else round here,' he says. 'Since I was questioned no one's had any time for me.'

'Why were the police questioning you again?' I sit down, then realise that I haven't made a drink for myself.

Mr Cavanagh holds an arm across his waist. 'I was seen walking through Ashfall Park after I'd collected from Barbara. That's where they found her purse. And I was the last one to see her alive.' He takes a sip, wincing slightly, it must be too hot. 'I just liked to cut through the park between the estates sometimes when collecting. I hadn't done anything.' He blows on his drink then takes another sip. 'Everyone's got the wrong end of the stick.'

My mouth goes dry and I really wish I had a drink with me now. I run my tongue over my chapped lips and try to stay focused. While I believe him to be honest, a little suspicion is creeping into me. What really are his intentions for being here? I glance at the door. Maybe I shouldn't have let him in.

'People always think there's no smoke without fire.' A resigned dejection in the flatness of his voice.

I picture Barbara in front of the flames. What was she doing?

'No one trusts me enough to let me clean their windows now. The slightest suspicion and they don't want you near their house.' He slumps back, the cup dangling by one finger. 'I've had to give up my job but I've a wife and three kids to feed so I'm gonna try and start a round elsewhere. I'm finished here. That's all I came to tell you. That I won't be cleaning your windows any more.'

His eyes portray a disconsolate incomprehension. I'm caught between compassion and doubt.

'It'll be hard building up another round. Times are tough with people cutting back.' He gulps a mouthful of tea, Princess Diana shaking. 'Paying for your windows to be cleaned ain't exactly a priority.'

'Well, I think it's essential. If you're house isn't well-presented it can bring down the tone of the neighbourhood.'

I always insisted on having our windows cleaned, didn't I, Albert? Even when you said you could do it yourself to save some money. I wasn't having you clambering up a rickety old ladder.

Mr Cavanagh stares at the dregs in his mug like a tea-leaf reader. 'I'll never get any work round here again.'

It doesn't seem fair that his livelihood, his future, should be affected without proof of wrongdoing. Innocent until proven guilty, aren't we? But then he was the last to see Barbara, and was where her purse was found.

He sweeps his shoulder-length hair back, just like James does. Could I give him some hope until there's certainty?

'You can continue to clean my windows if you like and it's possible there may be some jobs around the house that I can pay you to do in the future.' There's lots needs doing. That cupboard door for a start. Maybe he could do what Matthew's not up to.

'You sure, Mrs Winterbottom?' His face and voice lighten. 'People won't like it if they see me coming round. They'll think you're mad for employing me.'

'That's their problem.' I waft my hand. 'I'll employ who I see fit.'

I take the empty cup from him, Diana drained dry. His shoulders have lifted.

I get him to scribble his number on a scrap of paper.

As I see him out, he stops on the doorstep. 'More importantly, you think City can do it? Reckon they'll pip United and win the Premier League for the first time?'

'Oh, I think it will go to the wire.' I give him a wink.

He thanks me for everything. I look around our street as he leaves, a deep uncertainty troubling me, that the finger of blame might be pointing in the wrong direction. For a moment, I am lost in the past.

'Mrs Winterbottom?'

A young man walking along the pavement has paused. He ventures over. It's typical: hours of solitude, then suddenly I'm in demand. A notebook's stuffed in his coat pocket, the tiny metal spirals that bind the paper protruding upwards, unwinding a little, some of the pages starting to tear free. A couple of pens stick haphazardly out of a top pocket.

'How are you?' The voice added to the image equals his identity dawning on me.

'I don't have any more information.' Anything I do know I'm not telling a reporter.

'There's something I wanted to check with you. I spoke to a witness who saw a youth running away that night and wondered if you'd seen anything?'

'No, I didn't notice anything untoward.'

'Your grandson around?' He looks past me to the hallway, then pulls a pen from his pocket and frees the notebook.

James? Why would he be asking about James? 'He's not here.'

The reporter jiggles the pen between two tobacco-stained fingers. 'Do you know his friends?'

I think of seagulls squawking. 'We've never been introduced.'

'OK, never mind. I was just thinking with that sighting and

the victim's purse being found in a wood nearby.' He points the pen past Barbara's house towards Ashfall Park. 'That maybe . . .'

He doesn't seem to know how to finish the sentence. I look at that house, the curtains closed like the eyelids of the dearly departed.

The reporter puts his pen and notebook away, then takes a small, rectangular card from his top pocket. He pushes it into my hand, the name Lee Spade embossed in black on creamy white. Senior reporter it says and a string of numbers. Senior! I tell you!

'Maybe James could call me, or if you hear anything.'

He strolls away.

I stare at the card, my fingers running along the sharpness of its firm edges. I need to ask James about that crowd he's been hanging around with. I do hope one of them hasn't got themselves caught up in this.

CHAPTER 19

Guilt is a parasite that worms within you, slowly eating away from the inside out. A tradesman's tuneful whistle makes a shadow stir under the surface of my consciousness. What have I done?

The locksmith, busy at work on my front door, changes his tune, the new melody light but equally haunting. Something weighs heavy in my pocket. I feel the smooth leather of my purse and the guilt bursts through, hot on my face. I know Shirley doesn't believe there was an intruder the other night but even the slightest possibility was enough to convince her to have new locks fitted. At least it makes it less likely that someone can get in, but I can't tell her about finding the purse now. I must push it out of my mind. How can the murderer bury what they've done deep inside and carry on as if nothing's happened?

Needing a distraction, I click the radio on in the kitchen. A song I don't know fills the air. Or maybe I do know it and it's become lost to me. I take a satsuma from the fruit bowl and begin to unpeel it as I listen out for a recognisable bar or lyric. Nothing. The next track is instantly familiar as Bing Crosby's smooth baritone sings 'You Are My Sunshine'. One of your favourites, Albert, from 1941. Your gentle voice, I'm safe in your arms, feeling somehow both giddy and secure.

The song fades, the sunshine goes. I look down and see that I've torn away tough layers of orange peel and white pith that are scattered at my feet like rose petals. I split free a segment of the naked fruit and push it into my mouth hoping to feel and taste the tang of juice bursting out. It's all dried up and wrinkled, it must have been left out too long. The skin gets stuck in my teeth and I struggle to get it out. No longer vital or longed for, I throw the satsuma in the bin. The radio crackles as it dips out of frequency.

James lurches into the kitchen. I'd forgotten he's here to keep an eye on me, as well as on the locksmith in case he does anything to warrant us adding him to our suspects. He's free, seeing as it's a Saturday.

'You've always got the radio on, Gran.' James scoops up the peelings and tosses them into the bin. 'Why not just put a CD on?'

'I've grown up with the radio, it's been an important part of my life.'

Radio wasn't just entertainment, it was vital for communication in the war, wasn't it, Albert? Crucial messages disguised and passed using radio waves. You had to make sure the enemy didn't intercept them, but what an advantage if you could crack their codes.

A sizzle of static prompts me to twiddle the dial to reconnect it. Is it me or were the frequencies much clearer when we were younger? A tune emerges.

James smiles, his long hair bobbing on his shoulders. What I wouldn't give for his carefree existence. And his blond locks.

There's something I need to tell him. Ahh, yes, about the window cleaner, I haven't told him about my chat with Michael Cavanagh. And I need to talk to him about those friends of his and what that reporter was saying.

Before I can speak, a commotion drowns out the music, footsteps pounding the hallway. A pale-faced Shirley bursts into the kitchen, two stern policemen following her. For a moment, I think they're here to tell us they've caught the murderer. Then I see the look on Shirley's face, her composure dissolving. James scrunches his hair inside a shaky fist.

'James, the police want to speak to you.' Shirley's voice crumbles as easily as a biscuit dunked in tea.

The two uniformed men move towards James. I instinctively step in front of him. They halt, their shoulders jerking back, granite faces cracking.

'Can you move out of the way please, madam?'

Everything seems to happen in slow motion as if my brain can't work fast enough to keep up with events. I stumble aside. See them flank James, whose jaw is clenched. One holds up handcuffs that glint in the sunlight streaming through the window.

'James Stone, we're arresting you on suspicion of murder and theft. You do not have to say anything, but it may harm your defence if you don't mention when questioned something you later rely on in court. Anything you do say may be given in evidence.'

A monotone delivery. The words echo as I try to make sense of them.

'There's no need to handcuff him, he's just a boy.' Tears form in Shirley's eyes.

James stretches his arms out behind him, head down, hair draping his face. I can't move, everything's underwater. I hear a muffled click of cuffs locking, a flash of silver encircling skinny wrists. They march James away and I follow dumbly behind, past the startled locksmith, his mouth gaping. Out the door. Down the garden path. Through the gate. To a police car, outside our house once more. They push James's head down, shunting him onto the back seat.

'Shirley, what's going on?' I find my voice but it's frail.

'Just go back inside, Mum.' Shirley gets into the car as well. 'I'm going with him.'

The door slams shut behind them.

As the car pulls away, I see James's face through the window, his expression the same as when we took him to nursery for the first time with his fingers gripping my hand. My heart is hammering.

Across the road, curtains twitch. A glimpse of short, white hair and a puffy face, beady eyes triumphant. My blood boils. I will put this right.

I turn around and go back inside, pushing past the locksmith in the doorway. I grab my coat off the hook by the banister. Button it up. Storm out.

'Where you going?'

'Somewhere important.' My voice trails behind me.

'But I've nearly done here.'

'Can't stop.' I've already reached the pavement.

'What about your keys?' An exasperation that's become familiar to my ears.

'Just finish the job and wait,' I shout. 'We'll be back soon.'

They'll have gone to the main police station in the town

centre as most of the others have been closed down. I plough on as fast as my legs allow. No time to consider the route or dwell on what's happened, I'll let instinct guide me. All I need to do is point out their mistake. I should have brought my stick; pain from my hip is shooting up my body. I grit my dentures. I won't slow down. A biting wind howls around me but I'm not turning back. I pull my coat tight. My legs grow heavy, my eyes watering, my breathing becoming quick and shallow. I can't stop. I walk on and on and on, oblivious to the pain.

Just as I think my legs and lungs will seize up, I see it: a big blue sign on an ugly seventies concrete slab. My brain hasn't let me down, adrenaline must have sparked it into life, like a key in an ignition. I make my way through the automatic doors.

I expected commotion but it's eerily quiet. The reception desk is shielded behind a giant see-through box of floor-to-ceiling plastic. Is it to keep us away from them? Does it become a holding pen if we go berserk? The desk isn't manned. This isn't the cosy station of my youth, no friendly sergeant beaming from behind a wooden counter.

There appears to be a door to enter but no handle. I spot a sign on the wall instructing me to wait my turn then to press a giant button to open the door. I notice a few other people slouched on blue plastic chairs in a waiting area. Is everything made of plastic now? They look pasty under the harsh strip lighting. There's no time to wait for them. I press the button but nothing happens so I press it again, then a third time for luck. A female officer emerges from a door behind the desk. A buzzing. I push the door and it swings open, allowing me to enter the plastic cage. The woman gives me a faint smile. She looks harassed, reminding me of

Shirley. She's of the same age and height. I have to talk to her through the plastic shield.

'They've made a terrible mistake.' The words splutter out.

'Slow down, love.' It's not easy to hear what she's saying from behind the screen. 'What's the crime?'

'They've got my grandson.'

I have so much to say it's as if the words are jammed together like ketchup in a bottle.

'A kidnap? Who's taken him?'

'Your colleagues.' I glare. 'They've arrested my grandson over the murder but he's done nothing wrong.'

'You're not here to report a crime?' Annoyance seeps from her.

'They must have brought him here.' I need someone with authority and influence. 'I need to speak with the chief constable.'

'Not possible I'm afraid.' Said so casually, so dismissive. 'So, your grandson's been arrested?'

'Yes, but he didn't do it.'

'No, none of them ever have.' A flicker of a smile on tight lips.

My face almost against the screen, I say as clearly as possible: 'I know who really did it.'

Taken aback by my conviction, she studies me, as if trying to work out a difficult puzzle.

'What's your grandson's name?'

'James Stone.'

'Wait a moment.'

She disappears. Maybe I'm getting somewhere. But the minutes tick on. How do I get out of this transparent structure? Am I incarcerated here now? Just as I'm beginning to think I've been forgotten about, a young man in a smart suit emerges at the door I entered. He presses the button to release me.

'Follow me, madam.' He doesn't bother to smile, just swipes some sort of card through a device next to another door, then holds it open for me. We wander into a corridor that has lots of rooms leading off it. I follow him as he leads me to a small door, which he again holds open. Inside is a tiny room, containing nothing more than a basic wooden desk and chairs. He gestures at one of the chairs and I sit down. The room is stark with its grey walls bare apart from a white clock that I'm not sure is telling the right time. It feels constrictive. My breathing quickens again.

I think he says he's in the CID, but I'm so disconcerted I can't hear him properly. He's not very old and mumbles his words. When I think he's ready I speak quickly, it all comes tumbling out of me as if that ketchup has spurted free. I tell him everything: about the murder, James's wrongful arrest, Jean falling out with Barbara and her hatred for her and her violent temper and how she 'discovered' the body and is probably trying to frame James. I am breathless by the end. He listens, nods sternly every now and again, but does he understand? He twiddles his pen and his eyes seem to glaze over at intervals.

The policeman glances at his digital watch. 'I need to speak to someone.' He leaves the room.

Good. He'll have gone to fetch a superior, someone with brains and the authority to sort all this out. The clock ticks on, the seconds hand seems very slow, perhaps it's broken. I'm not too concerned, it will take him a while to explain it all. Then I begin to wonder if he'll ever come back. What is it with this place? Am I now trapped in this claustrophobic room forever?

The door finally opens and there he is with Shirley behind him, her eyes red-rimmed.

'Let's get you home, Mum.'

I follow her out of the building, glad to be out of the place. I assume they'll be releasing James to us. Shirley guides me to a taxi but there's no sign of him. I get inside with her and she tells the cabbie my address. She must know what she's doing. We set off and I look behind at the police station shrinking into the distance.

'Where's James?'

'They haven't interviewed him yet as we're waiting for a solicitor. Matthew's sorting it. I didn't want the duty solicitor.'

She runs a hand the length of her seatbelt. 'He'll need a good solicitor,' she adds, quietly.

'Why aren't they releasing him?' I shout. 'Why aren't they arresting Jean instead?' I look behind again but the police station has gone, with James still inside. Nausea rises in me.

'Jean Brampton?' Shirley shakes her head. 'James's friends have admitted stealing those purses that went missing. Police found some in their rooms. They've told them James was involved and that he took Barbara's purse on the night when . . . you know.'

'But he's denied it.' They must be lying.

'He's not said a word yet. We need the solicitor to speak to him.'

I sink into my seat. How do I fix this? 'We've got to go back, Shirley.'

'I need you to be safe at home, Mum.' Her lip trembles, tears welling. 'Can you just do that for me?'

The cabbie peruses us in his rear-view mirror, his black, bushy eyebrows raised. So many questions. I can't argue though. We can't speak freely with others listening and I don't want to upset her any further.

'Everything will be all right,' I say, gently, though that nausea is bubbling inside.

'He's in a lot of trouble, Mum.' Shirley leans into me and I wrap an arm around her. With her head on my chest, I stroke her hair as I used to do when she was a little girl. Back then, with a soothing kiss on her forehead, I could make anything all right, could salve any bruise or cut, could dry any tears.

'It will work itself out,' I say.

'What must people think of us?'

'Why would that matter? What business is it of theirs?'

'I don't even know who I am any more. Carer, parent, teacher, daughter, colleague. They're lead badges weighing me down. None of them are me.'

'You need to focus on James. That's your priority. He needs you the most right now.'

I feel her shake within my embrace. I hold her until the taxi pulls up outside our house. Shirley sits back up, brushes finger-tips across her cheekbones and dusts down her blouse. 'Let's get you settled and then the taxi's going to take me back to the police station.' She seems calmer. 'The solicitor should be there by then.'

'And he'll be able to resolve this,' I say, firmly.

My front door is locked, the locksmith nowhere to be seen. We find a note stuck to the door saying that my new keys are with that couple at number twelve. At least he didn't leave them with Jean. Shirley won't go until she's retrieved them and made sure I'm sat down with a cup of tea. Her parting smile falters in the corners.

'Go and get him out of there,' I tell her. I hear the taxi pull away. As I slump in our chair, waves of exhaustion crash over me, my limbs lead weights. But how could I ever rest with all these questions and thoughts clashing in my head, with the jigsaw pieces breaking and re-forming into a picture I can't bear to look at?

I watch the sun dip below the horizon.

As nightfall creeps in, I decide to head for bed. I must at least try to get some sleep. I don't have the energy to change into my nightwear; instead I lie fully clothed on the duvet.

My brain wears itself out, a fogginess obscuring the questions, the thoughts fading.

A rattling breaks through. I'm alert. Metal clinking against metal followed by the noise of our front door handle being yanked. It's happening again! I can hear more clanking and the door being shoved but it stays steadfast.

What if it's *him*? I thought Harry was long gone, a splinter in my memory, someone my family don't mention so as not to aggravate the wound that I won't fully reveal. But what if he has returned? That man who I've seen twice now, he looks just like my brother. Why would he come back after all this time? The answer is ice cold. It's hiding in the wooden box in our bureau downstairs.

Maybe I should confront him and end this once and for all. But I feel unable to move, never mind tackle the past.

Everything is quiet. The door remains closed. I am alone on the bed in darkness. Where are you when I need you most, Albert? More than ever, I wish you could respond.

CHAPTER 20

A row of trestle tables stretches down our road, all covered in red, white and blue. The street's closed to traffic so that people can sit safely outside, the tables heaving with food and drink: little triangular sandwiches on paper plates, plastic bowls of crisps and sausage rolls, and mountains of cakes, chocolates and sweets.

I take a seat directly outside our house so that I don't have far to walk; my hip's not good and I'm exhausted after yesterday. No one's sitting at this table yet. I wish James could be here. He's been granted bail but Shirley won't let him out the house and she's confiscated his mobile phone. How could he be involved? It doesn't seem real.

A sunny Sunday afternoon, neighbours have poured from their houses like a stream after a thaw to occupy the other tables. All this food, but I don't feel hungry and, anyway, it seems rude to tuck in on my own. I twist my wedding ring on my finger; no Albert, I'd never take it off.

Too many things to brood over. The churning thought of Harry being back and trying to get into our house. I keep checking the wooden box to make sure it's still in there.

I try to focus on the present, on what's around me. Some children are playing hopscotch further up the road and a bit of a singalong breaks out three tables away. It was the local residents' association who organised this fifties-style street party to bring people together and encourage community spirit. They've provided the tables, chairs, decorations and music, and wanted everyone to join in and bring out something they'd baked or created. Just as it used to be: everyone mucking in and sharing to have a good time.

Vera's heading this way. She's wearing a blue and white dress to match the occasion and a little Union Jack hat perched on perfectly coiffured hair. She somehow manages to make even that look glamorous. I give her a wave but she walks straight past and sits down a few tables further along. Maybe she didn't see me. I can't get her attention; she's immediately engrossed in conversation with what looks like that new couple, the Martins.

I picture James stuck in his bedroom, all alone, going out of his mind. He's practically in prison already. Shirley and Matthew couldn't come as they're too busy dealing with solicitors, and I don't think they'd let James out of their sight. I still can't believe he's caught up in it. I know he has his moments, he is a teenager, but, well . . . he's always been the same sweet boy to me.

I watch Vera in her outfit and think about royalty. It's the Diamond Jubilee in June and the Queen's just announced that three towns will be granted city status to mark the occasion. Chelmsford will be to do with the racing, but I though Perth was in Australia and I can't remember the other one. How I love all the glamour and ceremony around the royal family. I was proud to serve King and country, though I couldn't tell

James any of that, of course. While I'm slightly older than the Queen, it feels as if I've grown up with her and now it's sixty years she's been on the throne. When I was James's age, 2012 seemed as far off as another planet. It would have been our sixtieth anniversary this year too, Albert. Sixty years! Oh my!

I gaze at the Union Jack tablecloth and blink away the moisture in my eyes.

I must pull myself together. I spot Irene two tables away and send her a welcoming smile. She acknowledges me with a brief nod but doesn't come over, just turns her back and finds conversation elsewhere.

It hits me with a stinging slap.

Word has spread.

I am an old boot with dog muck imbedded in the grooves of its sole. No one wants to come near even a whiff of me. Yet again, life has changed in an instant.

Oh, Albert, why do I feel that my world hasn't stopped falling apart?

I listen to the music to divert myself, but it doesn't take me back as it should do, doesn't stir any memories. It's what's considered famous now, all Vera Lynn and Elvis Presley, not what I remember listening to at the time. It feels like a cheap reproduction, like these plastic flags people are waving around or a photocopy of a painting, the colour, texture and vibrancy lost. There's no evocation of the street parties we had.

I hear a chair scrape back, someone finally taking a seat opposite me. I look up, preparing to give them a wide smile and a kind word, and see a black tracksuit top zipped up to a wobbly chin.

'All on your own, Margaret.'

Jean Brampton! The last thing I need! A wicked smile splits

her face, making it resemble a cracked walnut. She picks up a pink fondant fancy and bites off its buttercream topping. 'You enjoying yourself?'

I say nothing, it's not worth the energy.

'Heard your grandson had been arrested, who'd have thought. All your snooping and questioning and he was responsible all along.'

Every molecule is urging me to defend James, to snap back, to put her in her place, but I don't know what to say, I don't know how to prove her wrong. Everything is as sticky and fragile as a spider's web.

Jean devours the rest of the cake in one gobful.

'Tainted by association.' Crumbs tumble out of her mouth. 'Nobody will have anything to do with you now. They'll all presume you knew and that you've been protecting him.'

I think of the dejection on Michael Cavanagh's face and him having to give up his job. I think of James imprisoned in his bedroom, and his prospects. I think of Barbara suffering a heinous crime and a broken promise.

'Not like you to be so quiet, Margaret.'

Even starved of company, I would rather be alone.

Jean leans across the table, the stench of body odour drifting over. 'You know why they're doing all this, don't you?'

I take an intense interest in a pork pie, knowing she's going to tell me regardless.

'To take our minds off the murder,' she whispers, 'to show we're a community not cowed by what's happened.'

Only in Britain can tea and sandwiches be regarded as an act of defiance.

'And . . .', she wags a finger, 'it's a practice run for the Queen's

Diamond Jubilee later this summer. They already had the furniture, the bunting, these silly little plastic flags, the fifties music. We're guinea pigs for the main event. They'll be worried stiff that something gets broken or ruined.'

I guess she has a point. I stare at the slab of jellied pie, but I've no appetite.

Jean rocks back in her plastic chair. She shunts it so it's sideways and she can look to the right and see her house and Barbara's house.

'Broken or ruined,' she repeats. She glazes over, as if she's watching a film, and I wonder what's in her mind's eye. Is she trying to picture the smoke rising above Barbara's house, just as I am?

Jean faces me, her beady eyes scrutinising. 'You really don't know what went on, do you, all those years ago?'

I give her a disapproving look, but she'll be used to that. 'I know about you and Don. No wonder Barbara hated you.'

'Me and Don?' Jean splutters like a backfiring exhaust pipe. 'You've got it completely wrong, you daft old bat.'

She shakes her head, muttering obscenities, then piles an array of treats – some tuna paste sandwiches, a few cocktail sausages, cheese and pineapple skewered on sticks – onto a paper plate and covers it with a couple of napkins.

'Me and Don!' Jean repeats. She stands abruptly. 'I'll leave you and your imagination to enjoy yourselves.'

She stuffs a slice of Battenberg in her mouth, then saunters off back to her house. Of course she'd deny it. I imagine she only came outside to taunt me.

Even though I'm not hungry, I might as well try that pork pie anyway, some comfort food.

I lean across to pick up a slice but knock a bottle of sparkling elderflower with my elbow. It wobbles, then falls from the table, smashing on the ground, glass shards glinting in the sunshine as the contents flow down the drain. Everything goes quiet, all eyes suddenly on me. The clack of tutting. It's not the attention I was hoping for.

I drop back down to my seat and the hum of happy chatter continues, another song starting in the background.

I look again at Barbara's house and feel a need for confirmation. I make my way up her drive and along the narrow, gloomy path between her property and Jean's. In the back garden, a patch of grass and a section of varnished fence are black, as if eaten away. I inspect the scorched remains.

An eerie feeling causes me to spin around. I almost jump at the sight of someone in the shadows, a man, watching me. He darts back, though I've seen enough to feel the chill. I follow but I'm not quick enough. By the time I've reached the front he's merged with the crowd.

Harry prowls my mind. What if the murderer isn't someone in this community? What if the killer was searching for something and thought that Barbara knew where it was? What if they're prepared to do anything to get it?

I've no one to turn to.

The sky becomes overcast. This party is no longer inviting. If I'm to be on my own, I might as well be inside where I'm warm.

I hobble to our house, glancing behind me after each step.

CHAPTER 21

James is as quiet as you, Albert, not said a word since he got here, just sitting morose on the sofa, me adjacent in our chair. Shirley still won't give him his mobile phone so he can't contact his friends and it's left him with nothing to do. We're prisoners together in a silent room; I'm to make sure he stays grounded, he's to make sure I don't wander off. Both guard and captive. Shirley's not told me anything more. She just brought James round after he'd finished school and then shot off, saying she had an important meeting. More solicitor talk I would expect.

Outside, it's cold and grey.

'Want anything to eat or drink, James?'

He shakes his head, hair flopping. It's not easy to get someone to open up. With a machine you can take it apart to understand its workings, how it functions and fits together. Humans are infinitely more complex. Words have to be your tools to prise them open.

'You know you can tell me anything.'

James picks at his black woollen jumper, pulling out bits of thread and rolling them between finger and thumb. Silence is even more unnerving with company than when you're alone.

Can I remember what it was like to be a teenager and to feel what he's feeling?

I was so young when I met you, Albert, but all this coldness takes me back to the cottage where I first saw you, where it seemed as permanently frozen as my memory of it. I swear there were icicles on the windowsills inside, the windows hazed with frost, some magical winter wonderland. I came to you with a problem, just as James has a problem now. The chill that greeted me when I stepped through the door, the predicament I needed help with, it feels so similar. I would have been eighteen, only a few years older than James.

I didn't know if you'd help me; as hesitant as a fawn in my approach. Our eyes met and I saw warmth in yours and felt my cheeks flush. You listened patiently as I stumbled over my words, then showed concern. It was a puzzle in need of some lateral thinking. My stubbornness, determination and competitiveness didn't make seeking help an easy choice. You had to be like that, in the environment we found ourselves in. But your intelligence impressed. Is that what first attracted me? And your generosity. Your handsomeness didn't hurt either. Together we solved it, forged a bond, formed a team.

If I was in James's position, how would I have reacted? I'd be mortified at being in trouble; I've always tried to do the right thing. But I'd be equally resolute to put it right. Is he of similar character? It certainly seems easier these days to lose a reputation, with so much more scrutiny and awareness. A constant pressure to achieve, condemnation if you do wrong. Will that make him more willing to prove himself?

'We can fix whatever you've done.'

I look at the grandfather clock. I've had to put all the clocks forward for summer time and it's been bewildering, as some change automatically these days, like the television, while others need a manual adjustment, leaving me uncertain as to which one's correct. I've been left with them telling different hours, making me disorientated, with even time confused and out of sync.

Looking at that giant clock takes me back as well, to that place in our past and to my favourite anecdote, something else that's stuck in my mind through the decades. I have an idea.

'Which way round do the hands of the clock go, James?'

He looks across with puzzled scorn. 'Clockwise, obviously.'

Ah, he speaks. 'Not necessarily.'

'It's the only answer.'

'Not if you're inside the clock. From that viewpoint they turn anticlockwise.'

A wry smile brightens his face.

'I used to have a clever friend who would ask people that,' I tell him. 'You have to see things from the other perspective. It was his way of making sure you think laterally and that you consider all the possibilities.'

The sun breaks free from the gloom to shine through the window, illuminating the room. James nods slowly.

'It also teaches you not just to look at a machine how you see it but to figure out what's going on inside,' I add.

'How does that help us?'

'If we're going to catch this killer, we have to think how they think.'

He seems sullen again, slumping back. 'Everyone thinks it's me. They know I stole Barbara's purse and they'll presume I killed her to get it.'

'I don't think that at all, James, but you need to tell me what did happen so that I can understand.'

He sighs heavily and for a moment I fear he may keep it all bottled up. Then he relents.

'We were being stupid.' He shrugs. 'It was just a dare, an initiation.'

James runs a hand through his hair before gripping it at the nape of his neck. I stay quiet to give him room to speak. It's like waiting for a tortoise to emerge from its shell. Eventually, he continues.

'Three of us. Started out as a challenge to see how far we'd go.' He yanks more thread from the hem of his jumper, which unravels into his hand. 'Liam sneaked into Vera Smith's house and took her purse. We egged him on. Never thought he'd actually do it.'

I can't hide my dismay.

'We didn't do anything with it, he just kept it. Said it was a buzz. Then it was Gaz's turn to prove himself.' He twists the thread around a finger. 'So we came back another time and he got Dora Singleton's purse. Couldn't believe how easy it was.'

Even though I love him dearly I can feel anger building. How could he be involved in doing something so hurtful to my neighbours? For once, I hold my tongue.

'They dared me too. After those two had done it, I couldn't back out. We'd be quits then.' The way his hands are working, I fear he'll completely unravel his jumper. 'We'd seen Barbara go in her house and not lock her door. I crept in, saw her purse in the kitchen, think she was upstairs, grabbed it and ran.'

He rips a strand of wool free and it falls into a little bundle in his palm.

I can't contain it any more. 'How could you steal from Barbara?'

James hangs his head.

'She's always been so kind to you, James, and the last thing you did in her life was to rob her. What a wicked thing to do. I should get your friends round and box all your ears.'

'We didn't think.' He rolls the wool into a ball with his thumb and forefinger. 'It was just a joke, we didn't mean any harm.' He flicks the ball away. 'Just wanted to see how brave we were.'

'It isn't brave, James, to steal from an old lady.'

He keeps his head down, hair hiding his face. 'I know. It was stupid. Sorry.'

James sweeps his hair back and looks me in the eye. 'I never touched Barbara though. Never even saw her. The kitchen was fine when I went in, she must have been killed afterwards.' Those bright blue eyes pleading. 'You've gotta believe me, Gran, I wouldn't do that.'

I know others will see someone on the brink of manhood, capable and strong enough to cause real harm. But I see only the boy that I read picture books to after tucking him up in bed, the boy who always listens to me, the boy who comforted me in my darkest moment of grief. And, despite what he's done, I see your kindness and sensitivity in him, Albert.

'I know you wouldn't, but look where your actions have got you.'

'Didn't think anyone had seen me but someone must have. Now one of my mates has grassed me up.'

'The truth always comes out.'

It breaks my heart to see him looking so distraught; I cannot fuel the anger against him for long, it dissipates like a cloud.

'I panicked and chucked the purse when I heard what had happened, but the police found it. Now I'm worried they'll have evidence of me going in the house and I'll get framed for murder.'

I know he wouldn't lie to me. A calmness washes over me. I have to do what I can to help him.

'If you tell the truth, then everything will be all right.'

'They'll fit it around what I did.'

I stroke our chair's armrest. The lad has put himself in a bad position.

'We'll find a way to show it wasn't you.'

'That's why we've gotta solve it.' Desperation floods his voice. He hauls off his jumper and throws it onto the back of the sofa where it lands precariously. 'It's roasting in here, why do you always have the heating full blast?'

It still feels cold to me, I'd be shivering if I turned the heating down.

'That window cleaner,' says James, 'he reckons he collected from Barbara at five p.m., but that's when I took her purse and we made sure there was no one else around; he hadn't even started collecting on this street then.' The colour is coming back to his cheeks. 'I couldn't say anything before without landing myself in it, but his story doesn't stack up. He must have called later, after I'd taken Barbara's purse.'

'I'm not sure he did it.' I remember Michael Cavanagh visiting and tell James all about it.

'But how could Barbara have paid him if I'd taken her purse? He could have called round soon after and maybe she accused him of nicking it and they argued and he lashed out.'

All this talk of theft makes me think of my own situation.

'My purse went missing too. Are you sure none of your so-called friends took it?'

He snorts. 'They wouldn't dare do that.'

I have a confession of my own. I have to be honest with him too. 'I did find my purse later, but I'm certain someone had taken it as it wasn't where I'd have put it.'

'Why would a thief give it back?'

'I don't know.' It's my turn to sound forlorn as it certainly seems unlikely. 'There's been lots of strange things happening. I'm certain someone got in here the other night and was looking around until I disturbed them.'

James tucks his hair behind his ears. 'Could have been the window cleaner. Maybe he nicked your purse, and then put it back cos he was worried about getting caught.'

I scrunch my lips. 'I still think Jean's involved. She's a nasty sort. Might have been trying to get to me as she knows we're on to her.'

'We're no nearer to solving it.' James rocks back, causing his jumper to fall to the floor. 'I look guiltier than any of them.'

'Don't despair.'

'But what can we do? They might as well lock me up now.'

We sit in companionable silence.

James turns to me. 'That memory of Barbara, has anything at all come back to you?'

My expression answers for me. I feel as much use as a lead parachute.

'I thought of something else,' says James. 'Have you got any photos of Barbara?'

I retrieve some photo albums from the cardboard box and we flick through them, pulling out the odd one that Barbara appears in, at special occasions and gatherings. James lays them on the floor, so that several Barbaras are staring up at me.

'Do you have anything that belongs to her?'

I'm a little concerned as to where this is going, but I recall a silk scarf that she lent me for a trip out that I hadn't returned, and I'm so pleased at having remembered it that I hurry to retrieve it and hand it to James.

'Great.' He places it around my neck as I sit back down. The Barbaras watch me from different directions.

'This time, instead of closing your eyes, focus on Barbara, taking each photo in turn. Feel her presence around you.'

I'm not sure about this, but I humour him, looking at Barbara in different situations, different times, different surroundings. One photograph in particular catches my eye, she looks curvier in it than I can ever remember. That same anxious expression as in my memory.

I hear her voice: *Whatever will you think of me, Margaret?* I repeat it aloud.

James edges forward. 'Anything more?'

The scarf's softness feels comforting, but there's something unsettling about it being hers. I concentrate really hard on each picture, but with all these Barbaras, with her property wrapped around my neck, with a molecule of her citrus scent in the air, it's starting to feel eerie.

I shake my head, then take the scarf off, fold it up and lay it on the armrest. 'It's gone, James.'

'It felt like we were getting somewhere.' He tangles his left hand in his hair. 'I won't give up on that memory.' A spark of determination, that's the spirit.

I scoop up the photos and arrange them in their respective

folders, which I put back in the cardboard box, carrying it to the bureau. The wooden box catches my eye and a thought arrives with it, of a time when someone tried to pin the blame on me and I did the wrong thing, letting everyone down.

'These friends of yours, James, what if there's a reason behind them telling the police about you?'

His face morphs from a downturned-mouth sullenness to an inquisitively raised eyebrow. 'You think they're setting me up?'

'They seem keen for you to take the rap. What if one of them went back after you'd gone?'

'It couldn't have been Gaz, he ran off in front of me and was well ahead, but I didn't see Liam move from his hiding place.'

'Perhaps he went looking for something else he could take and poor Barbara tried to stop him.'

'Liam did go back to Dora's house when Gaz took her purse. Thinking about it, I don't know why he did that.'

'What's this Liam like?'

'He's a bit, erm, dodgy.'

That situation I found myself in rears itself again. 'He could be looking to frame you to save himself. What do you think, James?'

There's one photo of Barbara still lying on the carpet that I must have missed, a friendly smile warming her face. James contemplates it intensely.

'I think we've got a new suspect.'

CHAPTER 22

I have long dreaded this day.

A raw wind whips around the cemetery, stinging my cheeks, numbing my fingers. This harsh winter seems everlasting. I stand in front of your grave, Albert, a bunch of white carnations gripped in my hand. It's never seemed real to read your name on the gravestone, precious words etched in white on black marble. My breath becomes mist that disappears into the pale blue sky. I run my fingertips over the engraved words as if reading Braille, as if it will help me understand them, as if they will permeate my skin to somehow make sense inside of me. I trace the shallow ridges of the letters, their curves and edges. They are cold and hard, still alien and bewildering. We spent so long choosing the tributes but how could they ever do you justice?

You're so far away out here, but never far from my thoughts. I can't believe it's been a year; time is jumbled and confused. It could be only yesterday, the pain still intense, yet feels a lifetime since I last saw your face, felt your touch, heard your voice.

My rock for sixty years.

A sob builds inside me but I swallow it down. Why is it the painful things that I can remember so clearly? A solitary tear escapes, rolls down my cold cheek and drips to the ground, soaking into the soil.

No. I must pull myself together. You wouldn't want me to give up, to just wallow in self-pity. I think of our life together, as if a film on fast forward. A courtship of laughter and dancing, wedding day bells, the wail of a newborn, sports day cheers, colleagues slapping you on your back at your retirement party. All over too soon. Time speeds up as you get older, a train you can't stop. But at least these memories warm me, a glimpse of sunshine through the clouds.

I wipe my cheek.

I wish Shirley was here. She will come to pay her respects later, my love. She couldn't bring me this morning as she's dealing with James and the solicitor. Matthew was going on about it costing him a fortune and that it'll bleed them dry. Shirley fears James has gone feral. What was it she said? 'Great, now I have a delinquent son on top of everything else.' I presume I'm the 'everything else'.

Shirley arranged for Mr Braithwaite to bring me, not trusting me to get here by myself, even though I've made the journey many a time on the bus. She'd prefer it if I was chaperoned everywhere. He's waiting in his car.

I stoop as far as I can to place the flowers gently upon your grave.

'For you, my love,' I whisper, the words lost in the wind. The bouquet softens the stark black. The cemetery is well maintained with pristine paths and clean, smooth gravestones and the ornate church standing majestically behind us. In front, there are pleasant views of rolling hills and bare trees, the tranquillity only broken by the odd caw of a crow.

You can truly rest in peace here, Albert.

The rows of neatly positioned gravestones make me think of Barbara, another cherished life taken so cruelly, hers unresolved with too many questions that must be answered.

Promise me you'll do it, Margaret.

I swear, I will find out who murdered her and then we can all rest in peace.

It's time for me to leave you. I blow a dry kiss that the wind snatches.

'Until we're together again, my love.'

Trudging back to the pathway, I notice a tall, slightly stooped figure, leaning against a wall, studying me. A coldness runs through my blood. I head in his direction but he bolts, his long strides too quick for me. I feel forever watched, forever chasing shadows.

I shake it off as much as I can and return to the car park.

Mr Braithwaite is by his car. 'Sure you've finished?'

I nod. 'It's time to go home.'

He doesn't seem to be avoiding me like everyone else. I don't recall seeing him at the street party and he hasn't mentioned James, so maybe he hasn't heard about the arrest. I'm certainly not going to bring it up.

Mr Braithwaite holds the passenger door open.

'I do appreciate you bringing me, though I'd have been quite all right coming by myself.'

'I'm sure you would have.' He winks. 'But it's for Shirley's sake as much as our own, to stop her worrying.'

I give a knowing smile. 'Have you any family, Mr Braithwaite?'

The briefest grimace on his face, like a candle flickering. 'Afraid not,' he says quietly.

I ease onto the leather seat. I know nothing about cars but this does seem a lovely vehicle. You'd be impressed, Albert. I don't know the make but I'd definitely describe it as luxury with its long, slender bonnet and sleek, shiny bodywork. It's very spacious and comfortable. Mr Braithwaite slides himself behind the wheel and turns the key, the engine purring into life. He puts the heaters on to make it even cosier, pointing them in my direction. The dashboard is full of buttons, dials and displays. Cars these days are more computers than machinery, controlled by microchips and wires as much as cogs and mechanisms. They're a long way from your first car, which just had an analogue speedometer and Bakelite radio.

Mr Braithwaite is clean-shaven and wearing a very smart suit and elegant grey coat, like a well-groomed chauffeur. A taste of how the other half lives. Perhaps I have been too hasty to judge him as other neighbours speak well in his favour.

'You're looking very smart today, Mr Braithwaite.' We slowly pull out of the car park.

'I've a meeting with the bank later.' He slips through the gears, a brief smile fading into seriousness. 'How are you managing without Albert?'

'I'm soldiering on, thank you.'

'Must be very difficult keeping on top of things.'

'I cope. Mustn't grumble.'

'If you ever need help, I'm happy to lend a hand. Don't feel you always have to call for Shirley and Matthew if anything needs doing. I'm only next door.'

'I'll bear that in mind, dear.'

We pass the bus stop where I would've got off if I'd come alone. It's only a few minutes' walk from there to the cemetery so I'd have managed that no problem. My hip doesn't feel too bad today, so thank heaven for small mercies.

We're turning right into King George Avenue, I recognise the route well. It's only about thirty minutes on the bus even when they go round the houses.

A moment of silence. I succumb to an urge to fill it. 'I don't think I've ever asked you much about your job, Mr Braithwaite. What is it that you do?'

'Please, call me Steve.' He turns the wheel effortlessly as we curve around a bend. 'I work in finance and have my own franchise of a very prestigious firm.'

'How's that going?' I should take an interest, it's only polite considering he brought me here.

'Have to admit it's tough at the moment. Not a lot of money out there to invest.' I don't really follow the economy, it's all double Dutch to me. 'Not that we don't do a good job. We've a lot of very happy and successful clients and a good reputation.'

He turns down Shaftesbury Avenue and over the roundabout, skirting around the town centre to avoid getting stuck in traffic, I presume. We're not far from home now. Another ten minutes.

'It's not something I know too much about.'

'Basically, I invest people's money in stocks and shares so they get a good return. You have to get it right. You can't be losing people's savings so we don't take gambles. We ensure you get a reasonable return without any risk.'

'I don't know anything about stocks.' And no real interest either.

'Take yourself, for example. You must have a pension, a tidy sum tucked away to give you a comfortable retirement.'

I don't like questions about money. 'I never got involved with the money side of things. Albert dealt with all that.'

'I presume Albert made sure you were well provided for?'

'Albert was always very good with money and made sure his family wanted for nothing.'

'I'm sure he did,' Mr Braithwaite says, breezily. 'Only, these things change, you see. Shares go up and down. Companies can go into liquidation. Investments can lose money. That's why you need to stay on top of things.' It all sounds a bit of a fuss. 'The markets can be very volatile.'

He pulls up at a red light and starts tapping the steering wheel with one finger. The only markets I know about are where I get my fruit and veg. I leave Matthew to deal with things like that. Can't say that I like leaving it to Matthew; the bluntest tool in the box is hardly going to be a financial whizz-kid. He seems to be taking more control, dealing with things that he says I don't understand. Shirley tells me he's being helpful and spending his valuable time saving me money.

Tap-tap-tap. The amber light joins the red light. The car revs. 'Well, if you ever need someone to look over things for you, an objective viewpoint, a professional's opinion, just let me know.'

It's not a bad idea. Someone to make sure that Matthew's doing a good job. 'I might take you up on that.'

The green light beams and the car pulls away. He turns right. I'm not sure of this road. Oh heavens, maybe I'm lost again, I do feel disorientated. These houses look familiar but I'm not sure where I am. I was certain we were heading the right way home and weren't far away. The car jerks over a speed bump, the sensation making my stomach lurch.

'So sorry, Mrs Winterbottom.' Mr Braithwaite holds up a hand. 'I took that far too fast.'

He slows down and it feels as if we're barely moving. I peer out of the passenger window, recognising the street now, the familiarity bringing a sharp sense of relief. We're back at Garnon Crescent.

Mr Braithwaite pulls up outside his house, opens his door and steps out. I glance down and something glistening next to the foot mat catches my eye; hadn't noticed it before, perhaps it rolled from under the mat during the journey. I bend down and pick it up. It's the small silver brooch you gave me, Albert, the butterfly with little jewels on the wings that twinkle in my hand, as if brought alive by the sunlight. When I'm not wearing it, I keep it in my purse so it's nearby. It must have fallen out earlier. It has a lot of sentimental value as it was the last present you ever bought me. You remained romantic even into our twilight years, buying me small items of jewellery or little gifts without special occasion or reason.

Mr Braithwaite opens the passenger door. I put the brooch in my purse, which I shove into my coat pocket.

'You all right there, Mrs Winterbottom?'

'I'm fine, thank you.'

I make my way up the garden path to our front door and unlock and open it. I'd like to look over our photographs with a nice cup of tea to bring the good memories flooding back.

CHAPTER 23

He's late. I can't abide tardiness, as you well know, Albert. Making people wait is arrogant and thoughtless.

I sit on the swing, the tough seat digging into the flesh of my hips, my backside no longer svelte enough to fit its curvature. James is pacing the edge of the rubber rectangle around me like a tiger encaged in a zoo. I don't have the energy to waste. I don't have time to waste either, which I'm beginning to think that this is. We should have known he's not the type to keep to appointments. The slate sky, with its threat of a bone-chilling downpour, darkens further. I'm wrapped up as warm as can be in a winter coat and a bobble hat that wouldn't look out of place on our teapot, but the wind still gives me a shiver.

James escapes his enclosure and sets off again to the brink of a slope to cast his eyes down a gravel path. It's the third time he's ventured off to act as lookout. He can't be away from home for too long in case Shirley checks up on him.

I place my stick on the ground, my joints groaning. Gripping the cold metal of the swing's chains, I consider how little the park has altered over the decades: the copse of trees behind me where we'd enjoy woodland strolls bathed in sunshine and birdsong, the expanse of grass often filled with football or cricket matches, and this small playground that's never been modernised. Nothing's changed.

I propel myself with a flurry of steps and push forward, my legs free from the ground, the briefest soar through the air, then rocking back and forth until my journey dissipates. The seconds of play only add to the churning in my stomach.

We used to bring Tom and Shirley here and it's only a few years ago that James would be running rings around us too. You'd be on that field, Albert, kicking a ball with him or bowling at a steady pace then making sure it was James that ran to retrieve it when he hit it for six. On this very swing you'd push him as he shouted 'Higher!', his little legs pointing towards the sun, giggles bubbling from him. 'Hold on tight,' I'd warn, worried that he'd go too far, too fast, and fly free to land with a crunch on the path and a trip to A & E, or worse.

No, it's us that have changed, not the park, so steadfast in its stability. There's no birdsong today, just the wind tormenting the branches.

'I can see him.' James jogs back from the slope. 'He's coming.'

Peering down the path to one of the park's many entrances, I spy a figure on a bicycle passing through a wrought-iron gate. He speeds towards us, looming larger and larger as he nears. I stay seated, James fidgeting next to me. We glance at each other and I try to give him a reassuring look.

Liam skids to a halt as he reaches the swings, jumping from his battered BMX in a movement as practised as a gymnast's leap from a pommel horse. He props the bicycle, its red paintwork flecked with mud and rust, against the swing's frame, then takes in both of us in the slow sweep of a glassy stare. He thrusts his hands into the pockets of his sweatshirt, its hood up and casting a shadow across his face. He's lean and lanky, wearing black tracksuit bottoms and trainers. Wisps of dark hair sprout from his lip and chin, not unlike myself really. He's a few years older than James, at least. This is no school friend. Liam stands there in silence, legs wide apart, chewing gum. For a moment, I think we're in a stand-off.

'What's this?' Liam nods towards me. 'Thought she was your bird, Jay, or you her carer? You wipe her arse for her? You get off on that sort of stuff?'

I pick up my stick and grip the handle tight.

'Don't speak like that in front of Gran.' A quiver in James's voice belies his boldness.

Liam sneers. He's clutching an object in his sweatshirt pocket, his knuckles bulging against the cotton. I can't quite tell what it is, though I don't like the look of it.

'What you want?' Irritation grinds the gravel of his voice. He glances around at the empty park.

I suddenly feel ridiculous. Two teenagers and an old woman gathering furtively at the park swings. It must resemble the world's least likely drug deal!

'About that night, five weeks ago today.' I can almost hear the words ricocheting around James's head like snooker balls as he tries to frame them. 'What did you tell the cops?'

'Heard you got arrested. Just told the pigs the truth, didn't I.'

'Which was?' James pulls himself to his full height but it lacks certainty.

Liam studies me as if I'm an undercover agent.

'It's OK. Gran knows everything.'

Liam scowls. 'It was just a dare. All right, we took those

purses but we was just messing about and didn't know what would happen to that old woman. That had nothing to do with me.'

'What did happen to her?' James adds a sliver of steel to his tone.

'Dunno, Jay, you tell me. Was you that went into her house, took her purse, then she winds up dead. All I know is that you came running outta there as if your arse was on fire and now we're all in trouble.'

'I didn't do anything to hurt her.'

'You nicked her purse. How do I know what you did to get it? You could have done anything.'

'You know I wouldn't do that.'

'I dunno what you'd do, that's what I told the pigs. The kid's gone in there and for all I know he's wrestled that purse off her and throttled the old woman.'

'Why'd you tell them that? I didn't do it.' James spits out the words, his face hardening. I can see him falling into the web of Liam's logic, entangled in the stickiness of its condemnation.

It sends me back several decades. To a cold hut, my manager sitting stiff-shouldered and stern-faced at his desk asking me over and over what had happened to the transcripts, how I must know something about where they were, how things don't just disappear. Eyes fixed on the woodgrain knot behind his left ear, my face reddened.

I return from inside that hut to the park, my brain switching slickly from past to present. I look at James, now shrinking as the enormity of his situation kicks hard, and see myself stood there, albeit another era, another world.

Liam still has hold of whatever is in his pocket. I try again to remember my conversation with Barbara, visualising her anxious face. Was she somehow warning me about Liam? Could he be connected to her or have been threatening her in any way?

'May I ask, young man, did you know the deceased at all?'

Liam turns to look at me as if he'd forgotten I was there, the polish of politeness slipping him off guard. 'What you say?'

'My neighbour, Barbara Jones, did you know her?'

'No.'

'You hadn't met her before.'

'Never seen her in me life.' The face behind the shadow scrunches as if considering every possibility to a complex sum. 'Why you wanna know?'

'I'm simply curious as to whether you had interacted before.' Liam glowers, but I have his full attention. He's so covered up and defensive, that it's hard to tell if he's lying. 'And what did you do after James left Barbara's house?'

'You what?'

'When I legged it, what did you do?' James picks up my prompting. We ask the questions, I'd told him, we lead the way and get under his skin, we don't allow him to intimidate us. That was the plan.

'I hid round the corner for a bit after seeing you run off.'

'Then what?' asks James.

'Then I just went home.'

'Where were you hiding?'

'Down that ginnel, behind the fence with the missing post.'

'How long for?' I can see James rising in stature as he fires each question.

'Dunno, ten minutes or so.' Liam scratches his hood with his free hand.

'You didn't go over to Barbara's house?'

'Why would I have done that?'

'To see what had gone off.' James shrugs. 'To check it out.'

Between the shadows, I catch a glimpse of genuine bewilderment in the contortion of Liam's features. 'Have you been chatting to your old man?'

'What's this got to do with him?' James's expression matches Liam's and they freeze as they analyse each other.

'Look, I didn't go anywhere near it.' Annoyance rises in Liam's voice, but it appears it's not just the hood that's hiding something.

'When Gaz took that other purse, you went back to the house he'd got it from,' says James.

'To make sure he'd took it and it weren't still in the kitchen. That he hadn't just shown us some purse he'd got from his auntie.'

'Rather than take his word for it, you went back to a crime scene.' James is in full flow now in his potential career as a barrister.

'To make sure Gaz hadn't neshed out of a dare.'

'So wouldn't you have done the same with me?'

'Didn't feel the need.'

Spots of rain splatter around us.

'I think you'd have done the same.'

'What you saying?'

'That you had plenty of time and opportunity to go back to Barbara's house.'

The raindrops increase, we could get soaked.

'You saying I killed that old woman?'

Suddenly, I picture James as a boy on the swing and wonder

if I'm letting him fly too high. I stand up, stick in hand, but neither of them notice me.

'Why would you have hung around?' asks James. 'Did you go in her house to see what else you could get?'

Liam moves forward and James's foot lifts as if to take a step back but just hovers. Liam's knuckles twitch in his sweatshirt pocket.

'Go on, say it.' Liam grabs the neckline of James's jumper with his free hand.

I move forward, lift my stick, push it between them and then use it to shove Liam away from James. Liam lets go and glares at me like a growling terrier. I steady myself, the stick grounded again as my prop.

'I think you did it,' Liam snarls at James. 'You were in that house, summat went off, you took her purse and then you fled. That's what everyone thinks.'

James pulls his jumper into shape, then shakes his head.

'That's what I'm gonna tell everyone. The pigs, the papers, our gang, anyone what wants to know. They'll all believe it was you cos it all adds up, don't it?'

Liam grabs his bicycle and hoists it in front of him, his eyes darting between the two of us. 'This is just weird, mate.'

Then he's back on his bicycle and riding into the distance without a goodbye.

'You OK, Gran?' James gives me a hand as we walk from the playground. It's still spitting with rain.

'I'm fine. We'd better get back before the heavens open.'

'What you reckon?'

'He has a temper, he's insecure, he certainly has a nasty streak, he was in the area after you'd left so had a window of opportunity, and he's definitely trying to pin the blame on you.'

Concern sweeps across James's face. 'He's right everyone will think it's me. And he'll add fuel to that.'

'Don't worry, we have him in our sights and we'll get to the bottom of this.'

'Don't know why he brought Dad into it.'

We wander from the park, James trudging, me wobbly with my stick, my hip stiff from sitting on that swing for too long. It no longer seems the peaceful place of family fun that it once was. The park hasn't changed, I remind myself, it's us. I think of my own situation all those years ago and how Liam could be shifting the blame. And I think of Barbara and our meeting that's lost in my brain and wonder, for what feels like the millionth time, what it was she was trying to tell me.

CHAPTER 24

I really need to go food shopping, I'm like Old Mother Hubbard. If it was up to me, even though it's a Sunday, I'd grab my trusty shopping bag and set off for town, but I don't think my warden will allow that. She's in my home, waiting for me to make mistakes to justify more unnecessary medical tests. Since James's arrest, Shirley's been either too busy dealing with legalities or asking me endless questions on how I am and things that seem to have nothing to do with anything, as if I'm back in school being tested. She's either not available or draining.

I step into the kitchen. Shirley and James glance sharply up at me, and their low voices go silent.

I narrow my eyes. 'I have to go shopping.'

'Whatever for?' Shirley's voice reaches the pitch of a soprano.

'There's no bread, milk, butter or cereal.' I tick them off on my fingers. 'And I'm low on teabags and cheese.'

It'll cost me quite a bit to buy that lot as prices are always shooting up. They're putting the cost of a first-class stamp up from 46p to 60p and a second-class from 36p to 50p. It's astronomical. How do they think us pensioners can afford that?

'Nonsense.' Shirley makes the high note. 'You've plenty.'

I know what is and isn't in my own house. I open a cupboard as if about to say 'ta-da'.

It's full of tins and packets. I swear it was empty this morning. I check the caddy and it's stuffed with teabags. An unsettling feeling rises in me. I open the fridge door expecting empty shelves and a lonely light. Cartons and containers are neatly stacked. Maybe I should be pleased, but it's like seeing summer when you know its winter.

Noticing the look that Shirley and James give each other, I scuttle around the kitchen opening cupboards and drawers.

'These were all empty this morning.' Even as I say it, with the sensation of a million ants crawling over me, I know it sounds daft. 'Who's filled them?'

'Mum, we did your shopping yesterday, you helped us put everything away. I didn't want you tempted into going out on your own again, remember?'

'I might have wanted to buy my own things.' I search for the memory but there's nothing there, only dead ends and blind spots. 'Or I might have fancied a change of brand.'

'Don't get upset, it's saved you having to go out.'

'Teabags, I don't have enough teabags and you know I like several cups a day.' Where's the caddy? I must show her.

'Mum, you've just this second looked. You've enough to last you weeks.'

James gives her a scowl. I don't know why he's getting annoyed, it's not his things that keep disappearing and reappearing as if I'm living with a malevolent magician.

'I don't know how they got there, Albert.'

Shirley's face blanches, her lips opening to speak then puckering instead.

'It's OK, Gran.' James's voice is soothing and he puts a gentle hand on my shoulder that steadies me. 'We won't let you go hungry or thirsty. Anything you need, I'll sort.'

Shirley takes a deep breath. 'Why don't you go and sit back down in the lounge, Mum?' Her tone is warm but frayed like a well-worn jumper.

I'll go back to my crossword. Leaving the kitchen, I see again their furtive glances. They're up to something. I stop in the hallway, just out of sight.

'Why'd you have to talk to her like that?' James's voice bristles with anger. 'There's no need to humiliate her.'

'It's hard to stay patient, she can be very trying.'

'Leave her alone. She can manage.'

My ears are burning, my cheeks flushed. A spark of pride within the heat, that James is sticking up for me. He's right, isn't he, Albert?

'She can't, James.' Shirley's tone is resolute. 'We've been lucky so far, it's only a matter of time before something bad happens.'

'Were you serious when you agreed with Dad about putting Gran in a home?'

'I said I thought he had a point that it would be the safest place for her and that we'd look at what's available.'

I should have known Matthew would be behind this. I steady myself against the wall, one hand stroking the wallpaper, and look at all the framed photographs lining the hallway, this house the backdrop in each one. My heart thumps.

'Then you are gonna put her into care.'

'It wouldn't be packing her off to some awful institution. It'll be somewhere nice, somewhere safe, somewhere she'll like.'

'See, you've already made your mind up.'

Everything I know is here. There'd be no coming back. She might as well send me to Mars.

'No, I'm saying let's see what there is and then we all, including Gran, can decide.'

Silence hangs in the air. The grandfather clock chimes and I have to put my shaking hand over my mouth to stifle a shriek.

'Mind. Made. Up.' I hear the soft squeak of James's trainers on the lino. 'She's happy here and won't want to leave.'

'Doesn't mean it's the best place for her.'

'She could live with us.'

'Me and Dad have to go to work. Gran needs someone to look after her.'

My brittle nails scrape at the textured wallpaper. I don't want pity or people doing things for me.

'She can get better. She . . .' I think he's about to tell her something else but then his voice trails off.

'That's the problem, she's only going to get worse. I told you what the doctor said. There's no cure, they can only, hopefully, slow it down.'

Shirley's talking about that awful GP. So, he thinks I have a disease.

'All these things she's been doing and the way she did the test. It's Alzheimer's, advancing rapidly. She'll have had it a while, she's not been right since Granddad . . .' She falters, the rest of the sentence gone.

My heart sinks to my stomach. I remember the doctor trying to explain something to me but I was too distracted, too annoyed, too lost in the mist, to make sense of it.

'That's just one opinion, another doctor might say different.'

He won't give up the fight, but something dark and ugly that I've avoided looking at is staring me straight in the face.

'My grandmother was the same, James, it started with her forgetting things and got worse. She died before we really knew what it was. These things can be passed down.'

'She doesn't seem ill.'

'She won't be forgetful all the time, she'll still have good moments. Believe me, she can be as sharp as ever.'

'But she can't get better?'

'She'll forget more and more. There are . . . her mind's like . . . that sieve. Full of holes.'

No. It's not like that. When I'm trying to remember something it's the same as when we're doing those crossword puzzles and you know the answer but it just won't come to you. You know it must be in there but you can't force it back. Then there are parts of my life just wiped slate clean from my mind like chalk from a blackboard, the dust scattering. I thought it was just old age.

'Does it matter? It doesn't change who she is.'

'It's only the start.' Shirley's voice is flat. 'One day she'll forget how to look after herself completely and who we all are and it'll become so difficult to communicate or care for her.'

I bite my lip, hard enamel digging into soft skin.

'That day could be far off.' James sounds so sad.

'I hope so, I really do, but we can't let her keep putting herself in danger.'

Only the wall holds me up. Blood thundering in my ears, the rest of me ice. My brain a time bomb, nothing to stop its pathway to destruction. I'm as dependable as a stranger to them, and they will become strangers to me. Memories vanishing, as if never there. I'll never forget you, Albert. I can't forget you. I won't.

'She'll always be the same person to me,' says James quietly. His footsteps again. A tap running, splashing. The crunch of teeth through crisp flesh, molars munching. A pause. 'Like this apple. The core remains.'

'Maybe,' says Shirley. 'But we have to accept that the person we know will no longer be there.'

A strange sound, a sort of snuffling followed by a jagged outtake of breath.

'Oh, James!' Shirley's tone is now full of compassion.

'I don't want to lose her too.' His quavering voice wet and nasally.

I haven't heard James cry for years, not since he became a teenager. Another piece of my heart shatters. I can't bear it. That I should be the cause of this pain.

'I know how much she means to you, James.'

I can't listen to any more, I don't want them talking about me, being upset over me. I want it all to stop.

Pulling myself up straight, I take the deepest breath, then march into the room. 'I can still hear, you know.'

Shirley freezes then reddens.

James's face is as crumpled as his clothes, tears coursing his cheeks. A string of snot dribbles from his nose and bits of apple tumble around his open mouth. He pulls himself together, wipes his nose on his sleeve. He's just a boy. Just a boy. I give him a hug, his arms limp at first, until he reaches around and holds me too. After an age we pull silently apart.

Shirley hands James some kitchen roll and he blows his nose like a foghorn.

'I thought you were in the lounge.' She picks up a dishcloth and starts wiping the clean worktop. 'How long have you been listening?'

'Long enough.'

'I'm so sorry, Mum.' A note of anguish pierces what remains of my heart. 'You weren't supposed to hear that.'

Shirley focuses on scrubbing at a faint stain near the dish rack.

James has dried his eyes. He's wearing a black T-shirt that looks too big for him, its long sleeves almost reaching his fingertips. 'MCR' it says in fading white, next to an emblem of a melting candle. He takes another bite of his apple, chews, then swallows. 'It's only right Gran knows what we're saying about her and what you're plotting.'

'James, enough. I'm not plotting anything.' Shirley stops her scouring and throws the cloth into the sink. She faces me, her eyes watery. 'I was going to talk you through everything, Mum, when the time was right. It's just visiting a residential home to see what you think.'

'I don't want to move.' Quiet but determined.

'It wouldn't be far.' Gentle yet wary.

'I won't leave this house.' This is where we've always lived, Albert, where we belong and where we'll stay.

'You understand you're not well.' Like a teacher to a simpleton. I'm not a child. She is mine. I can still remember changing her nappies, wiping her blooming backside, mollifying her tears every time she fell and grazed herself. Always there for her. I've never let her down.

'I heard and understood everything.'

She steps forward, her fingers interlocking mine. 'So, you appreciate it will get worse . . .'

I have no reasoning left to argue with. Everything is out of my control. Decision-making, independence, freedom – slipping from my hands into hers.

'. . . That we can't ignore it.'

She's always had to be proactive, determined to organise everything, to make preparations. She can't just let things be.

'We should tell a couple of neighbours and friends as well, so that they can look out for you.'

I push her hands away. 'I don't want anyone else to know.' I didn't mean to shout, but my voice is ringing around the room. 'It's no one else's business.'

The atmosphere is as thick as rain clouds.

Shirley's the first to react, her jaw unclenching. 'If you feel that strongly. I don't think it's right though.'

I don't want to cause them grief, but it's *my* health, *my* home, *my* life.

Shirley leans back against the worktop and looks to the ceiling. Her face is puffy, more lines appearing on it by the day. For a horrible moment I think she might cry too. I haven't seen her cry since . . . well, you know when. She inhales loudly through her nose. 'I'm doing my best, Mum.'

No, I don't want to hurt them. I know they care for me and they're my world. Whatever happens to me I will have to live with, but the worst part is knowing that this thing, this disease, this whatever it is, will also bring pain to my family.

I don't want to be a burden on them or for them to suffer because of me. That's not fair. I can't stand to see them upset.

'I know, Shirley.' If I'm sinking, I can't take them down with me. 'It's OK.' My hands ball into fists behind my back. 'We can look at a care home.' Shirley's face brightens a touch. 'Just look, mind. I'm not saying I like the idea.'

'That's all I want.' Shirley clasps her hands together as if in prayer.

'I just want you to be safe and happy, Shirley, that's all I've ever wanted.'

'Likewise.'

'It'll be all right,' says James, putting the apple down on the sideboard. 'Gran's still clever, I've seen what she can do. She remembers stuff that happened donkey's years ago.'

Shirley manages a half-smile. 'I'm glad you've bonded over your Life Story project but it's short-term memory that's the problem.'

'Not just that. Gran's been great at investigating the murder.'

The grandfather clock ticks on in the other room.

'What do you mean?' I can almost hear Shirley's mind ticking over too. Her lips purse and her eyes fix on James.

'She's been brilliant at investigating people and getting evidence. You wouldn't know there's anything wrong.'

He digs us deeper into trouble.

'What are you talking about, James?'

Like a bird sensing a storm, I take a step back towards shelter. 'It's not really an investigation,' I say.

'James, what've you been doing?' There's nowhere to hide from the tempest that's about to blow through.

'We needed to do something to clear me.' He hesitates,

realising too late the trap he's wandered into. He picks up the apple, its exposed flesh yellowing. Takes a bite. Chews slowly. 'So, we've been trying to work out who did it.'

'How, exactly?'

She's very good at asking questions herself, the Spanish Inquisition would be proud.

'I've been trying to help Gran bring back that memory of meeting Barbara.'

'For crying out loud, the pair of you, stop obsessing over that conversation, it probably didn't even happen.' She eyeballs him. 'What else is there?'

James munches for a while then gulps it down. 'I just went to a press conference to find stuff out and Gran's been speaking to people, you know, jogging . . . er . . . memories.'

'James, you'd better not have been interfering with police work.' That high pitch is back. 'You're on bail, get into any more trouble and they'll lock you up.'

'I only listened.' He really should have kept his trap shut.

'It's a murder investigation for heaven's sake, it's incredibly serious. It could ruin your defence.'

She turns to face me, a steeliness to her features now. 'And you should know better, Mum. You can't be snooping into people's lives and encouraging James to get into more trouble. You're supposed to be keeping him safe.'

'The point is, Gran's been as good as any detective.' He's nibbling but there's nothing much of the apple left.

'You're not detectives. It's not a game.'

'Someone has to prove I didn't do it.'

'Which is exactly why me and Dad are forking out for a legal team. Leave them to make your case, don't go making it worse. What's going on in your heads? You're not Poirot, Mum.'

'I was thinking more Miss Marple actually.'

'That's it, I've had it up to here.' She waves her hand well above her head. 'This stops now, I'm keeping you two apart.'

James tosses the remains of the apple into the bin. Our investigation is definitely being wound up now and I think we're both grounded. At the age of eighty-nine, Albert.

Shirley grabs her handbag from the kitchen table. 'We need to get going, James. You're going to pack up these daft ideas and concentrate on your schoolwork.'

She looks at me. 'And you're coming with me to look around a nursing home with an open mind.'

She turns back to James: 'And don't think I haven't noticed that tattoo. I'll have words about that later.'

'Parents,' mumbles James, shaking his hair around his shoulders, his hands disappearing into his sleeves. 'Who'd have 'em?'

That's it then. Suddenly, the loss hits me with a wave of panic. I'm fading away and this thing that's been keeping me going, this investigation, will be no more. If we can no longer solve this murder then James could be blamed, his future destroyed. Both of our destinies are narrowing into darkness.

What can we do, but do as she says? I can't cause a fuss and upset them any further. As they walk away from me, I brace myself as best I can, choking back the dread.

CHAPTER 25

The sweet tea wets my cracked lips as I slurp. Placing the steaming mug on the mantelpiece, I submerge into our chair, feet propped on a footstool. A heavenly sigh as the chair moulds around me. I can see why you liked sitting here, Albert, the only downside is it's not the best viewing position for the television. Our old, boxy set sits in the corner and this chair is at too far an angle to see it properly. Matthew tried to persuade me to buy one of those large plasma things, thin as a crisp they are, so I've no idea where they put the tube and all the workings, but there seems no real point and I hate to throw away something that's still in working order.

I phoned James on his mobile this afternoon, or it might have been this morning, I'm not quite sure. He said he felt like he was already incarcerated being kept hidden away at home. I tried to give him hope, but what can I do?

I feel a bit guilty sitting here all snug in my towelled dressing gown and slippers, a fat caterpillar ensconced in its cocoon. I flick through the channels to find one of the soaps. I know you were never that interested, but I still like to keep up with them. Your head would bob above your newspaper every now and again to enquire about the latest plotline or character and I'd answer as best I could while trying to listen to what was going on, but you'd shake your head in confusion, mutter something, then disappear behind the print again.

My stomach rumbles. What did I have for tea? Have I eaten today? I'm too comfortable to get up now anyway. Another slurp instead.

Corrie comes on, rain lashing the cobbles, drenching the poor folk arguing outside.

'Get indoors,' I tell them, 'you'll get pneumonia out there.'

They're too busy yelling at each other, the spittle and tears mixing with the rainwater skating down their chins. I feel quite smug in my warm, safe home.

Something wet bounces on my hair. The subtle splash of a single raindrop. Must be my imagination, I've become so absorbed in their story that I'm feeling what they're feeling. Two men shove each other, anger steaming from them like the heat from my tea. A woman tries to separate them, I forget her name, think she's the one who works in the café. Her blouse is saturated, poor love, mascara zebra-striping her pale face.

Another drop, almost imperceptible, my hair cushioning the impact. Then a third, a tiny plop before a dab of coldness seeps onto my scalp. I run my hand through my hair and feel a smidgen of wetness. How strange!

The men grapple, tumble, roll about in puddles grunting, their clothes torn and wet. The woman shrieks, the deluge relentless. I feel the pain of a punch, the anguish of her cry. I want the smaller, handsome one in the blue jeans and navy shirt to win, he's a regular.

'Go on,' I say, 'you can beat him.'

Drip-drip-drip. I look up and another drip slaps the top of my nose before running down the bridge. It's raining in here as well. I don't want to move but I'll get soaked too if I stay. I haul myself up, toddle over to the front door and pick up an umbrella resting beside it. With a click it spreads open, its dark petals released from the bud in a rapid flowering. Returning to my seat, I hold it above my head. The downpour drums against concrete and the regular – is it Tony or Peter? – has managed to restrain his foe in a headlock. They both look exhausted, panting, rain arrowing across their bruised and bloodied faces. An increasing splish-splash on my umbrella, the nylon shuddering. The drips come quicker, trickling from it to kiss my bare knees. A cold static prickles through me. *I'm indoors.*

I drop the umbrella onto the carpet. More drops strike me. This is weird and wrong and I'm getting wet. A waterfall could soon cascade down.

I lurch to the front door where a Fort Knox of fortification confronts me. Shirley ensured that locksmith made everything secure, though heaven knows how I'm supposed to get out quickly in an emergency, or how someone's supposed to get in to rescue me. I ease the chain off, then stoop down to slide across a new bolt that's been fitted to the bottom. I'm nagged to make sure I always use them. And where's the key for the new lock? Shirley insisted that I couldn't just leave it in the keyhole in case some unscrupulous type was to push it out and somehow lever it through the letterbox. I think she saw that happen on *Crimewatch*. Now where did I put it? Ah, yes, under the doormat by my feet. I retrieve it from its hiding place and unlock.

I grab my purse from the little table, I'm not losing that again, and step outside. It's raining out here too. I'm one of those cartoon characters followed by a black cloud, there's no escaping it. At least Noah had time to build an ark.

I shuffle down the path, icy water lapping into my flimsy slippers, numbing my feet. I can't stay inside, it's too bizarre, anywhere is better. I reach the road, my nightie and dressing gown clinging to me, goosebumps on my skin. My garments are getting heavier, weighing me down and I've left my umbrella in the house. I won't go back. I just want it to stop.

Barbara's house stands dark and empty. My sodden hair flattens around my head. A light shines from the house to my right. I wade along the street and up the pathway towards it. The front is in darkness, it's the kitchen at the back that's lit up. I approach a side door, the yellow glow behind frosted glass, and rap hard, then rattle the handle. I knock again. A silhouette looms larger until it blocks out the light. The door swings back.

Thick eyebrows curling down towards a scrunched nose, the mouth a perfect zero.

'Mrs Winterbottom?' Mr Braithwaite's eyes scan me from behind wire-framed glasses. 'What are you doing out here?'

'It's raining,' I splutter.

'I can see that. Why are you out in your nightwear?'

'No, no, it's raining inside.'

'Whatever do you mean?'

I search for the words to explain, water thudding against my back.

He shakes his head. 'Never mind, get inside. You'll freeze to death.'

Mr Braithwaite moves out the way and I step into his kitchen, immediately feeling its dry heat.

He shuts the door, then positions me onto a brown, bristly

doormat, the fluffy whiteness of my sodden slippers now a flattened beige.

'Wait there.' He holds up a stiff palm as if sign language is the best way to communicate.

I stand still, gripping my purse in both hands as little pools of water collect on the floor, the doormat becoming an island.

As he's about to open a door, Mr Braithwaite stops and turns around to face me, a shadow of concern falling across his face. 'Don't wander off.'

He leaves the kitchen and, shivering to the steady patter of dripping, I survey the room. This is Terry and Mavis Miller's house. I've stood here many a time, nattering to Mavis while marvelling as she cooked like a chef, a whirlwind of pots and pans and knives. I've supped gallons of tea and savoured mountains of delicious cake with her. Seems only yesterday. But something's not right. Something's changed. The floral wallpaper has gone, replaced with a dark shade of green paint. Mavis wouldn't have liked this colour in her kitchen; it doesn't complement the surfaces at all. The cupboards, sink and worktop all look the same, but other things are wrong. The oven is new and the fridge-freezer larger and a shiny silver rather than plain white. It's also bare, unadorned by the colourful fridge magnets that Mavis collected. The familiar appears odd, unsettling my stomach. I feel out of place, out of time.

The door opens and Mr Braithwaite strides in clutching several towels. He wraps a large one around me and throws another to the floor for me to stand on. It squelches under my slippers, my damp feet now tingling with pins and needles. He passes me the remaining two and I use one to rub dry my soggy hair with one hand, holding the second towel and my purse in the other.

'What were you doing out in the rain dressed like this?' The tone of a father to a wayward child.

Clenching the purse under my armpit, I wrap the smaller towel around my hair, twirling it up into a bun.

'It's raining inside my house.'

The satisfied smile of the well-informed. 'You've got confused and stepped outside. That's why you're wet.'

'I'm telling you it's raining in my lounge.' I pat dribbles from my face, then hang the remaining towel around my cold neck. 'I couldn't stay there any longer.'

His eyebrows don't know whether they're up or down. 'How could it be raining inside?'

'Go and see.' I cross my arms. 'I can't go back until it's stopped.'

Mr Braithwaite studies me, his head tilting to one side. I huddle in the soft warmth of the towels.

'I'll take a look.' He pulls a coat from a hook then opens the front door. Rain thunders the driveway. 'Don't go anywhere else while I'm gone, just stay there.'

He disappears into the downpour. Having stopped dripping, I take another look around. The wooden dining table is recognisable, as is the washing machine that has lasted the Millers so long. Why didn't Mavis tell me she had a new oven? She must have worn the other one out with all that baking. I wonder where they are? Maybe they're in another room. I lift my feet free from my waterlogged slippers as I don't want to upset Mavis by muddying her house. I'll see if she's in the lounge, just through this door here. There's only darkness. I can't traipse around searching in this state. Another door on the far side leads to Terry's study where he keeps his stamp collection. He's often shut away inside, studying and logging each one. A strip of light shines beneath the door. Maybe he's there and can tell me when Mavis will be home.

I amble inside, bare feet silent on the carpet. No one's here. Wherever can they have got to? I vaguely remember this room, but it seems different too. Terry didn't own a computer, or the desk that it's on. There are also lots of binders and files and a bottle of Scotch with a near-empty glass. That's not Terry's tipple, he only drank wine. I swirl the remnants in the glass and sniff its whisky fumes, an image of a crowded pub coming to me. I drop my purse and it unclasps as it clatters onto the desk, its contents spilling out.

A noise makes me jump. I shouldn't be in here. I scoop up my belongings and cram them back into my purse. I return to the kitchen just as a man enters from outside. He's all wet, he really should have taken an umbrella if he was going out in the rain. Oh, it's Mr Braithwaite. That's right, he'd gone to check on my house. He doesn't notice that I've come from Terry's study; he's too busy removing his coat and dragging his feet back and forth across the doormat. He takes his glasses off and wipes them dry on his checked shirt before putting them back on.

'I've sorted the problem.' He sounds smug, as if something that had eluded me was quite simple to him. 'You'd left the bath running and it had overflowed and was leaking through the ceiling.'

I clasp my mouth. I remember wanting a relaxing hot bath; do you recall, Albert? I was telling you about a dear, old friend of ours who would swear by a good soak to get the brain working. Such a character, did his best problem-solving in the bathtub. Did I put the plug in and turn the taps on?

'Was there bubble bath in the tub?' I would have poured plenty in to get the water all fragrant and foamy.

Mr Braithwaite laughs. 'Not that I saw.'

Might not have been me then. What a strange evening, but it does explain why it appeared to be raining in my lounge. Oh, I do hope it hasn't proved costly. 'Is the ceiling damaged?'

'It'll be all right.' He looks like he could do with a towel. 'I stopped it before there was any real damage. I've emptied the bath and put towels on the floor to soak up the water.'

'I see.' A lucky escape. 'Thank you.'

He steps towards me, crossing the room in long strides that seem to eat the space between us.

'Where are Mr and Mrs Miller?' I ask.

He stops dead. 'I'm sorry?'

His forehead creases with befuddlement, bless him.

'Mr and Mrs Miller, are they out?'

Mr Braithwaite's temple smooths as realisation dawns. Maybe he's a bit slow.

'The previous owners.' He shakes his head, his short hair glistening. 'They don't live here any more. It's just me, on my own.'

It doesn't feel right, this place belongs to them and they belong to this place, they should be here. A giddying disorientation rocks me. Change and familiarity have bled into each other like different-coloured paints mixing into a messy pattern. I just wanted a quiet evening in front of the television. That uneasy feeling in the pit of my stomach again. Illness. I'm not well. Is this what will happen to me more and more and more? Queasiness, exposure, my nightie still stuck to my skin. I need to get home and change. I need fresh, dry clothes. I need to hide underneath my thick, warm duvet.

'Are you all right, Mrs Winterbottom? You're acting a little strangely.'

I slide my feet back into my slippers, giving the sensation of pushing them into cold custard. 'I must be going.'

I'll have a bath when I get home to heat me up and wash the grime of this evening clean away.

'We never got round to checking your finances.' Mr Braithwaite adjusts his glasses, rebalancing the frame on his nose. 'I'll call round tomorrow to see how you are and we can go through them.'

I squelch towards the door.

'Just a moment.' He disappears, then returns to hand me an umbrella. 'Use this, you don't want to get soaked again.'

I open the door, put the umbrella up and step outside into the swirling night air, the rain receding into drizzle. Clutching my purse to my chest, I hunch into myself with every squishy step.

CHAPTER 26

'This is the lounge.'

It's a vast room, too big really, all that open-plan space means everyone can see what each other's up to. No cosy togetherness. No privacy. Cushioned chairs circle the perimeter, an arena with no entertainment.

The girl showing us around the nursing home beams at me, as if her eager friendliness proves what a pleasant place it must be. But her bright cheerfulness is at odds with the dreary lack of animation. The room is mostly filled with women, just a few men dotted around. Over by an upright piano, one old lady sits staring into space. Another shuffles past to take a seat closer to the television. It's not even on. They move in slow motion, no sense of purpose, just lethargy. The girl's swamped in a shapeless, navy uniform. Even without make-up she's pretty and I imagine her away from here, perhaps going to a ball in a sleek cocktail dress where she would giggle as she turned heads.

A hand touches my arm. 'Isn't it wonderful, Mum?' Shirley's energy is out of kilter with this place; she's already done several laps of the building in the time it's taken me to meander around the lounge. 'It's so peaceful.'

Lifeless. Only murmuring and the scuffling of sensible shoes and the scraping of wooden chairs perforate the silence.

'I'm sure you'd enjoy being here.' Shirley's glazed look of rapture covers an anxiety that's never far from breaking through the surface. The journey over was silent; me annoyed, her apprehensive, the car clouding with tension. I was a dog being taken to the vet's. It's a waste of a Saturday.

We were greeted enthusiastically by this girl, 'Ellie' the name badge on her lapel says, before being escorted inside. The front door has a lock on with a code and keypad. *To stop people escaping!*

'Some of our residents have a tendency to wander.' Ellie spoke as if divulging a secret. 'We want them to have the freedom to roam in safety but obviously won't let anyone get lost.' I'd wondered if we were entering a safari park.

The reception area was as functional and polite as the receptionist, its only feature a small table bearing a simple vase and flowers. The blooms released no sweet fragrance, probably plastic. The whole building has a chemical stench of TCP and air freshener that scratches at your throat, and a suffocatingly thick warmth. Every wall is beige.

Ellie had taken me into the lounge while Shirley shot off to do her laps.

'It's cosy isn't it, Mum?'

Now Shirley's back by my side, the mask of smiles and pleasantries not fully covering a seeping nervousness. Those warning looks flashed at me every now and again, especially when I'm about to open my mouth. *Please don't embarrass me*, her eyes plead.

'It's all open-plan to make it as spacious as possible and so our staff can see if anyone needs any help.'

Ellie talks to both of us, but her words are directed at Shirley. Underneath those baggy clothes, she must be a slip of a girl. Only in her twenties yet she seems to be running this place. She's not really my cup of tea: too sweet, too milky.

I look around for other staff members. They're either helping some old dear sit down or tidying things away. They all look too young. What life experiences have they had? What do they know about caring for people? Irene said a while back that they're all Eastern Europeans, paid such pitiful wages that they take no pride in their jobs and become lazy and careless. It can't be very easy to communicate with them, resulting in all kinds of frustrations and terrible misunderstandings.

I think I'd rather live in that doctor's surgery.

'Here's the dining area. We have schedules for meals and bedtimes so that our residents have regular routines.'

Ugh! It sounds so monotonous.

'What do you think?' Shirley whispers in my ear.

I grimace.

'We have plenty of activities to keep our residents stimulated. Lots of games for everyone to join in and gentle exercise classes for those that are able, you know, to keep people active. There are crafts classes and help with knitting or embroidery to keep hobbies going. And quizzes, film nights and music to get the mind engaged.'

Sounds like a crèche.

'Relatives and friends are welcome any time.'

Once they're talking to me again, I'm not inviting the neighbours here. What would Irene think? And could you imagine Vera visiting?

I shudder.

'Trained medical staff are available at all times.'

The smile is fixed to the girl's face as she continues with her script, Shirley nodding like a mother encouraging a child.

'You'll be safe here,' she says.

'I hate it.'

Shirley's eyes narrow so much that they almost close and her jaw clenches hard. 'Don't be daft, there's nothing wrong with it.' Her teeth scrape her bottom lip. 'And not so loud. They might hear.'

I'm too old to listen to a salesman's blarney. I've heard the horror stories about these places, where they torture or neglect you. This girl seems soft enough but I bet there are nasty types lurking among the staff who can't wait until all the visitors have gone. Irene says there was a terrible scandal uncovered at the place where her older sister lived. Two staff members supposed to be looking after the elderly were bullying and abusing them instead. No one had any inkling as to what was going on, she said, not a clue. What other travesties go unseen?

'Over here is a conservatory connected to the lounge. You really get the sun in here on a summer morning, it's a lovely spot to relax.' It's the same stifling temperature no matter which part you're in. I think they're trying to boil away the germs. 'It's got great views of the garden.'

'Isn't it pretty, Mum?' It's just a stretch of brown lawn. I try to picture it in full bloom, but I can't imagine anything as supreme as the garden you created, Albert. 'You love sitting outdoors chatting to whoever's passing and there's lots of like-minded people here to get to know.'

People with no minds more like, all sedated and stultified on medication and platitudes. Drooling old biddies sat doing nothing. It's not for me, I can't sit here on my backside all day, just knitting and playing dominoes. I've no time to waste and I want to contribute to society. Shirley might have put a stop to our murder investigation but I can't get it out of my head. I can't just leave it; Barbara was relying on me.

One of the staff, I suspect he's Polish, helps an old woman put her cardigan on. Another inmate is struggling with a shoe. I don't belong here. I can still cook and clean, dress myself, tie my own shoelaces. Yes, yes, Albert, I'm aware that's not always going to be the case, I was listening. I realise there's no way of defeating this disease, that it's not something physical I can battle and recover from. I'm still functioning though. I'll patch over those holes in my memory before they get too large and I fall through them.

'Any questions so far?' asks Ellie in a sing-song voice.

'How much does it cost?' I ask.

'I've given your daughter leaflets with all the information on pricing so you can discuss it privately.'

Bet it costs a packet. It'd mean selling our house just to pay for the privilege of being incarcerated here, and kissing goodbye to the children's inheritance. Everything we worked so hard for gone, just so I can be kept an eye on.

'Let's look at one of the bedrooms.' Ellie's off and I trundle behind her like my shopping trolley.

We pass through so many double doors and corridors that I fear I'll never be able to find my way back. The bedroom is basic and no bigger than our spare room. A single bed with a solitary pillow. A tiny chest of drawers. A small wardrobe. A lone window.

'It's nice and clean.' Shirley glances at me for approval. I frown back. That scratchiness in my throat is getting worse and my nose feels a little bunged up. Could be the start of a cold.

The 'en suite bathroom' isn't big enough for the three of us to enter at the same time. No window, just a fan that whirrs when Ellie turns the light on. A toilet, sink and tiny bath with a plastic shower attachment and flimsy shower curtain are crammed inside. I'd be living in a budget hotel for doddery guests.

We leave the room. Shirley takes advantage of Ellie being several steps ahead of us. 'It's not bad.' She gives me a friendly nudge with her elbow. 'There's everything you'd need.'

No one's getting out of here by their own free will. I've read that in prison they're allowed satellite television, computer games and fresh food.

Shirley's face is all puppy-dog eyes, big and pleading, her eyebrows raised in expectation, a twitch to one corner of her mouth. That's it. If her mind is set on this, I'll have no choice. I'm stuck here. We won't be able to solve the murder and James will be in deep trouble. Perhaps she's right. Who was I to think I could help? I don't really know what's going on. Maybe it's better for everyone if I just accepted my fate and lived out the rest of my days here. All I want is to see my time out with dignity.

We reach the lounge. One of the prisoners shuffles towards me. Stooped, her white hair straggly, she stops in my path and looks me up and down.

'Hello, Brenda.' A surprisingly cheerful tone.

'My name isn't Brenda,' I snap.

'Course it is.' Her thin eyebrows jerk with indignation, her gaze questioning. 'What took you so long?'

'We've never even met.' My cold isn't helping my irritation, I can feel the mucus blocking me up.

'Why would you say that?' The woman lifts a wrinkled hand to her mouth, bony fingers trembling against dry, flaky lips. 'And to your own sister.'

'I'm not your sister.' Heads turn towards us, eyes examining. My cheeks burn hotter than the room. I was someone's sister once, but not after what happened.

'What kind of game is this, Brenda?' She touches my arm, as if checking that I'm really there. Her eyes are glassy, reflecting like a mirror. I feel the world shift beneath me and have a sudden urge to get away from her. I'd run if I could, put her far behind me, forget I ever saw her.

'I think you might have the wrong person.' Shirley moves towards us, her voice soothing. The woman doesn't even acknowledge her presence, those hollowed eyes, deep pools about to burst their banks, are fixed on me no matter how much I try to avoid them.

'Disowning your own sister.' Her fingers clutch my arm.

'Look, I don't know you.' I shake off her weak grip. Her arm wheels back, her mouth a gaping black hole. She reaches out again, her hand grasping but finding nothing but air. I feel as though I've swallowed sand. I begin to cough, hoping to clear it, while waving the woman away.

'It's all right, Gloria.' Ellie puts her hands on the woman's shoulders. 'It's not Brenda, your sister isn't visiting today. She'll be here tomorrow.'

Ellie guides Gloria towards an armchair. I try to cover my coughing fit with my palm. Gloria looks around as if uncertain of her surroundings and not quite sure what to do. I can't stop coughing, it's so arid in here. Or the growing realisation that's crawling through me as I watch the old woman shuffle in her seat. She is me and I am her. The names don't matter. I may as well be Brenda.

'Sorry about that,' says Ellie on her return to us. 'Gloria gets a bit confused. She isn't good at recognising faces.'

I'm bent double now, my hands on my thighs, hacking like a cat with a furball. Shirley pats me on the back. 'You OK?'

My eyes water but my gullet stays bone dry. I'm struggling to breathe.

'Here.' Ellie hands me a glass of water.

I gulp it down, feel its cold relief. Ellie waits patiently until my coughing stops, then takes the empty glass. I take a long breath through my nostrils, releasing it through quivering lips.

'I think that's everything,' Ellie says. 'Any questions? Anything I've missed?'

'Can't think of anything,' says Shirley. 'It all seems lovely.'

That's it then. Her mind is made up and I am one of them. I don't want to be a nuisance, so I'll just have to accept it. I might as well make myself at home. I look for the comfiest chair nearest the television and park myself on it.

'Do you need a rest, Mum?'

'This seat isn't taken, is it?' I glance around.

'No, but we aren't staying.'

'I know I've not packed but you can bring my things to me later.'

I lean back. The chair doesn't mould around me, it sinks a little too low, something digging into my left buttock. I rub the armrest but it's coarse, no soothing scent, just a fustiness. I'll just have to get used to it.

Shirley crouches down in front of me, holds my hands in hers and says softly: 'You're not moving in straight away, Mum, it's only so we could see what it's like.'

'We can go home?'

'Of course.'

Let's get out of here while I still can! I push myself from the chair and march towards the exit.

'We can have a chat about the pros and cons later,' says Shirley, following me.

While I know that this is my future, for the moment I am free. The sky is overcast with frail, wispy clouds, but the cool breeze is a tonic after the stifling heat. During the drive home, I wind the window right down to feel the wind against my face, to get the fresh air flowing through my lungs.

Shirley winds it back up. 'Best not if you've got a cold coming.'

I'm not sure of this route. Oh, I hope she isn't taking me to visit another home on the way.

'Just popping to ours first,' says Shirley. 'I've got some cough syrup you can have.'

That's a relief. We pull into the driveway. Two figures seem to be arguing by the front door and the knot in my stomach returns at the thought of more trouble. One of them is James, snarling, a look I haven't seen in him before. Shirley pulls on the handbrake and is out the car in a flash. I recognise the other person, it's that reporter, is it Luke? No, it's Lee ... Spade, I think, his surname. I fiddle with my seatbelt, finally unfasten it, then lurch out.

James is squaring up to the reporter, looking burlier; no longer a boy but a young man. They stare at each other, inches apart, like boxers at a weigh-in.

Shirley steps between them. 'What's going on?'

'Just after a response from your lad.' A haughtiness to the reporter's tone.

'And I was telling him where to go.' James sounds breathless.

'Response to what?' Shirley glares at Mr Spade and, suddenly surrounded by three people, he backs away.

'Police had a breakthrough.' Mr Spade smiles and I notice stains on his hands, like the smudges of a psychiatrist's inkblot test. 'A reliable source tells me they've got a DNA sample from Barbara Jones's kitchen. Who do you think they'll match it to?'

That's not right, is it, Albert? It won't incriminate James as he didn't do it. But he did go in that kitchen and take her purse. My throat's dry again. The reporter's eye has a gleeful glint. That knot in my stomach tightens.

I look across at our grandson whose face contorts as he works out all the possible permutations, then settles on the worst.

Shirley looks as if another millstone has been added. 'Please kindly leave us alone,' she tells the reporter through gritted teeth.

He marches down the drive and we're left standing there, statues of gloom.

Shirley breaks free, pushing past us and into the house. 'I'm putting the kettle on.'

James drops onto the doorstep and sits there with his head in his hands. He's switched back to harmless grandchild in an instant, his eyes now full of fear. 'They're bound to match it to me. It'll send me down.'

'We don't know that.'

That prickly feeling of being watched returns. I turn to see a figure sitting on a wall on the other side of the road. Trainers, tracksuit bottoms, a hoodie, but this time with the hood down.

Liam stands up and swaggers over, stopping at the foot of Shirley's drive, like a vampire that's not been invited to cross the threshold.

'Bad time?' he sneers.

James looks up. 'You're not helping, trashing me all over socials and telling everyone it was me.'

'Well you made out that I might have done it.'

'What you doing here anyway?'

'Your old man knocking about?'

A memory resurfaces. 'You were looking for Matthew before?'

'And why did you mention my dad when we met in the park?'

We both frown at Liam, who has the expression of someone changing their mind about spinning a yarn.

'Might as well tell you now,' he says. 'You wanted to know what happened after you ran off that night.' He jerks his head in the direction behind him, as if it were towards Barbara's house. 'About five minutes after you legged it, your old man parks up and knocks on her door, seeming in a right hurry.' He looks James in the eye. 'That's when I thought I'd better make myself scarce.'

Liam laughs at our open-mouthed faces. 'Reckon it was you or him.'

He pulls his hood up and strolls away.

CHAPTER 27

A discoloured patch on my ceiling is gradually spreading and growing darker. Another problem in need of fixing.

I keep mulling over my conversation with James. We couldn't speak much after Liam dropped his grenade. Shirley was soon at the door wanting to know why we weren't coming inside; she never leaves us alone together for longer than two minutes. I was in a daze as we sat in their lounge having a cup of tea. I couldn't even find their bathroom when I nipped to the loo and was glad to be home after Shirley gave me a lift back. James managed to give me a quick, hushed call on his mobile phone that evening when he got a moment of privacy.

'Why did your dad go to Barbara's that day?' I asked. 'And why hasn't he mentioned it?'

'Liam might be lying. Just winding me up.'

'We need to ask your father directly.'

'How do I do that?' Apprehension had crept through James's voice, all tinny on the poor reception. 'What if he . . .'

His words trailed off and I imagined him contemplating the worst and felt it affecting me too. Are my daughter and grandson safe with that man? Should I tell Shirley? But we're not supposed to be getting involved in any of this; she'd just dismiss it and ensure that James could never spend any time with me. It's hard enough to envisage someone I know well, no matter how difficult I find him, being involved in something so horrific. But you never know what someone's capable of.

'How's your dad been?'

'He's always busy and stressed, and now there's all the legal stuff cos of me.' James's sigh was timorous and tired. 'I stay out his way, mostly.'

As I'd wondered what was the best thing to do, James had mumbled that someone was coming, he had to go, and the line went dead. And I'm still wondering now, without you to advise me, Albert. Both our grandson and myself alone in the gloom.

That patch resembles a rain cloud, growing murkier and more unsettling. I take a tissue from the box beside me and blow my nose. This cold is spreading too. I wonder if I should take some medication?

A banging on my front door. You become able to identify visitors by the sound of their knock: Shirley gives a few swift, impatient thumps; the window cleaner's is a clear, rhythmic rap; Barbara's used to be a soft, almost apologetic tap. This thumping isn't recognisable.

I open the door. Jean's standing there with a curious look on her face, an air of agitation. That dark cloud seems to spread to my stomach. I try not to show my discomfort, but I never have been an actress.

'You going to let me in?' Jean glances around as if she's on the run.

I look at Barbara's vacant house and hesitate, the hard edge of the door in my grip, ready to be slammed shut or opened wide.

'Oh, come on, I didn't do anything to Barbara, you daft cow. Just let me in.' Jean almost pushes her way past and I relent, stepping out of her way, but still not wanting her in our house, particularly with me alone. 'I've never assaulted anyone.'

'Maybe not with your fists,' I reply. Her tongue is as vicious as ever.

Jean snorts as she marches into our lounge. She plumps herself down in your armchair, Albert, the cheek of it, making herself right at home. She takes a tissue from the box on the armrest and gives her nose a good blow. I pick up the box and take it with me to the sofa opposite. It doesn't feel right sitting here, it's as if I'm the visitor.

She has a prolonged look around. 'Never been updated this place.'

'Bit like yourself,' I fire back.

Jean cackles. 'Look at that old TV. Does that thing still work? I've a Betamax in the loft if you want something to match it.' Then she sees the stain on the ceiling. 'Oh dear, had another accident?'

I rub the armrest but it's not the same, there's no remnant of you, Albert.

'To what do I owe the pleasure, Jean?'

She sits back, her grubby tracksuit scouring the preserved cloth of your chair. 'I've been stewing, ever since what happened to Lady Muck across the road. I have to tell someone.'

Is she actually about to confess?

'And after what you said about me and Don, I want to set the record straight, as they say.'

Oh. This isn't going in the direction I had briefly hoped. I grab a tissue just in time to catch a sneeze.

Jean looks at me expectantly. 'I think this'll do me good.'

I don't like seeing her sitting where she is, all haughty and dominant.

'Whatever you have to say, this isn't a church, Jean. I'm not a vicar able to absolve you.'

'No, you just think you're a saint. But we all have our faults and our sins, Margaret. We all have our cross to bear.'

My cross weighs heavy on my back. 'I suppose.'

'And you wanted to know how the problems between me and her started.'

It's important that I hear her out. 'Go on then.'

'Because you *really* don't know any of it.' She eyes me as if I'm an alien creature.

'Just tell me, Jean.'

'I always found Barbara a bit aloof. I know you got on with her better, birds of a feather and all that.'

I hold my tongue.

'Don was much friendlier. Always made an effort, asking how I was and offering help.'

'Don was a scoundrel who didn't treat Barbara well at all.' I can't help myself, she always gets things the wrong way round. 'He was controlling and manipulative.'

When I understood the full extent of Don's behaviour, I realised how Barbara had become trapped. It made me appreciate you even more, Albert. I picture you comforting me, bringing a smile to my face. My memories of you won't go, will they? I will retain them?

'I realise that now. But at the time ... I'm just setting the context for you, Margaret. I thought they were happily married. That's why what I saw was such a shock.'

Jean ambles over to the window. My shoulders slacken now that she's no longer in your chair. She looks at Barbara's house as if seeing it from a new perspective.

'I'd missed the bus so was walking home from work and took a shortcut through Ashfall Park – funny how fate works isn't it? – when I saw Barbara with another man. In broad daylight. Snogging by the swings as if they were teenagers, not a woman in her late thirties and a man even older who should have known better. Sometimes I think maybe they wanted to be caught. They didn't even notice me. Consumed with passion, I guess.'

My breath is held in my throat. My best friend and yet I had no idea that Barbara had been unfaithful.

Jean is fully focused on Barbara's driveway. 'Not even sure why I got so worked up about it. Probably cos she was always so high and mighty, looking down on my family like we were trash and there she was carrying on like that. I went straight round and knocked on that door, without thinking it through. Don had just got home from work and I told him every last detail.'

I wipe my runny nose with a fresh tissue. This will not end well.

'He was furious, as you can imagine. I went home thinking I'd done a good thing by helping someone who was being deceived. I don't know the full details, but I know Don put a stop to that little affair there and then, and obviously they stayed married.'

I shudder. Don would not have reacted well.

'Barbara never forgave me. She was all dramatic, claiming she'd had to end things with her fancy man, that I'd cost her the love of her life, how she'd never been happy with Don, that it had been her last chance of happiness.'

Why couldn't Barbara reach out to me?

Jean keeps her attention on Barbara's property. 'If she'd been that miserable and liked this fella that much, I'd have thought she could have divorced and gone off with him. But she was the religious type and I suppose things were different in those days.'

I doubt Don would have just let her walk away. He'd never have let her have any of his money and would have dictated things.

'Everything calmed down over the years, they both had little to do with me, embarrassed I presume that I'd caught a glimpse behind the mask of their marriage. But it was always there, simmering away, coming to the surface every now and then when we'd have some problem – that fence, cutting down a tree, an overshadowing extension. Resentment spilling out.'

It must have been awful for Barbara. I don't condone breaking her marriage vows, but I can see how she felt so unloved, how Don drove her to it.

Jean turns to me. 'Never told you anything, did she?' She has that look again, a scientist with a specimen.

'Who was the other man?'

'Don't know, didn't get much of a look at him.' Jean scoffs. '*Love of my life!* She was probably just one of many.'

What else did Barbara never tell me?

'I've always had regrets about it.' Jean nods to herself. 'I've wondered what would have happened if I'd kept my gob shut. Maybe it weren't my business. They'd have been found out at some point, but perhaps things would have been different between us all.'

There's something in her expression, in her tone, that seems sincere; an earnestness, a depth that makes me reassess. It wasn't her fault she got embroiled in all this, and who's to know what was the best way to handle it. Despite myself, despite her, despite everything, I have a sudden urge to give her a hug. But I know we'd both hate that.

'Do you feel better now?' I ask.

A slanted smile. 'Yes, I do, like you would after puking up.'

'That's lovely, Jean.'

'I'll let myself out.'

Jean leaves as noisily as she entered, my front door given a good slam shut.

I switch seats back into your chair and try to rebuild the shapeshifting jigsaw of my life. It's exhausting, attempting to put everything into place, to make sense of it all, on top of this rotten cold.

I sit and stare at that stain on my ceiling, wondering how to make it go away.

CHAPTER 28

We don't have long. James has to get home before his parents are back from work, so I need to tell him as much as I'm able. Something about Jean unburdening herself, and me comprehending my illness, has made me appreciate that I need to reveal things to him while I still can. I pull the wooden box from the bureau, its plain, simple structure hiding a stash of secrets. James has faith in me. He'll be my memory. I trust him.

Crouching as much as my back will allow, I prise off the lid and pull out letters, photographs and papers from a part of my life I've long pushed to one side, then gather them together like old friends. They are jewels that I must pass on as I would the family silver. When was the last time we reminisced about our past, Albert? The most exciting and fearful time of our lives. Impossible to forget? A sliver of fear at the box's near empty interior.

James peers at the faded photographs of us outside a mansion and yellowed paper bearing faint pencil markings. 'What is it, Gran?'

'Documentation and memorabilia, from a job when I was young.'

'Thought you were just a housewife.'

I stiffen. 'No woman is ever just a housewife, James.' I can see I have much to teach him before he can start courting. It's time I told him my full Life Story.

'I turned eighteen not long after the start of the Second World War. Men were called into service, and I wanted to do my bit too. I was good at languages, I'd learned German, so the powers that be thought I could be useful.'

James's eyes light up. 'Were you a spy?'

I laugh. 'No, never glamorous enough for that. Bit more boring, I'm afraid. I'd always enjoyed puzzles and crosswords, and had a way with words, so I was ideal for codebreaking. I worked in London, perusing newspaper personal columns for coded messages. I must have shown some promise because they soon sent me to Bletchley Park, or Station X as we called it. It's where a lot of great minds of the day were based, all trying to break new cipher systems.'

The radio playing from the kitchen is Morse code tapping a memory into me. I'm walking into Bletchley Park for the first time, the Victorian Gothic mansion looming, geniuses all around scurrying to their posts, my footsteps uncertain.

Something scraping drags me back to reality. James has pulled up two chairs from the dining table. We sit down.

I tell him how coded messages transmitted by wireless were intercepted and sent to codebreakers. We had to work out the ciphers and translate the code in a race against time as Hitler's forces advanced, and then stop what they were up to without giving away how we knew. It all flows back to me with the ease of water returning to a dried-up stream.

'We became so successful we'd even read Hitler's orders before the German generals at the front.'

'So women could crack codes too?'

I roll my eyes. 'There were thousands of intelligent young women at Bletchley. We were just as good as the men at solving puzzles and a damn sight more spirited.'

James leans forward. 'Was it like hacking mobile phones?'

'I suppose so. Any system can be hacked, as you call it.'

I describe how the Enigma machine looked like a big typewriter, your message passing through three rotors, bouncing off the reflector and back through the rotors to light up a replacement letter on the board. Twenty-six positions, three rotors, more than seventeen thousand different combinations. Plus a plugboard that swapped pairs of letters to scramble it further. Using Morse code, we'd send the recipient the starting position, order of rotors and plug positions to decode the message on their Enigma.

'How would you ever crack a code?'

'There are flaws in every system. One of Enigma's weaknesses was that a letter could never be coded into itself. And you could guess common messages that were used to eliminate thousands of potential rotor positions. Think of it as a sort of crossword technique of filling in where letters would go.'

I can see he's absorbing everything like a sponge.

'And people make mistakes. I'd look out for any changes in coding styles. One slip and key information could be missed but equally one slip from the enemy and we'd be onto them. You had to concentrate very hard to spot patterns.'

'What did you uncover?'

'I made a big breakthrough. In one mass of jumbled-up letters, I noticed that L was the only letter missing and realised the operator had been lazy, just repeatedly pressing the L key, the rightmost button, to send a test message. With that discovery I broke the main Italian Navy Enigma. It meant we could decipher more messages about the Italian Navy's plans to attack British ships off the Greek coast. We worked for three days and nights until we'd unscrambled their battle orders and that led to the Royal Navy's victory at the Battle of Matapan in 1941. And we went on to help with the success of the D-Day landings in 1944.'

I remember the surge of elation after intense tiredness, the celebrations as the wine flowed and I was congratulated. Me. Just a naive and giggly teenager. Me. I had made a difference, I had helped our sailors to a historic victory, I was part of the war effort. Me. It was all as heady as the vinegary wine.

James grabs my arm and shakes me back to 2012. 'You won the war, Gran.'

I smile. 'No single person won the war, James. Millions of us all did our bit, including incredibly brave men on the frontline. If you like, I was just a tiny cog in a colossal machine. Lots and lots of clever folk at Bletchley all worked hard and other countries helped.'

And I let them all down too. A shadow obscures my achievements. That nagging feeling that weighs on me.

'Why haven't you told me before?'

'I had to sign the Official Secrets Act and was told I must never ever say where I was working and what I was doing. It bound me for life. Information has been slowly released over the years but I stayed true to my word and kept our secret.'

Oh, the irony of having to forcibly forget for decades. But we never cracked.

'Wouldn't happen nowadays, it'd be all over Twitter in a flash.'

I only talked to you about it, Albert, and Barbara learned parts. Now you're not here, it's good to spill the beans to James, to keep these memories alive, passing them from my head to his.

'So you didn't even tell Granddad?'

'Granddad was at Bletchley too. That's where I met him.'

'Granddad was a codebreaker as well?'

'One of the best.' I wink. 'Almost as good as me.'

I can picture you laughing at that, Albert, your blue eyes sparking, that chuckle rumbling from deep within. That memory returns, the one I surely can't ever forget.

'I was alone on an evening shift struggling with a particularly difficult problem.' I can see the scene, feel that frustration gnawing. 'I decided to seek the help of one of the clever Cambridge mathematicians also working that night.'

Me: pacing the floorboards, arms flapping, like a bird trying to take off.

You: still and patient as a rock, talking me through it until we reached a solution.

'We put our heads together and worked it out.'

A thought lights up like a letter on Enigma. I scrabble through the bundle of documents.

'Here it is.' A scrap of old paper, the pencil markings almost invisible. I'd held it up to you, Albert, to show you my workings, and looked at you properly for the first time. Something fluttered in my stomach. You reached out to pull the paper closer, your fingers brushing mine, a tingle of electricity, the paper trembling. The gorgeous blue of your eyes. Was that the moment you really noticed me too?

A touch on my shoulder. 'You still with me, Gran?'

I nod and search through the papers, brittle in my fingers as leaves after the autumn fall. I stop, heartbeat thumping. The handwriting so familiar, the letters neat and assured with intricate flourishes. The year we met, 1940, sloping into the corner. My hand trembles again some seventy-two years later.

I haven't seen your handwriting for so long but it's as if you've written it today.

My Darling M, how wonderful it was to spend the weekend in your company.

Even now I can remember first reading it, all those decades ago. You'd sent it while you were away visiting family, just a few months after we'd met.

How delightful you looked as we walked by the riverbank in the moonlight, where I stole a kiss by the water's edge.

My heart aches. The words swim in and out of focus, I catch only snippets.

My work was my existence, my whole raison d'être. Now I have a new devotion, a better purpose, a real reason to live.

I smile at the thought that someone once considered me beautiful. A tear hits the page, a letter blotting outwards in a tiny explosion of blue ink. I dab the paper with my cardigan sleeve to dry it; I don't want to lose the words.

When I received the letter, I read it over and over and over and now it echoes again. I am there and I am here. My heart in the past, my body in the present. I knew then that I was going to marry you. What a wise decision for someone so young! My love for you is as strong as ever, not a moment of regret. I glance at the final words beneath your name.

I cannot wait to see you again.

I hold the letter away from me as the tears fall fast.

James holds my heaving shoulders. 'What's wrong?'

Like a rough sea, it takes me a while to calm. Once my tears have run dry and my breathing steadied, I can look up at him.

'A letter from your granddad brought everything back. Happiness and sadness.'

'How can it be both?'

'You'll understand when you're older.'

'Let's not get too soppy, Gran.' James pats me on the back as if I'm a soldier. 'We've still got our own war to win.'

He's right, I cannot live in the past. I put everything back in the box. There's one item at the very bottom that I can't even share with James.

'I'd better get back before Mum wonders where I am and interrogates me,' he says, ambling to the front door. 'Pity she's not on our side.'

'How are things with your dad?'

James's face pales. 'I've not spoken to him. Do you think there's a way we can find out anything more?'

'I'm not sure. I just worry for you and your mum.'

He hoists his bag onto his back. 'I've been trying not to think about it.'

Then he slopes away.

CHAPTER 29

Opening the lounge curtains, I face a heavy coating of pristine snow. Icy tentacles creep up the window, the glazing frosted in the corners. It's a siren, its deadly beauty sparkling with enticement but carrying a lethal chill. For a moment I think it's December, then I look at the date on the newspaper: Wednesday 4 April 2012. The snow's come down thick several times already this year and now it's snowing in April! Even the weather is confused, the seasons muddled. I do hate it when the winter drags on, and there seems no end in sight to this freeze. All these weather predictions and alerts make you fearful.

The smooth covering, like icing sugar on a cake, is picturesque, but I can't possibly venture out there. One slip and I'd be stranded, shattered, with hypothermia setting in, or I could fall victim to a vehicle skidding onto the pavement as though a drunken elephant on roller skates. Delighted children may frolic in the flurries and build sturdy snowmen, but winter is no time to be old.

Icicles hang from the gutter at Barbara's house. A splash of colour against the whiteness catches my eye, like drops of blood on a blank page. Bunches of flowers, I think, resting against the front door. For a second, I'm tempted to investigate. But no, it's too hazardous.

I sit in our chair, stare at a crossword, guess some answers that won't fit, then glance at the window. No, I mustn't. I blow my nose, I'm so full of mucus.

Perhaps I can tell if they're flowers with another look. I shamble over. The view is no clearer.

A movement in my peripheral vision. That spider is watching me, its body seemingly a little hole in the ceiling, its legs tiny cracks in the paint. Good heavens, how's it surviving in this weather?

'You'll outlive me at this rate,' I tell it.

I look back at our chair. At the gold pendulum swinging hypnotically in the grandfather clock. At the dungeon of the lounge. Then another peek outside. The snow looks crisp and crumbly, not slippery, you know, the firm sort that your shoes crunch into, soft not hardened. If I wrapped up well . . .

Damn it, I will not be trapped inside our house, it's just crossing the road. I know it won't do my cold any good, Albert, but I can't stay sniffling inside forever.

I button up my chunky cardigan and swathe myself in a padded coat and woollen scarf, then heave on thick, rubber-soled boots. I unfasten my prison door, every bolt, lock and chain, and step outside. The brisk air nips, my sharp breath billowing before me. Slow and steady, I crunch into the snow that's settled on my path. Dark clouds curtail the morning light. The road is deserted, everyone tucked away in the comfort of their homes or having already ventured to work. Smoke coils from the odd chimney that's still in use. I won't stay out too long, love, just enough to see if, and why, there are bouquets lying outside Barbara's house.

The snow is lighter on the road, snaking tyre tracks pressed into it. I cross carefully, arms stretched out for balance, my footholds firm. See, nothing to worry about.

I trudge up Barbara's driveway. Three bunches of flowers are propped against the front door. They have withered, curled, once colourful petals now an earthy brown yet frozen into place, their cellophane surround tinged with frost. I stoop down to pick one up and pull its crinkled cardboard tag open, holding it in front of my nose. The writing has washed away, just a blur of black ink streaking downwards. I imagine the carefully chosen words, the expressions of sorrow, love and loss. They must have been here a long time; I wonder why I didn't notice them before.

Tributes are often left close to the scene of death these days. I prefer to leave flowers where the dearly departed are buried, where I can feel their presence. Otherwise, it's a constant reminder, marking the spots of tragic road accidents and crimes, screaming out the loss and pain. Do you remember Princess Diana's death, Albert? A torrent of flowers that swept London's streets. I shiver a little inside my thick clothing.

Bending down to inspect another one, my foot begins to slide. No grip. It slips upwards and I lurch backwards. My body rattles with the surge, right arm wheeling, fingers grasping air. My hand whacks the door handle, fingers find it, grip tight. Bearing my weight, the handle clicks, drops. The door swings inwards, taking me with it, and I stumble over the doorstep, falling inside Barbara's house. The door clatters against the hallway wall and I somehow manage to steady my tumbling body. My clammy palms resting against the wall and splayed legs, like a suspect about to be searched, keep me upright.

I take deep breaths, my heart thumping. The hallway's dark and empty.

I pull myself up. Why on Earth is the front door unlocked?

My breathing and heart rate steady. I shouldn't be in here. I'm lucky I didn't cause myself a terrible injury, blundering in like that. I take my hand away from the patterned wallpaper, grateful for thick carpet to balance on. *No one* should be in here. It should be locked and secure.

'Hello,' I shout out. 'Is anyone there?'

My eyes adjust to the darkness. I can't understand how it was possible to get in – surely the police wouldn't have left it unlocked? I look behind me to where the door remains wide open in confirmation.

The silence is oppressive. This house used to be so welcoming; a warm, friendly place I was always pleased to visit. So many happy memories of being invited in to chat to Barbara over a cup of tea and a plate of biscuits. It's barely recognisable: cold and gloomy with her presence drained away. The soul of this home has gone.

I know I should leave, Albert, but, despite my trembling hands, you know I'm going to explore further. I take a few hesitant steps forward, towards the darkness, towards the kitchen. My heartbeat increases its drumming.

A noise from behind the kitchen door.

'Who's there?' My voice shrill.

Silence.

I inhale, hold the breath, release it slowly. Nothing to fear.

I turn the handle. The door creaks open. I step into the kitchen.

Light spills through the window, a black-clad figure silhouetted against it. I catch my breath. It doesn't move. It feels surreal, in this place, in this moment. Is it real? My imagination? A ghost?

A pair of eyes glare back. Is it one of James's friends with another stupid game? The figure's masculine, doesn't look like a teenager.

We are as frozen as the flowers. His height, his round-shouldered stance. A coldness chilling me from inside out. *Those eyes.*

Harry is here, in front of me! He's back, hunting for what I've hidden in that wooden box. How far would he go to protect himself?

I advance out of the doorway and he leaps towards me, fast as a cobra striking. I instinctively close my eyes, throwing my arms in front of my face.

A whip of air, something brushes past me. I open my eyes. He's gone. I'm alone, shaking in the same spot where Barbara was . . .

A wave of nausea.

Then a thought carves through me. *Why would Harry run? Why wouldn't he just demand it back, now that his cover is blown?* I think of my illness. I think of Gloria in that care home. Harry was here, wasn't he, Albert? The nausea threatens to erupt.

Through the window I can see the once beautiful garden seemingly frozen in time. In the shadow of the house and blackened fence is the dark patch of singed grass, untouched by snow. I imagine the flames dancing, Barbara stood before them, lit by their glow. She's holding something, her hand raised as if about to toss it into the inferno, and I try to picture what it is.

I blink and she's gone. Just the charred remains of a once lush lawn.

The urge to leave becomes overwhelming.

I head back along the gloomy hallway to the front door that's still ajar. I can't get to it quickly enough. I peer outside, but there's no one there. I close the front door behind me, then look down to place my steps carefully. A fresh set of footprints are flattened into the snow, larger ones than mine. I follow them to the road where they disappear in a thinner layer of mush. The street is as deserted as it was before.

Too many questions without answers. I should never have come out. I just want to get back home, back in our armchair, a fresh brew, the television on, whatever the programme, it doesn't matter.

How could I explain to anyone what just happened? They'd think me mad, would question what I was doing snooping around, why I went in there. No one will believe me any more.

The snow sucks my steps like wet sand, slowing my movements, the cold beginning to penetrate my bulky layers. That eerie sensation of being watched is ever present, this road's aura of security long gone.

In fact, the whole world's gone wrong since you left it, Albert. Crime and murder on our street, suspects and suspicions, memories taken from me. What's even real any more? I can't even rely on myself. Am I not the sum of my memories? Does my brain's accumulation of education and experiences not define who I am? If we're shaped by memories but mine are vanishing then what have I become? Am I as vacant as any ghost?

I don't look back when I finally reach the safety of my own home, and then lock and bolt the front door.

CHAPTER 30

The whirr of a drill and the hammering of nails drown out the radio, but it's good to see and hear a man at work. Michael takes a screwdriver from his toolbelt, which he now has instead of a bumbag. He no longer wears that funny hat, his long hair flowing free.

'Nearly done,' he calls out, as he secures a screw into place on our cupboard.

Compassion got the better of me, made me believe him and think of his family without a breadwinner, so I offered him extra work. And I wanted a chance to ask him the questions that I've been repeating in my head to keep them there. I'm keeping a healthy distance but mainly as I don't want anyone else catching this blasted cold. I'm feeling worse than ever.

'There's something I've been meaning to ask you.'

'Go ahead.' He makes sure the screw is tight.

'The evening that Barbara died – what was it, nearly seven weeks ago? – you said you collected from her at five p.m.'

'That's right.'

'Might it have been later?'

He returns the screwdriver to a pocket. 'Possibly. It was

always around five p.m., but it varied. Sometimes I lost track of time nattering to people.'

'So it could have been twenty or thirty minutes later?'

'Guess so. Though I thought it was five.'

'And when you collected from Barbara, how did she pay you?'

'She always had the coins ready. She'd put four pound coins, or sometimes a fiver, on that sideboard in the hallway in advance. It's funny how things become habit.'

'She didn't have her purse on her or have to fetch it?'

'Nah, there was no need.'

The telephone rings, but I think that's all I need to know. I head into the hallway and answer it.

'Margaret? It's Lisa Wardle.' Her voice is full of agitation. 'I've heard about your grandson's arrest.'

'He's innocent, he didn't so anything, well, he didn't do that, but—'

'Is that why you both came round, trying to find someone else to blame?' She's so indignantly loud that I inch the receiver away from my ear.

'It's not like that at all.' Why is everyone continuing to get things wrong? I hold the mouthpiece closer to my lips. 'If you'd let me explain. James would never—'

'I want you and your grandson to stay away. I hope the police have enough on him.'

I squeeze the receiver so firmly that I fear the plastic will leave a permanent indentation. She just won't let me speak. A thought clangs in me louder than the grandfather clock sounding the hour: *the lady doth protest too much.*

'One other thing.' The angst tangoes in her tone.

'Go on.'

'Do you know anything about Aunty Barbara's will?'

'No. Why?'

'It's missing. I know exactly where she kept it. I asked the police family liaison officer to locate it earlier and they found her front door unlocked and the will wasn't there.'

My cheeks burn. I can't mention going into Barbara's house. How will that make me look? 'Won't the solicitor have a copy? Anyway, she'll have left everything to you.'

'Not if she changed it. And at best it will delay things.'

'Why would Barbara have changed her will?'

Silence.

I eventually have to break it. 'There's something I need to tell you.'

'Have you remembered something?' Her voice softens.

'It's more a question really. Someone reminded me of an event decades ago.' I'll just come right out and say it. 'Did you know that Barbara had an affair?'

I just want confirmation. While I believed Jean, it would be reassuring to have someone corroborate it.

I can hear Lisa breathing down the telephone. 'Do you think that's connected to what she was worried about?' she asks, finally.

'I don't know. Do you?'

'I don't want to speculate about Aunty Barbara's private life. All that was a long time ago. If you remember anything specific or hear about the will then call me.'

'Lisa, if there's something you're not telling—'

But the line is dead. I glare at the telephone as if the world's ills are all its fault.

I return to the kitchen. Michael is testing the cupboard door, which swings smoothly.

'All finished.' The cupboard looks as good as new. He's done a much better job than Matthew would have done. 'You want me to take a look at that damp patch on your lounge ceiling?'

'Maybe next time.' I just want to rest. 'You've already been a great help today.'

I show Michael out. James is coming the other way and gives him a glacial look as they pass.

'Good timing,' I say. 'Saves me having to unlock and lock this blooming door again.'

'You OK, Gran?' James glances back at Michael as he disappears down the street. 'He didn't try anything?'

'He's fine.'

I tell him about Michael's answers, while I can remember them.

'Suppose it makes sense,' says James. 'Barbara might not have noticed her purse was missing at that point.'

I think of another visitor to Barbara's house. 'What about your dad?'

James shakes his head. I can see the trepidation in his eyes, the fear of finding out something life-changing greater than the fear of the unknown.

'I'll help you raise it with him. We need to find the right moment.'

James nods, hair covering his face. His black T-shirt has a picture of a military-clad skeleton dancing with a young woman who's wearing a ballroom gown, red flames igniting their backdrop.

My stomach grumbles. Thankfully, this cold doesn't seem to have dampened my appetite, though I may have missed lunch. 'What time is it?'

'It's two.'

'Shouldn't you be at school?'

'Easter holidays.'

They really are never there.

'Your mum with you?'

He laughs. 'No chance.'

'Does she know you're here?' I don't think she'd like us being together without supervision.

James disappears into the lounge. 'She's out and what she don't know won't hurt her.'

I follow him. The lounge spins a little, like the end of a fairground waltzer. Coldness clutches me. The fire's gone out, taking the room's heat with it. Grey coals crumble in the sooty grate. 'Not sure she'd be best pleased if she found out, James. She wasn't happy with what we'd been up to.'

James kneels by the fireplace, strikes a match from the box I keep beside it, lights a scrap of newspaper and throws it onto the coal.

'That's why I'm here.' He prods the black chunks with a steel poker. 'To show she's wrong.'

'Mothers are never wrong, James.'

The coal smoulders, then catches light. 'Everyone makes mistakes, Gran.'

I have to take a moment as dizziness makes me wobble. I settle back into our chair, the fire flickering into life, and stretch my hands towards the heat.

'You want anything?' James paces the room so much that I fear he's beginning to take after Shirley.

'No. I'm fine, dear.' The hunger can wait, I'll make a sandwich later.

'I'll make you a black coffee. Read how it's really good for boosting memories.'

James disappears into the kitchen, returning a few minutes later to hand me a mug containing something gloopy thick and strong smelling. It reminds me of that awful sludge we called coffee at Station X. It doesn't look like a miracle cure.

'Thanks.' I give a weak smile, then place the mug on the mantelpiece. I am heartened, though, as it reminds me of when he cared for me after you departed, Albert. 'Best you tell me quickly what you have to say in case your mum catches us.'

'Mum don't get it.' Agitation stalks his face and voice. 'She says leave it to the lawyers but what will they do? Just sit in a dusty office studying legal books.'

James fishes his mobile out of his pocket. The rips in his jeans seem to gape wider. He jabs the shiny glass screen. The whole world is made of glass these days: tables, doors, buildings, and now telephones. But it's so fragile, can shatter so easily.

'The internet.' For something that I'm told contains colossal amounts of data the internet is awfully small. 'The latest stories on the murder criticising the police for not solving it. People don't get why no one's been charged. It's putting pressure on the police to solve it, and quickly. They'll be desperate to wrap it up and get some good headlines.'

My stomach becomes a dead weight. What if he's right?

'We've gotta solve this.' James sweeps his hair out of his eyes.

I don't know if I have the strength. This cold is dragging me down. It's difficult enough to make sense of what's around me. 'As your mum said, we're not detectives.'

'It'll be good for you. I've read about it, keeping mentally active is the best thing. Keep that grey matter working, Gran.'

Something about that visit to the care home won't leave me. I can't hide from reality. Do you remember when Dora had cancer, Albert? Too many friends we've lost to that terrible disease. But hers was treatable, they stopped it spreading, cut it out. *They can deal with it*, she told us, *if they catch it early.* There's nothing they can do for me. As my disease grows and spreads, I will recede and vanish, my abilities disappearing with me. I feel the holes inside me, the blackness expanding, the emptiness left behind. I will just have to accept I'm not the person I was.

'I realise now that I'm not well.' A swell of emotion rises in me, my eyes prickling. I swallow it back down. 'And I'm a little bit frightened of what's going to happen to me.'

'Don't be scared, Gran.' James takes my hand, the conviction and certainty of youth in those blue eyes. 'Anything goes wrong, we'll put it right.'

I almost laugh. Oh, to have the blasé confidence of the young again. But it does stem any tears.

The spider's scampering across the ceiling, still buggering on. I've grown used to it, it's part of the fabric of the place now. Maybe I have no greater right to live and exist here than it does. Maybe it's just nature. Why should I treat it any differently to the birds or the butterflies? I give it a nod.

James is still looking at me attentively. 'I'm always here, Gran, if you ever need to talk about it.'

I pat his warm hand. 'I appreciate that, James, but I don't think there's anything we can do, so I'll just keep plodding on.' I smile. 'You know, my generation didn't have talking therapy or counselling, we just got on with things.'

'Then that's what we'll do, get on with it.'

'We've no choice now,' I say. 'We have to confront him.'

James gives the expression of someone faced with challenging a headmaster.

We stare at the document. It's all there, in black and white.

CHAPTER 31

The parish church always makes me marvel. The stone walls, the symmetrical turrets, the spire pointing to the heavens. It's obstinately endured centuries of change with little alteration to itself. I'm dwarfed by the giant doorway beneath its broad arch.

Shirley and Matthew are by my side and James is somewhere nearby. He seems to be keeping a distance from his dad. We need to have that conversation with Matthew urgently, but today is not the day. Everyone's dressed in black; shadowy figures drifting around. Clouds meander across a grey sky, break into wisps, then evaporate. That final conversation with Barbara is still haunting me. I want to think about happier times.

I close my eyes and picture a brighter scene: sunshine, floral dresses and sharp suits. Church bells chiming and lively conversations. I'm all in white and you're next to me, Albert, your grin set, your aftershave strong, your shoes buffed into a shine. Confetti flutters, colourful fragments clinging to my hair and veil as cheering echoes around us.

My mind reaches further back with you at the altar, waiting

for me, wanting to be with me. I'm arm in arm with my father, our steps rhyming. You glance behind, your face lighting up. I stumble when repeating the vicar's words until your warm smile relaxes me and then you gently slide a ring onto my finger that has remained there ever since.

'You all right, Mum?'

My eyes open to greyness as if a colour film has been drained. Shirley gives me a look of concern.

'Do you have a headache?'

I shake my head, my lips rise briefly then fall.

Shirley nods knowingly.

I know where I am. In a scenario that's become way too familiar. Far more funerals than weddings now. It's an overcast Tuesday afternoon in April to finally say farewell to Barbara. As much as I'd like to stay with the celebrations inside my mind, she deserves nothing less than my full focus and respect. It's taken a while to have the opportunity. James says the police couldn't release the body until a post-mortem and numerous tests were done to collect evidence. How awful for the grieving to have to wait to give their loved one a proper send-off, a painful prolonging of injustice.

'Do you recognise anyone?'

Shirley's loud, distinct voice shakes me. I need to concentrate on the here and now. People are wandering into the church to take their seats and I strain to see who I can identify. A sea of faces bob past, a ripple of recognition quickly washed away in the sheer volume. Maybe I know them, maybe I don't. The wind scatters leaves around our feet. I wonder how much I've lost and how much more I've still to lose.

A figure I can distinguish, with a small comfort in the

identification. Vera with her flowing funereal coat and black pillbox hat. Are the rest strangers or a new blank? A cruel game, attempting to put a name to a face as the identities try to escape me like cunning spies in disguise.

Shirley's having no such trouble. Taking Matthew with her, she heads off to talk to a couple whose faces are familiar, but I can't for the life of me remember them.

James approaches, wearing his best suit – his only suit, which is navy but at least he's made an effort – hair bouncing around the collar. His mum nagged him for ages to put it on, spent even longer ironing his shirt. His tie is still skew-whiff.

'Look who it is, Gran.' I follow his gaze to the cemetery wall where a figure is perched on top, legs dangling, like a child on a swing. 'Liam's come to gawp.'

Even though his hood is up, I can tell it's Liam, watching with the intensity of a vulture following a pack of lions.

'Quiet now, your parents are coming back.'

'What you two up to?' Shirley almost pounces, a lioness indeed.

'Nothing,' I say.

'We'd better get inside.' Shirley turns to lead the way.

I see someone else several yards away, standing adrift from others. A tall figure, partly reduced by a stoop, wearing the regulation dark suit and coat. My breath seems to freeze in my open mouth.

'Just a moment,' I say.

He is statuesque as I step towards him, then it's as if he's sensed my interest, like a deer suddenly raising its head, its ears pricking, and he swivels. I stumble in his direction, but he is always a pace ahead. He curves around a crowd of people heading my way and they swallow me up, I cannot get around them, apologies muttered as we become entangled in a slow dance. I break free into space. But he's gone.

Scanning my surroundings, I can't see him anywhere. There's just Liam sitting on the wall, watching me with a smirk.

I hobble back to my family who are waiting with an air of bemusement.

'Was there someone you recognised?' Hope fights with irritation in Shirley's voice.

'I thought so.'

I look again but most people have gone inside now. How do you know if what you've seen is real or a figment of your imagination? There's nothing I can do. I must focus on Barbara.

'We definitely need to take our seats.' Shirley takes my arm, possibly to guide me safely, but maybe to make sure I don't venture off again, and as we pass through the doors the vast interior spreads out before us, still breathtaking. The glimmering gold surrounds, the aged wood, a sense of peace.

A long strip of red carpet covers the stone floor that we step along, yellow square patterns around its edge. The worn, wooden pews are nearly full. Kneeling at them to pray would be impossible for many of us here. At an organ near the pulpit, the organist is ready to strike the first hymn. Above it a rare glimpse of sunlight streams through a stained-glass window to scatter colourful patterns.

Shirley takes control of where we sit. James is on the edge of a pew, his eyes flitting around the congregation. Shirley and Matthew are either side of me, like sentries. More people stream in. Barbara was very popular. The organ reverberates and we're soon in song, 'How Great Though Art' rumbling through the church. During the vicar's sermon, I try not to be reminded of your funeral, Albert.

Lisa takes to the pulpit to give a reading. I focus on the words, their meaning, their significance, but in the circumstances it's difficult not to scrutinise her manner, her appearance. She looks suitably shattered, emotion playing with her vocal cords like fingertips on a violin's strings.

When the funeral's finished, the final hymn sung, the last tribute given, the closing word of prayer, I spot James still surveilling everyone. We follow the flow heading for the exit, where the vicar is stationed.

'Lovely service, Reverend Brown.' I shake his outstretched hand.

'Thank you, Margaret.' His balding pate shines like a halo. 'It's good to see so many people here.' He keeps hold of my hand, draws me closer. 'Including yourself.' He fixes his gaze on mine, his expression both serious and softening. 'How are you keeping?'

'Very well, thank you. Mustn't grumble.'

Rev. Brown hesitates, seems to take a moment choosing his words. 'You know we've missed you here, Margaret.' My hand remains clutched. 'It would be lovely if you were to return.'

I release my hand from his. I can still feel that anger, deep down. At God, for taking you from me, Albert. At the world, for carrying on without you. Even at you, for leaving me. There was even anger at this poor vicar, for continuing to preach when I thought everything was hopeless, pointless, even though I knew how stupid that was, how self-pitying, how futile. Many people visited to comfort me and there were many kind words and gestures, but I couldn't come back and sit here every week and pray. Not after that. Perhaps that anger has cooled now. Perhaps I have more perspective.

'Maybe,' I mutter. 'Maybe.'

'If there's anything we can do to help.' His voice gentle. 'You're always with friends here.'

I nod my appreciation, my tired eyes watery. I wonder if I could find the strength to pray again. 'I don't think I'm over it yet.'

Rev. Brown is close by my side, as if in my confidence. 'You know, I don't think you ever get over it, Margaret. You just learn to live with it.'

In a moment of stillness, the old stone building seems to breathe as his words settle around me.

'So sorry but we need to find Vera,' says Shirley. 'Please excuse us vicar but we said we'd give her a lift to the wake. I don't want her thinking we've forgotten.'

'Not at all.' He smiles. 'You go off to do your duty.'

We say our goodbyes and walk along the path that winds through the churchyard. We've barely gone a few yards when we bump into Mr Braithwaite.

'A fitting send-off,' he says.

'Yes, a nice service considering.' Shirley is suddenly patient and sunny amid the gloom. 'Glad you could make it, Steve, you didn't seem sure when we spoke yesterday.'

'Didn't know if I could get out of some important business meetings.' A fleeting smile. 'I really did want to pay my respects so, thankfully, I was able to rearrange.'

'Good. Wonderful to see so many people here.'

He turns to me. 'How are you, Margaret?'

'Very well, thank you.'

Something catches his eye and I follow his gaze to the butterfly brooch on my lapel.

'That's a very pretty brooch, Margaret. How did it come to be in your possession?'

'A gift from my late husband. It's of huge sentimental value.'

'Albert clearly had wonderful taste.'

'There's Vera!' Shirley's cry makes us all jump. 'Come on, gang, let's not lose her. Do excuse us, Steve.'

'Not at all.' He steps aside. 'I'll catch up with you later.'

Shirley's away, Matthew's long strides keeping up with her rapid little legs. James and I traipse behind.

I see Jean standing alone on the grass, staring at the gravestones, lost in a world of her own. She looks across. I hold up a hand and she acknowledges me with a tip of the head.

Then we notice Liam still settled on the wall, like a cinemagoer sitting through the end credits. Matthew whispers something in Shirley's ear. While Shirley catches up with Vera, and they pause to talk, Matthew scurries over in Liam's direction. We watch their animated conversation, Matthew pointing at something behind Liam, the teenager spitting on the ground.

James looks at me with an anxious expression.

'We'll speak to your dad as soon as we get the chance,' I say.

Liam jumps down to the other side of the wall, disappearing. We reach Shirley and Vera at the same time as Matthew, but no one comments. He seems able to put on a cheery disposition at a moment's notice. We head for the gate, Matthew's battered Fiesta parked nearby. We're almost there when James looks behind us.

'Uh-oh.'

I glance back too and see Lisa hurrying our way with a furrowed brow.

'Don't think there's any way of avoiding this,' James adds.

The five of us stop and turn in unison, as if a dance troupe beginning a routine.

'What's he doing here?' Lisa's a bit out of puff as she nears, though determined to get the words out. 'It's not appropriate.'

I sense Shirley bristle and strain to reach every inch of her full height. 'My son didn't harm your aunt. We just came as a family to pay our respects.'

What she doesn't add is: *and there's no way I was leaving him home alone or letting my mother attend unaccompanied.*

Lisa stops in front of us, the towering church her backdrop. James edges behind his mother. 'He shouldn't have come.'

'We didn't mean any trouble,' I add, soothingly. This is one place and situation where it's best to keep the peace. 'We all loved Barbara and wanted to be here.'

Lisa's hands settle on her waist, a black handbag swaying. She sniffs in reluctant acknowledgement. 'I'd like a word with you, Margaret.' She looks at everyone else. 'In private.'

Shirley appears to be about to protest, but I give her arm a squeeze and sense a little of her tension alleviate. 'We'll wait in the car,' she says.

'I'd like James to stay with me.' I need him as my memory and it's only right that we continue to work together.

Shirley and Lisa both look ready to complain. Shirley's brow cracks.

'I'll need his support and I don't have my stick.' I grimace and clutch my hip. 'He'll have to help me to the car.'

'Very well,' says Lisa.

'We'll be waiting,' adds Shirley. She leads Matthew and Vera through the gate and once they're out of earshot, Lisa turns to me. 'Has anything come back to you, Margaret?'

'She hasn't recalled anything of significance.' I think James is my spokesman.

Lisa looks around, but apart from a handful of people near the church, I think everyone has gone. 'Have you heard anything about Aunty Barbara's will?'

I shake my head.

'You're worried about your inheritance.' James stands straighter. 'We know you fell out with your aunty.'

Lisa glares at James. Then looks me in the eye. 'I did know about the affair.'

James's head jerks up and he glances at me with raised eyebrows. I've a feeling I might not have remembered to tell him about Jean's visit.

Lisa shuffles her feet. 'We'd had an argument about money, she wasn't herself, was anxious about something. She mentioned someone was trying to come back into her life.'

'Someone from her past!' I exclaim.

'What happened exactly on that night she was due at yours?' asks James.

'I'd invited her over to talk about it.'

'The meal and cake and her staying over.' James's eyes narrow. 'You were buttering her up.'

'I wanted to find out who it was and how she felt about it.'

'You don't know who it is?' I ask.

Lisa casts her eyes downwards. 'Obviously, she never arrived. If only she'd come earlier, she might still be alive.'

'Those mistakes you made over the timings and other things,' says James. 'Your plans changed that night. You panicked.'

'I was just making sure she was coming. She was having second thoughts.'

'You were tempting her and guilt-tripping her.' James is in full flow now. 'The inheritance. If this person came back and Barbara left things to them then you'd lose out and you need that money. You were going to make sure she had nothing to do with whoever it was. You wanted to keep things as they were.'

Lisa's face flushes. 'I've always supported Aunty Barbara. Her intention was for me to have that inheritance.'

'A murder case delays any inheritance. You want it solved quickly before anyone stakes a claim. You're desperate for it to be wrapped up.'

Lisa gives James a pointed look. 'This case being solved quickly is better for all of us.'

We're the only people left in the churchyard now, just the sound of cawing overhead.

'I have to get to the wake,' says Lisa. 'I've told you everything I know. If you find out anything, let me know in return.'

We walk in silence to the gate, where Lisa goes one way and me and James in the opposite direction. We reach Matthew's car. Shirley rolls the passenger window down and sticks out her head. 'What was that about?'

'Just a chance for me to explain and say sorry for what I did,' says James. I stay quiet; I'm not good at covering up.

Shirley's crinkled crow's feet suggest she won't be taking her eyes off us again.

I think of the past coming back to haunt us. What was Barbara trying to tell me?

CHAPTER 32

Shirley's house is neat and tidy, always seems recently vacuumed, it puts me to shame. A cherry-blossom fragrance lingers. I imagine there's freshly washed laundry in the airing cupboard, an emptied dishwasher, and a spotless bathroom. A large flat-screen television is hung on the wall as if it's a painting, a home entertainment system housed in a mahogany case. And they complain they don't have enough money, Albert! Still, I'd prefer to be sitting in your armchair amid the decay of our house than perched on this sofa; I've never really liked the navy colour and camelback style.

James is pacing the house from his bedroom to the lounge to the kitchen to the toilet. Such a waste of good energy. He dashes into the room.

'He's here now.'

I hear a car crunch across gravel and onto the driveway, then a handbrake squeak.

'Everything will be all right,' I say.

'How can it be if he's guilty?' James sprawls next to me. He's wearing one of those rock band T-shirts, a long-sleeved black thing with a big, yellow cartoon face that's sticking its tongue out of a wobbly mouth and has crosses for eyes. Nirvana, it says above the fluorescent face. Appears daft to me.

I follow Matthew's path by the sounds: the front door opening, shoes wiped thoroughly on the bristly doormat, footsteps along the hallway. He enters the lounge, looking smart in his shirt and tie.

'Oh, hello, Margaret.' He does a double take. 'What are you doing here?'

'Just seeing how James is.'

Matthew picks up some mail left on the mantelpiece and flicks casually through it. 'Thought Shirley didn't want you two left together.'

'She wanted me to check that James was all right and was staying home.' I fear I may be picking up bad habits from James as that little white lie came easily.

He looks at his fidgeting son. 'And where's Mum?'

'She's at that PTA meeting.' James runs a hand the length of his hair. 'Dinner's in the oven. Think I was supposed to turn it on.'

He disappears into the kitchen and is back in a flash, plonking himself back next to me.

Matthew glances at his watch. 'I can run you home, Margaret. I think we can leave James for five minutes without him getting into too much trouble.'

'There was something I'd like to ask you.' I pull a folded-up piece of paper from my purse and dangle it in Matthew's direction.

His cautious expression as he takes Barbara's bank statement suggests he knew there'd be more to my visit. 'What's this?'

He opens the paper up, it's got a tad creased and tatty, and his eyebrows dance as he takes it in. 'Crikey, Barbara had a fair bit of money.'

He scrutinises it, then me. 'What are *you* doing with this, Margaret?'

'I found it. Here.'

'In *this* house?'

'In *your* study.'

Matthew's eyes dart between the document, the ceiling and myself. 'What were you doing in there?'

'I stumbled in accidentally.' As is my wont, Albert. 'And saw it on your desk.'

'But I've never seen it before in my life.' He holds it at arm's length as if its very presence is tarnishing. 'It has nothing to do with me.'

Matthew hands me back the statement, then looks as if he's having second thoughts, as if I can't be trusted with it. Is he playing me? Is he taking control again?

'There's something else,' I say.

Matthew eyes both of us, a fox sensing traps. 'What's this all about?'

'You know my friend Liam.' James has found his voice. 'He was looking for you.'

'Liam's asked for you a couple of times,' I add.

'You stay away from him.' Matthew points a stern finger at James. 'He's nothing but trouble.'

'What does he want with you?' I ask.

'He's just trying it on. It's nothing.' Matthew puts the mail back on the mantelpiece, standing with his back to us. Tension clouds the room.

'We saw you talking to him at the funeral,' I say.

'I was telling him to sling his hook. He shouldn't have been there.'

'He told us he saw you go round to Barbara's after I took her purse.' James's tone is resolute. 'You've never mentioned that.'

Matthew faces us, his skin now pale. 'It's not what you think.'

'So what were you doing at Barbara's?' I ask.

'I just nipped round on my way home from work to ask her something.'

'What did you want to know?'

Matthew takes off his tie and throws it onto a chair. I suspect Shirley wouldn't like him making the place untidy. 'Shirley was worried about you, Margaret.' He undoes his top button. 'I'd been asking your neighbours how you were.'

I feel blood begin to thud in my ears. 'Did Shirley ask you to?'

'No, I did it off my own back. Just wanted to see if anyone had any concerns. As the person closest to you, I thought Barbara would know best.'

'You were gathering information to use against me.'

'It wasn't like that, Margaret. You've been a danger to yourself. Shirley was fraught. I wanted to see what Barbara made of it, if she thought you were safe at home or if she'd seen anything that we weren't aware of. And I thought she might talk to you, convince you that you really do need help.'

'You wanted me out the way, to put me in a care home so you could have my house.'

'I wanted to either put Shirley's mind at rest or work out the best thing to do for everyone. Listen, I'm not after your house, Margaret. I just want my family to be safe and stress-free.'

'What did Barbara have to say?' asks James.

'She was concerned about your health as well, Margaret.

She knew something was wrong. But, to be honest, she seemed distracted, it was clear something else was on her mind, so I said I'd call back another time. I was there barely two minutes.'

My muscles remain tense, that blood still thumping. 'Why did you never say anything?'

'I didn't want to worry Shirley, I was just trying to help, and I didn't want to upset you, Margaret. I knew you'd react like this. It was better not to say anything.'

Matthew turns his focus on James. 'Then that former friend of yours starts hanging around. He finds me and tells me he saw me at Barbara's around the time she was murdered and tries to blackmail me, the little toerag, saying he'll land me in it with the police if I don't pay him.'

'Have you?'

'Course not! I haven't done anything wrong! I told him where to go but he's a persistent little bugger, keeps harassing me. I've told him it'll be *me* reporting *him* to the police if he comes near me and my family once more.'

'But again, you didn't say anything,' I point out.

'I didn't want to drag anyone else into it or start people fretting.'

I look at the bank statement. 'It doesn't explain why this was in your study.'

'Either someone put it there or . . .' Matthew has the look of a schoolboy who's worked out a difficult sum. 'You're sure that's where you found it, Margaret?'

My stomach churns. There's now a large element of doubt in everything that I say and do. 'I was certain that . . . at least, I think that's . . .'

The memories aren't fixed, they roam and merge and clash like clouds.

'If you called at Barbara's after I took her purse and spoke to her then that proves she was still alive and I didn't kill her.' Excitement buzzes around James. 'Have you told the police that?'

'I know, son. I've told them I visited Barbara, but I'm not sure they believed me. I think they assume I'm just trying to protect you and I've no way of proving it. They're focused on the forensic evidence.'

As much as Matthew annoys me, I trust what he's told us. I look across at James and can see in his eyes that he doesn't doubt it either.

Trying desperately to work out how I found that statement, I envisage Enigma, its tiny bulbs flashing to signify a letter, which would send a spark of energy through me too. A code. A message. A challenge. But the wiring's wrong, the setting's incorrect, the message can't get through, snagged somewhere, stuck in the system. It's complex, this simple-looking machine. If just one thing goes awry in its mass of wires, then all the vital connections are lost.

'It would have been easier if you'd told us all what you were doing from the start,' I say.

'I know.' Matthew's voice and features soften. 'And I know we have our differences, Margaret, but I was just thinking of Shirley. I've been very worried about her, she's working herself to the bone, and the toll it's taking to look after you.'

I'm about to tell him that I can blooming well look after myself, but, no, I can see that's in the past, that I do need some support. And I can hear you telling me, Albert, that he's always provided for his family and treated Shirley well. I can see that he genuinely loves and cares for her, in his own, sometimes misguided, way.

'I understand. Shirley's important to me too and I don't mean to be such a pain. I really am grateful for everything you all do.'

A smile emerges on Matthew's lips. 'I'm glad that's all sorted.'

The room feels lighter, airier; a spring day after a storm. Another problem, another possibility, that feels as if it's been stalking me, getting ever closer, is a black cloud on my horizon.

'James can walk me home,' I say, giving his T-shirt a tug. 'I could do with the exercise.'

Matthew picks his tie up from the chair. 'You sure?'

'Yeah, we both need a bit of fresh air,' adds James.

'I have got stuff to be doing.' Matthew glances at his watch. 'Promise me you'll stay out of trouble.'

We both nod while having our fingers crossed behind our backs, though I don't think that's ever been a proper get-out clause.

'Shirley will kill me if you don't,' adds Matthew.

James follows me into the hallway.

'There's one more thing I need to show you about my past,' I whisper. 'There's someone else that could be involved.'

CHAPTER 33

I haul the wooden box from its shelter. This unburdening of secrets is contagious. It's important not to keep everything to yourself, Albert, I understand that now. I need to release this final piece of my past.

'There's something you need to know about your Uncle Harry.'

I pull out another letter, the paper fragile, its ink faded. It remains strong enough, the words still legible. James reads it over my shoulder:

My dearest Margaret,

I feel compelled to write to you about what has happened between us. It fills me with great sadness that our relationship, which meant so much to me, should be so strained. Please allow me to explain my actions so that you understand them.

I did not do it for money or for my own good. I did it because I believe in the cause. You know full well that I have long railed against the injustices of poverty and hardship. The details that I provided were not harmful to my country, I was merely helping an ally access information that they had a right to know and that helped them combat a great evil that threatened peace, security and everything we hold dear.

I was startled when you challenged me and simply had to act. It was nothing personal, Margaret, and I did not want to upset you. I hope that you can now see the bigger picture.

Your brother,
Harry

Even now, upon reading it for the umpteenth time, that letter sends a lightning bolt through me.

James pores over it. 'What went off?'

'Harry was working at Bletchley before me,' I explain. 'As a translator. He excelled at languages at Cambridge. There were always rumours circulating Bletchley that a traitor was leaking our work, but never any evidence. One day, I was due to meet Harry for lunch. He must have forgotten, more important things on his mind no doubt. While searching for him, I peered into Hut 3 and there he was, shoving the transcripts I had only just decoded down the front of his trousers.'

James's jaw drops. 'What did you do?'

'I didn't know what to think, so I followed him to see what he was up to.'

Should I have confronted Harry there and then, Albert? I had always been a little afraid of him. I remember you telling me later that it was impossible to know how best to handle it.

'I followed Harry as discreetly as possible to the railway station where he moved the transcripts into his bag. I knew then that those papers were going to Moscow. I challenged him, asked him what in God's name he thought he was doing.'

'Uncle Harry was a Russian spy?' A mixture of confusion and awe swirls in James's voice.

I nod. That memory has become such a part of me surely it will be impossible to forget. I'm there now, Albert. It wasn't cold like today, but imbued with an innocent warmth. I can feel Harry push me to one side, into the shadows of the station's wall.

White smoke clouds the horizon, the chug of a nearing locomotive.

'For heaven's sake, keep your voice down, woman,' Harry hisses in my ear.

'Those transcripts aren't yours.' I reach to seize his bag. 'Give them back.'

He grabs my wrist, a constrictor's squeeze. 'I've no intention of doing that. Besides, it's too late, Maggie.' I've always hated his pet name for me and now it stings with venom.

'You're betraying King and country.'

'You wouldn't understand.' His expression black as soot, he towers over me, every inch the big brother commanding his little sister. 'There's a greater purpose at play.'

Harry swings the bag away from me, takes a step back. I have to do something, I can't let all our hard work, our national secrets, our security, be handed over. But it's my charming, clever brother, who I've always looked up to. That lightning bolt has split me in two.

The toot of the train entering the station, passengers rushing to the platform.

'I'll tell them what you're doing.' The greater good has to prevail.

A red flash in Harry's eyes, his jaw clenching. 'You'd inform on your own brother?'

'You've left me no choice.'

'There are always options.'

I don't want to give him up and see him suffer. But I can't let him betray us.

'Think about it, Maggie. These are *your* transcripts, *you* created them, they bear *your* handwriting, were last in *your* possession. All I have to do is say that it was *you* that took them, it was *you* that passed them on, and that I wasn't involved at all.'

I shake my head at his audacity, my long auburn hair tumbling free from its grips.

'It will be *you* that takes the blame.' His voice assumes its usual coffee-rich smoothness, strengthened by his conviction. 'It will be *you* that's punished and shamed. You'll be throwing away your career and liberty.'

That manner, so self-assured, so superior. He's always had a darkness to him, but never this selfish and reckless. He's prepared to throw me under that train, which is screeching its arrival, smoke billowing.

Tears prick my eyes. But I won't cry in front of anyone, least of all this man masquerading as my brother.

'Think about it, Maggie, there's a good girl.'

Then he disappears into the haze.

*

The grandfather clock striking the hour brings me back into the land of the living. I rub my wrist as if Harry's fingers are still gripping my flesh.

'You OK, Gran?' Concern swims in James's eyes. 'You glazed over there.'

I repeat my story to him. The second time is no easier.

'What happened next?'

I told you everything, didn't I, Albert? You knew by the look on my face that something terrible had happened. I shook in your arms. Once you'd calmed me, we discussed the ramifications. You said you'd support me whatever my decision.

'I guess I was a coward who couldn't face the consequences. I stayed silent.'

You reassured me I was doing the right thing, that there was too much at stake personally.

I'm back in that hut with my manager demanding to know what had happened to my transcripts. I'd mumbled incoherently about how I was very, very sorry but I had no idea where they were, how I hadn't done anything wrong, how it wouldn't happen again. He must have known I was lying – how can anyone be so apologetic and chastened about something they claim to know nothing about? – and I'd wondered if I could somehow disappear too. I'd betrayed my colleagues, my King, my country. They were my transcripts of vital messages that real heroes had risked their lives to obtain. They were my responsibility. I've always wondered if there was more I could have done to change Harry's mind or resolve it.

James looks up at me. 'Don't think you had much choice, Gran. You did the right thing.'

He's the spit of you, Albert.

'Did you and Uncle Harry ever talk about it?'

You wanted me to cut off all contact with Harry so that whatever he did couldn't be connected to me. But it wasn't so easy when it was my flesh and blood and someone I'd loved for so long.

'Our paths crossed a few times, on family occasions, but we never mentioned it. I later discovered he was a Communist Party member who'd been recruited at Cambridge for the Soviet Union. I've always worried that if anything happened, Harry could still easily pin the blame on me.'

That fear grew inside me like a disease. It would take only a little loose talk or some documents to be discovered or a journalistic investigation for trouble to start, and Harry had made it quite clear what he would do to protect himself.

'Then I didn't hear from him for years. Until this arrived.'

I shake the letter. It had been pushed through our letterbox, not posted. A way of safeguarding the message inside or letting me know that he was close to where we lived? I recognised the handwriting immediately, felt the lightning.

'I realised this was my protection.' I shake the letter again. 'In justifying himself, Harry basically admitted what he'd done. He could no longer blame me when his confession was in my hand.'

'So you no longer had to worry about it.'

Fear does not disperse so easily. It simply recirculated through my bloodstream. I shake my head with the same sadness as when I confronted Harry. 'This letter was my only safeguard. I knew Harry would realise he'd been foolish in giving it to me. My concern now was that he'd try to take it back. And I knew how devious and ruthless he could be.'

'Has he ever tried anything?'

'I'm not sure. Lots of strange things have gone on. I know I'm not well and that my illness makes it difficult for me to be trusted. But an intruder has been able to get inside this house. And I keep seeing what I'm sure is Harry.' The letter quivers in my hand. 'Someone entered Barbara's house and killed her. What if it's Harry? He knew I was close to Barbara and would have told her things. What if while hunting for this he approached her first? Anything could have happened. And he could still be after this.'

'You're certain it's Uncle Harry that you've seen?'

I falter, shredded by doubt. 'I'm not certain of anything any more.'

James sees the anguish on my face. 'All this bringing back the past, Gran. It might have affected you.'

'You might be right.' Maybe my mind is my real enemy.

'Do you know where Uncle Harry went?'

'I know he fled the country at the start of the seventies when parts of Bletchley's wartime past were revealed but I can't remember the rest of that decade. I suspect he came back.'

I clutch the letter, tormented with images. 'I shouldn't have let him dominate me. I should have spoken about him sooner.'

'He was to blame, Gran, not you.'

James is right. And it's history now that I cannot change. 'I suppose it's easy to get people wrong. To put them on a pedestal when they're fallible.'

I see something dawning on James's face. 'You think someone's cool and clever and they're not. It's easy to get sucked into their bad ways.'

We say the name in unison: 'Liam.'

'I wanted to be like him,' says James. 'To be tough, streetwise, strong. He reacted to me the same way Uncle Harry treated you.'

'Liam's doing what he thinks he needs to do to survive, just as Harry did. Sometimes it's an act of bravado. People appear fearless and shrewd when they're actually scared and insecure. He's probably just a lonely and frightened little boy.'

I watch James's expression change as he digests it, and think how you never stop learning.

'I'd better get back,' he says.

We move into the hallway. In the background, the radio's playing some racket that's pretending to be a song. I feel better. I think I may be beating that cold. Maybe getting things off my chest has helped.

'We need to make sense of all this,' says James. He seems in a daze, trying to take everything in. 'We need to find out what happened to Uncle Harry.'

That song distracts me. The music is all screechy, but with a horrible whiff of familiarity. 'Why does that noise make me think of Barbara?'

I step towards the kitchen, just as the record ends.

'That was The Bilkers with their new single "Karma",' I hear the DJ announce. 'We'll be hearing more from them later.'

'The Bilkers!' I exclaim. 'That word.'

Promise me you'll do it, Margaret.

James is on his phone in a flash, thumbs tap-dancing. 'They're a local indie band. Hadn't heard of them.'

He holds up his mobile and presses the screen. That song repeats, the drumming frantic, guitars squealing. The clamour calms and I can hear the so-called singer drone over a lumbering bass.

What goes around, round, round . . .
. . . Coming back to you.

That bass is knocking on a trapdoor in my mind.

James's eyes burn bright. 'When did you say you met with Barbara, a few days before she was killed?'

James turns the song off and starts scrolling on his mobile. He has the look of someone who's discovered that their lottery numbers have just come up.

'I've got another lead.' He opens the door and steps outside. 'I'll report back soon.'

Then he's off, scampering down the path with an energy I wish I still had.

CHAPTER 34

The Crown and Anchor's metal-shuttered windows stare blankly, its boarded-up door impenetrable. I instinctively reach out and touch the cold and abrasive honey-coloured stone. I wonder how many hours of your life you sat inside these walls, Albert, drinking, chatting, playing dominoes and bridge.

'I don't understand, James.'

Our grandson has a backpack slung over one shoulder and the expression of a boy scout determined to secure the hardest badge.

'Hopefully, it'll all become clear, Gran.'

'But it's locked up, and standing outside doesn't help.'

'Follow me.'

He leads the way into what was once the pub's garden, the grass now overgrown, weeds and nettles creeping up the picnic benches as if reclaiming them. A tall, wooden fence at one end of the pub has a couple of sections missing.

'Think you can fit, Gran?'

James slips through the gap with ease. It's more of a squeeze for me. I breathe in and manage to avoid getting stuck. At the pub's rear is a narrow alleyway cluttered with rusting beer barrels, soggy cardboard boxes and strewn crisp packets.

'This way.' James approaches a battered door, its blue paint flaking, splintered scuff marks down one side. He grips the handle and I expect it to hold firm, but, as he pushes, I can see it's been kicked free from its lock.

James disappears into the darkness inside. I've little choice but to follow, taking tentative steps. It's a bit creepy, particularly when today is Friday the 13th.

In a gloomy corridor, ripped up cardboard, sheets of old newspaper and a mound of ragged clothes are scattered across the floor. Something drips rhythmically.

'How did you know how to get in?' I automatically whisper, uncertain as to whether that's because I feel like a burglar or because I don't want to disturb the place's settled remains.

'That's not important.' James takes my hand. 'Don't take anything in till I say.'

I am a child being led into the unknown. We weave along the corridor and through a swinging door out into the bar area. There's just enough light to see a portrait of decay: cobwebs in nooks and crannies, dust an inch thick on tables and chairs, wires hanging from where light bulbs once glowed. What was alive and bustling with people, chatter and laughter is now frozen into silence. The pool table's baize is grey and frayed, two cues still resting on it. The optics are empty. The clock has stopped. A musty, dour stench permeates everything.

James guides me to the front door, lets go of my hand, then turns me around so that I'm facing the room as if I've just entered it. 'I know it didn't look like this, but try and imagine what you saw the last time you were here.'

You liked the large, open bar area, didn't you, Albert, and that it could fit so many people in, everyone on view, no hiding places. The bar itself sweeping round, always a space to stand waiting to be served. In one corner is a small stage. Something about it causes my stomach to tighten.

'Over there.' James points to a wall adorned with posters, some torn and dangling, others faded. A distinct one in the middle displays three young men dressed in baggy clothes, their hair wild, black stripes across their eyes like racoons. Two of them are pointing guitars as if they're guns, making them resemble highwaymen. The third is holding drumsticks ready to lash out and hit someone. LIVE, TONIGHT, 8 P.M., it says above them. THE BILKERS.

I catch my breath, then look again at the stage. I can picture them on it: a drum kit wedged in at the back, the drummer flailing in fury, as though he wanted to destroy those drums, crush those cymbals; the lead singer thrashing his guitar and screeching into the microphone, spittle flecking the floor; the bass player, all long, loose limbs, more stilted than the rest, hunched over his instrument, bobbing awkwardly.

I turn back to the poster and see the date: Monday 13 February 2012.

I'm aware of James studying me, a hopeful smile spreading across his face. 'Where did you sit, Gran?'

I scrutinise the empty tables. Pieces of that night are floating back to me like flotsam on the tide. We hadn't realised the band would be playing when we met in the pub. We didn't even know it hosted live music. We'd moved to the furthest table away from the racket.

'That one.' I point to a small, circular table at the far end.

'Great.' James dashes over. He sweeps dust from its surface with his sleeve and positions two chairs facing each other.

'Please take a seat.' The tone of a waiter. 'Preferably the one you sat at that night.'

I move the chair to where I think it was and sit down. James pulls his mobile from his pocket. How will calling someone help? A drum roll bursts from the device, a bass line thudding behind it, then a squeal of feedback, followed by a thundering guitar riff. James places his phone in the middle of the table. A singer starts with the high pitch of a shrieking cat. I can't make out the words until a quieter part of the song when just the bass continues.

What goes around, round, round ...
... *Coming back to you.*

It echoes through me. It's the song on the radio. It's the song that I heard that night. Another piece of the wreckage inside my mind drifts into place. I can hear the hum of conversations as a backdrop to the music. I can see the young people pushing their way to the stage.

James switches his backpack to his chest, opens it up and pulls out a large bottle of whisky and a tumbler.

'Where on Earth have you got those from, young man?'

'Borrowed them from Dad's drinks cabinet, I'll put them back when we're done. You had a whisky that night, yeah? Your usual tipple.'

He pours a generous amount into the glass and adds: 'Straight, no ice.'

'Steady, James.' I hold up a palm. 'I'd have only had a single. We're supposed to be aiding my memory, not getting me tipsy.'

I think my cold has almost gone, so I can savour a drink.

The whisky fumes reach me: heady, smoky. I swirl the glass, the murky liquid eddying, then take a sip. It's warm and strong with a sweet finish.

James sits opposite me. 'Pretend that I'm Barbara. What were you talking about? What do you want to say to her?'

I visualise Barbara in front of me. It was a strange meeting place; we hadn't been in this pub for years. Remember, Albert, how we'd occasionally bring Barbara here. It wasn't her scene but it gave her a break from Don; he allowed her out every now and then with us two, the only people he seemed to trust her with. The barman poured the drinks as she poured out her woes. It's changed so much. Why did Barbara want to meet here? I remember our conversation.

'We thought it would be somewhere quiet and uncrowded to talk, not expecting the music and the audience. Barbara didn't want me to come over to hers or for her to visit me, she wanted to go somewhere separate, somewhere she wouldn't go again. And she wanted a stiff drink.'

The words are dredged from the depths of my mind. It really is as if I'm communicating with the spirits, her ghost speaking to me eight weeks to the day since she died. She'd ordered a cognac. I can see her now taking a gulp and spluttering as it hit the back of her throat. She was never a big drinker, barely touched the stuff, apart from an occasional brandy, usually to settle the nerves. I take another sip of whisky and breathe it in.

'Keep going, Gran, this is great.'

I see the anxiety etched all over Barbara's face. *Whatever will you think of me, Margaret?* She just couldn't get the words out. That music grating away, like a chainsaw ruining a summer's day, making it even harder for her to speak.

What goes around, round, round ...
... Coming back to you.

The chorus repeating, familiar now. I take James's hand, just as I'd taken Barbara's. I'd do anything to help her, to relieve her. 'Whatever it is, I'm here for you.'

'What did she say, Gran?'

My heart sinks. 'She couldn't bring herself to tell me.'

A guitar squeals a horrid squall of feedback. I see the disappointment hit James's face. The ruins can't be fixed.

Promise me you'll do it, Margaret.

Those words chime with the music. Before saying them, Barbara had handed something to me. I can see it now, her hand trembling as she passed it across the table, the shame evident in her closed eyes and wrinkled nose.

'A letter,' I blurt out. 'That was it. She gave me a letter.'

'What did it say?' James gawps, as if I'm about to give him the meaning of life.

'She asked me to take it home, saying she couldn't even bear to have it in her house. It would explain everything, she said, I was to take it with me, read it as soon as I got home, then keep it safe.'

James leans forward. 'So did you?'

'It was still in its envelope. I remember having it in my hand, not even daring to put it in my bag in case I lost it.'

Don't read it here, it's not private. You must keep it safe once you've read it. Promise me you'll do it, Margaret.

It all floods back to me. It had felt as if I was at Bletchley again, secret information in my hand, to be deciphered as soon as possible then secured.

An image develops of Barbara in front of the flames holding that letter. A thought pricks me: it was on the same night! She'd lit that fire in a moment of torment, wanting to destroy that letter. But then she'd stepped back and decided to hand it to me instead. I try to remember more. Was it to protect her?

Another sentence emerges: *It was him, after all these years.*

My blood freezes. *Harry.* I was right after all. It wasn't my mind playing tricks on me. He *is* back. I knew it!

James holds his hands in the air. 'But what did the letter say?'

'It was too noisy, too busy. We finished our drinks and just left. I gave Barbara a hug, told her everything would be all right, that I'd contact her. She was going somewhere else so I headed home.'

It suddenly hits me in the stomach, this punch of distress, anger, sadness. 'And I never saw her again.'

I take a nip of whisky and pull myself together. I recall hurrying away from the pub, that letter gripped tightly, head down, coat wrapped taut. A mission. A pledge. I even looked around to make sure I wasn't being followed.

'I got home and put the kettle on. I needed something to keep me calm and warm me up. I brewed a chamomile and sat in the armchair. Then there was a knock on the door.'

The drums pound, the cymbals clashing, the guitar and singer wailing; the song reaching its climax.

'Who was it?' James perches on the edge of his seat.

'I can't recall, it's not important. I just remember I was interrupted and didn't want to leave Barbara's letter, so precious to her, on display. So, I hid it.'

'And then you read it once you'd got rid of the caller?' James has reached a pitch the singer would be proud of.

'I never went back to read it. Whoever was at the door distracted me for so long I forgot all about it.' I want to kick myself, but I'd cause too much damage. 'It was probably your mum getting me all worked up about something else.'

I always meant to go back and read it, Albert. It just disappeared from my brain.

'But you must still have the letter. Where did you put it?' James sees my face and knows the answer. He groans. 'So close.'

A wave of exhaustion washes over me. It's been so draining, this scouring the past.

'The letter must be in your house, Gran. We can find it. How hard could it be?'

The song ends. I remember the audience applauding, whooping, my ears left ringing.

James lifts the glass to his lips.

'You're too young for that.' I snatch it from him and down the remnants. The hit and heat of alcohol are reviving. James takes the tumbler from me and puts it and the bottle back in his bag. He picks up his phone as the next song blasts out, and turns it off.

'Yes, that's enough of that racket.'

'I read that stimulating the senses can bring back memories, Gran. Didn't know if it'd work with your condition, but was worth a go. When I realised that gig was on the date you'd met Barbara and you'd gone somewhere unusual then it all clicked into place.'

If only my brain still worked that easily.

James leads me out of the pub. I'm a bit wobbly, hope the booze hasn't gone to my head. I'm glad to be out of there, it's so gloomy and fetid. For once, I'm pleased they might be knocking something down and starting afresh.

We rush home, duty's weight on our shoulders. I can barely get the key out of my purse and in the lock, my fingers trembling worse than Barbara's.

Then we search and search: every room, through wardrobes and drawers, underneath furniture, down the sides of the armchair and sofa. It's the same as when my purse went missing, it's just not there. My house is a Bermuda Triangle.

We sit side-by-side on the sofa, exhausted, the lounge a mess.

'We have to find it.' James looks at me with forlorn eyes. 'We just have to.'

But we've nowhere left to look.

He stares at our blank television. 'You never fancy a proper TV, Gran?'

'Everyone criticises our old box.'

'Oh!' James's eyes light up like a bulb on Enigma. 'I know where it is.'

CHAPTER 35

'Unlock the bureau, Gran.'

I take the little key from its hiding place, slide it into the lock and turn it with a sharp click. James opens up the bureau and glides out the wooden box. My instinct is to order him away from it, then I realise I don't need to.

James lifts the lid as though removing the cover of a pharaoh's sarcophagus. He rummages through the paperwork and photographs, sifting with the air of a historian documenting his discovery. A reverential hush descends. One by one, each piece of my past is considered then put to one side. Hope drains as the contents dwindle.

The letter isn't there. Foiled again. We'll never find it. Maybe I imagined it, Albert, another symptom of my illness. I can't bear this quashing of expectation.

Almost at the base, James pulls free an envelope, holding it up as if it's the Jules Rimet Trophy. It bears Barbara's name in thick, black ink. Exhilaration courses through me. Obviously, it was tucked away near the bottom, the last place you'd look.

'You'd have put it here the moment you needed to hide it,' says James. 'It's your safe space.'

I have no recollection, just as when you put down a set of keys then a minute later have no idea where they are and upon finding them have no memory of putting them there.

James opens the envelope, removes the letter and offers it to me. 'Barbara wanted you to read it.'

'We'll read it together.' I lean over his shoulder as we devour the words:

Dear Barbara,

I understand it came as a shock to you and that you're upset, but I'm hoping you've calmed sufficiently to read this letter and hear me out. You owe me that at least. After abandoning me, then having nothing to do with me for my entire life, I don't think it's too much for me to ask for your help. I don't think you realise the difference your support could make to my life.

It's always been there, in the back of my mind, this feeling that my real family, a part of who I am, remained a mystery to me. That feeling grows stronger every day, and that's why I acted on it to seek you out. I just want to know why you made the decisions you did and for us to build a relationship.

I never knew my father. I'd like to get to know my mother before it's too late.

I stare at the neat, joined-up writing.

'Barbara had a child?' I try to make sense of it.

'Is this who came back into her life?' puzzles James.

My world is reshaping again. My best friend of fifty years and she kept her secret from me her entire life, struggling to unburden herself until the bitter end. A spike of shock is developing into a bruise. Then I think of my own secrets, the things we're too ashamed for others to know, and my heart softens. It would have been so difficult for both of them. And Barbara did reach out to me, she did want me to know. It's there in James's hand. She trusted me and turned to me in the end. Was it not I that let her down?

James looks at both sides of the paper. 'Doesn't say who it's from. Do you recognise the handwriting?'

I scrutinise every word. 'No. I've no idea who wrote it.'

With a sigh, James folds the letter up, slides it inside its envelope and puts it back in the box. 'Let's leave it here where it's safe.'

'Should we take it to the police?'

'Let's think about it.'

My head and heart are too in turmoil to know what to do. I rummage through the albums in the cardboard box and pull out the photograph of me, Harry and Barbara. That bruise aches. Two people I thought I'd known so well.

James looks as bewildered as I feel. 'You said you thought you'd seen Uncle Harry hanging around.'

'A tall man, round-shouldered.' I wave the photograph. 'Just like this, just as I remember him.'

'But . . .' James hesitates, clearly weighing his words. 'How could it be, Gran?'

'I told you, he needs to get rid of that letter he sent me, to protect himself.'

'No.' James frowns. 'I mean, isn't he your older brother?' He points to me in the photograph – long-haired, slim, wrinkle-free. 'You don't look like this any more, Gran. How could it possibly be Harry if he looks the same?'

He's right. Heat tingles my cheeks. I'd convinced myself, but it couldn't have been Harry.

James's attention switches to his mobile phone. It reminds me of those *Doctor Who* gadgets that can do magical things.

He sees my interest. 'Just searching for anything I can find on Uncle Harry, to see what happened to him.' He holds up the device. 'You need a smartphone, Gran. It's got email, apps, all my music, photos and videos, maps, etc., etc. There's this audio recorder thing where we could record interviewing suspects.'

James presses the screen and brings up an image of what looks like an old-fashioned microphone.

'Did you write that letter?' he says slowly and loudly.

He jabs again and his voice booms back, making me jump.

'See. Just press this button to record. You try.'

He holds up the device and I press where he's indicating.

'Now speak.'

'How is this getting us any closer to the truth, young man?' I say in a stern voice.

'Press there to stop it.' I follow his directions. 'And there to play back.'

A shrill voice echoes my words. Is that what I sound like? My voice used to be strong and melodious, not thin and rasping. If only it were as easy to get back time as it is to preserve it on that machine.

'See, it's easy,' he says.

It could be a useful device for subterfuge. I would have liked to have been a spy, to have seen some action rather than toiling away behind the scenes.

I wander to the window. Barbara's garden, once so neat

and tidy, is growing wild and unkempt, thorns and weeds flourishing.

'I can't find anything.' Exasperation is snarled in James's voice.

I wish that garden was immaculate. I wish everything was how it once was.

Someone walks past my driveway. The flicker of a tall, slightly stooped, middle-aged man. My blood freezes, my wishes caught in my head.

'That's him!'

James dashes to my side. 'Where?'

'Walking down the street. He went left.' I gesture feverishly.

'I'll go after him.'

'Are you sure? Is it safe?'

'It'll be all right.'

When you get older, you realise that one day everything doesn't work out fine. Before I can say anything further, James has gone. I watch from the window as he scampers down the driveway and turns left.

I feel pathetic, standing here, doing nothing. I spot James's mobile phone on the sofa. What if he needs it? I slip it into my cardigan pocket. I hope he doesn't do anything silly.

What can I do?

You're not here to answer me, Albert. You're no longer around to help, you have no say or influence. I am useless, here on my own without you. Your loss is a black hole dragging me into the abyss. I sink into our chair.

Think, Margaret, think. Except, I can still hear your voice, those warm, playful tones. *Come on, my girl. Use what little grey matter you have left to come up with something clever.*

It's no good. My brain has become scrambled, a message in need of decoding. What's the key? What's the way in? Use another route. I focus on what you would do. You'd want every loose end tied up, nothing left uncertain. I take my purse from the other pocket of my cardigan. Open it. Take out Barbara's bank statement.

I retrace my steps. It wasn't in Matthew's study, it wasn't in Barbara's house, it wasn't in that care home. Another possibility appears, like Enigma lighting up. Things click into place, the wheel turning, the encryption emerging. The clarity of a cracked code never fails to take my breath away.

How can I get confirmation? How can I find out more? An idea floats to the surface of my memory.

A key! Ha!

You were right, Albert, there are nuggets of gold in the dark mine of my memory. And I was wrong, your influence hasn't gone, you still have a presence here to help me. I won't just sit here and wait for time to take my faculties. I'm on form in this moment, I must take advantage of my current sharpness. It's time to do some proper snooping. To solve one last puzzle. To have one last adventure.

I see the spider in its web, still and silent. I give it a wave goodbye as I leave our chair.

CHAPTER 36

Our bedroom looks as though a burglar's rampaged: drawers flung open, their contents emptied; the wardrobe doors wide, dusty boxes and bags pulled from deep inside; even items dragged from beneath the bed. Wheezing, I survey the scene with a sunken heart. Turns out remembering I had a key to that house was the easy part. Where I'd left it is proving more difficult to establish. I was certain it was in this room. To be fair, it's been a long time since I've used it. After several years, I think anyone would struggle to locate something like that.

I won't give up. Stubborn as a mule you'd mutter, Albert. I will search every inch of this house if need be.

In the lounge, the bureau stares at me. I wonder? Inside, hanging on little hooks, is a row of keys. I study each in turn. One has a key ring with *Shirley* scrawled on it, must be her spare, there's one for the shed, and one that I haven't a clue what it opens but doesn't look right. The fourth has a brown leather tag bearing the initials *MM*. I kiss the key jubilantly. You smile at me from the mantelpiece, your calm expression releasing a ripple of reassurance. No more time to waste. Wish me luck.

Leaving the house, I take my stick with me as my hip is

playing up. While today the mind is willing, the flesh is weak. Every step is painful. Pausing at the front gate, I make certain the coast is clear. My stick clacks against concrete as I hurry to the front door. Another glance. No one's watching. I knock on the door several times to make certain. Now for the moment of truth.

I try the key in the lock.

It turns smoothly.

Dearie me, seems someone didn't change their locks when they moved in. Not that clever on the home security front, are we? Just as well as I don't think I'm up to shinning the drainpipe and climbing through a window. Do you remember, Albert, that when the Millers lived here, they would ask me to keep an eye on the place while they were on holiday? I never minded checking that everything was all right, collecting the mail, watering the plants. It's only what a good neighbour should do. They left me a key so I could always get in, particularly if there was an emergency. It was never returned.

I scurry inside and close the door. The empty porch is sparse, nothing more than a white box. Where do I start? I'm going to have to focus to prevent my mind wandering like an unruly child. I'll keep repeating what I'm doing so that it stays fixed.

The hallway is unchanged since the Millers lived here. I'll start upstairs. The staircase isn't too steep, thankfully, my stick muffled by the thick carpet.

Mavis had created a lovely home. It's been redecorated and made as bland and charmless as the interior of a cardboard box. The warm colours Mavis used have been replaced with monotonous shades. Walls that once held patterned wallpaper are now a featureless white, as icy and welcoming as the South

Pole, all character lost in a blank void. No pictures or paintings to attract the eye, just a bare sheen. The carpets have been replaced too, from floral swirls to plain pastels. Something about it makes my stomach uneasy. Focus, Margaret. *This is not Mavis Miller's house, she's no longer here.*

I take a gander in the bathroom. A modern suite has been installed. It used to look so elegant and refined. The Victorian cast iron bath is now plastic and a curved shower unit occupies one corner. Mavis takes baths, not showers. She doesn't live here any more; I must remember that. Stay in the present. Concentrate. Keep repeating it, Margaret, keep repeating it.

The main bedroom is dark with sombre-grey walls. A king-size, wooden-framed bed is covered by a crimson duvet. The matching curtains are still shut in the daytime. Wardrobe doors along one side have full-length mirrors attached. I open one. Rows of neatly hung suits and shirts. Flicking through, I stop at a navy pinstripe suit and pull it out for a better view. Such a well-tailored outfit would look lovely on you, Albert. A button is missing, just a frayed piece of cotton dangling in its place. It needs sewing back on. A sensation like being splashed with cold water. That button found in Barbara's hand! Could it be? I shove the suit back inside and close the wardrobe door.

An engine grumbles, tyres rolling slowly to a halt. Is it him? There's no way of getting out of the house in time or explaining this.

I peep through a gap in the curtains, heart pounding. A car has stopped outside. My hand trembles.

The car reverses, backing away as if a frightened animal. It lurches into a three-point turn, then drives off the way it came,

'I'm not sure how reliable I'm going to be.'

'I'll be your memory, just tell me anything you need to remember.'

He's right, that is why I shared my past with him.

James paces the floor again. 'It's not going well for me; those dead expensive solicitors aren't looking hopeful. It's my DNA that forensics found in Barbara's kitchen, from touching the counter, and it was on her purse in the woods. Liam and Gaz have given statements that I went in Barbara's house and came running out. Everything's against me.' His voice rises. 'Do it for *me*, Gran. We need to prove that I didn't do it and who did.' He bangs a fist into a palm. 'As well as for yourself and for Barbara.'

The fire sizzles, the sparks dancing again. He does strike up a very convincing argument. I can't just sit here feeling sorry for myself, James needs my help. We need to clear him and this crook needs catching. Justice, security, are important. He may actually make a good barrister. And they're very well paid, so that's promising.

We were a brilliant team, you and I, Albert. Your mathematical skills, patience and calm confidence together with my determination, reasoning and tenacity made us a formidable force. There was no dilemma we couldn't solve. You're no longer here to help me, but here's somebody that needs my aid and who I need support from.

'Are we gonna solve this thing, Gran?'

His eyes wide, beseeching, challenging. Look how he's grown, a couple of years ago he was playing with toys and wouldn't have said boo to a goose. The room is toasty, my lethargy dissipating.

'Go on then.' I sit upright. 'If it'll keep you quiet.'

'Fab.' He shakes a fist in triumph. 'We're back in the game.'

My purse is on the mantelpiece. I pick it up to put in my cardigan pocket so that I don't lose it. It seems unusually full. Unclasping it, I pull out a piece of scrunched-up paper, which I unfurl and hold up to the light.

'It's Barbara's bank statement.' I hand it to James, my hand shaking again. What's it doing in my purse?

'One thing's for sure, Barbara definitely wasn't poor.' James contemplates the piece of paper. 'Why've you got it?'

My mind stumbles down blind alleys as I try to retrace my steps. I've hardly been out. There was that strange incident in the snow when I stumbled into Barbara's house and saw . . . No, it's not from there, I was barely in the place two minutes and went no further than the kitchen. What about that care home? No, I think it was after that.

A light comes on in the alleyway. I reach for the memory.

'I think I picked it up when I was at your house after visiting the care home.' Yes, that's it! I visualise it. 'My mind was as scrambled as a coded message. I couldn't remember which door was the bathroom and I went into your room first and then your dad's study.' I see a desk covered in paperwork. 'It was in there. I must have seen Barbara's name and thought this doesn't belong here I'll return it to her. I really was very confused. You know what happens. I put it in my purse for safekeeping and must have forgotten all about it.'

James's eyes widen. 'Why would Dad have it?'

His features distort as the permutations play out in his mind. I think of Matthew: brooding, controlling, obsessed with money. Each thought darkens the whole.

presumably lost or now heading to a different destination. My breath tumbles from me.

I need to search that study by the kitchen where I went when I was here before. I find the room. Again, curtains shut, cave-dark. I put the light on. Sparse, tidy, everything is in its place. A computer and printer on a desk, a bookcase filled with tomes on accounting and management, ring binders and DVDs. As exciting as an accountant's office.

Déjà vu confirms my suspicions: this is where I must have picked up Barbara's bank statement, that night when I was soaked and confused. A desk full of paperwork. I remember scooping up my belongings. In my haste, I will have rammed that document into my purse with them.

In one corner is a metal filing cabinet containing six drawers. I lean my stick against it and try to pull the top one open but it won't budge. There's a little keyhole at the top but no sign of a key, or little pots or ornaments to hide one in or under. He wouldn't take something so small and easily lost with him. It must be here somewhere. We used to keep a key under the doormat, not as concerned about security in those days. There are no rugs and I'm not ripping up the carpet.

There's a mouse mat by the keyboard. I lift it and something glints. Holding up the small, silver key, I think of Enigma. That would have a key of the day to set the machine to, so that the encryption was always different. Today's key is in my hand.

In the lock, the key is so tiny and fragile I'm frightened it might snap. It turns easily, the top drawer slides open. Inside are marked pieces of white card, alphabetised, separating grey folders within.

I pull one out. *Irene Broadbent*, it reads. I look inside and there are financial documents detailing transfers from Irene's bank to Mr Braithwaite's. It looks as if he's been fleecing her. Suddenly, her reticence and remarks make sense: she didn't want me to know she'd been making bad investments.

I pull out several more. Each bears a name, more of my neighbours. Within are bank statements, letters and forms detailing transactions. Lots of big numbers in rows and columns. There are personal items, letters from banks addressed to account holders with passwords and reference numbers. It doesn't look right.

Then I see my own name staring back at me. It's like seeing yourself in a photograph of a place you don't recognise. The folder's empty. Something about it disturbs me.

One folder is labelled accounts. Inside are Mr Braithwaite's latest bank statements: debt, debt, debt. An overdraft at the limit. I certainly wouldn't take financial advice from him.

I have an urge to get out of this house but curiosity compels me. This is my opportunity to find as much as I can. I gaze at the computer. Think of all the information it can hold that can be retrieved in an instant. I sit down on the swivel chair in front of the desk, grateful to take the load off my feet.

First thing: how to turn it on. I look for the on switch. It's so cold in here; he must never have the heating on. I rub my arms as I search. It's a similar model to Matthew's computer. I try to remember when he showed me how it worked. Ahh, the button with a circle and a line going through it – on and off in binary coding. I press it. The computer plays a happy little tune, the screen flashes into life.

A message appears asking for a password. What could it be? I remember Matthew changing his. He said a lot of people just left the automatic password on, which was lazy and foolish as it meant hackers could get in easily. The same as that Enigma operator, just pressing the same key over and over again, unwittingly giving the game away. Mr Braithwaite couldn't have been so lax, could he? Well, he didn't change the locks. What was that basic password again? Oh, yes, simple. I type in 'password123'. Access denied.

I rub my hands together hoping for a spark of heat and inspiration. It's as cold as the cottage at Bletchley. Do you remember that small white building in the stable yard next to the mansion? It was somehow more freezing than the wooden huts we worked in; I'd have my woollen coat and mittens on. The concrete floors sent the chill right through your feet and into your bones. The sour, earthy smell of rising damp. The blackout curtains made it as dark as this room. So basic, just a wooden trestle table, light bulbs with no shades and inefficient electric heaters. During those twelve-hour shifts, I'd fend off the stench and tiredness with that bitter coffee.

I was never told what to do at Bletchley, but learned to think for myself. I wasn't trained in mathematics as you and your friends were, Albert, but then you mathematicians had no imagination. I used the psychological approach. To me, crosswords and codebreaking are about getting inside the mind of your opponent. It was people, not just an inanimate machine I was trying to crack. I began to recognise individuals encoding the messages by their styles. To test the day's settings the Germans would often use their girlfriend's names. I worked them out trying different options, as I would a crossword, and then recognised them. That gave me enough letters to get started. People make mistakes. That's how you catch them out.

Hunched over the desk, it's as if I'm at Bletchley now. What would Mr Braithwaite choose as a password? What's important to him? Wealth. Success. Status. I look for clues. The books and DVDs. My eyes stop on one.

I type in 'Wall Street'. Access denied.

I'm not giving in. That determination to find out the truth was forged at Bletchley and has never left me.

How does he see himself? I type in 'Top Dog'. Access denied.

It has to be something personal. I remember James saying that with 'his green eyes, thick eyebrows and strange stare', Mr Braithwaite looked like something out of *Twilight* or 'that old film' *An American Werewolf in London*. I thought watching such a movie would scar his impressionable mind but James claimed it wasn't even scary. Is that how Mr Braithwaite sees himself, every time he looks in the mirror? He's a financier with no family and no one else in his life. Those files, is he preying on others? Something clicks in my brain.

I type in 'Lone Wolf'. The screen glows green. A thrill surges through every single molecule. There's nothing like cracking a code.

Now what? A blue screen emerges with little symbols on it. One is a picture of a folder. That must contain files. I use the mouse as Matthew showed me. An arrow flits around until I get it to stop over the icon. Click. The screen goes white and is covered with files titled with people's names. One stands out: Barbara Jones. Another click and it opens. I hope I don't delete anything. Crucial information I need is retained in all that memory.

There are more options. I choose one and open up an image of Barbara's will, a decent sum of money, her niece and some charities the beneficiaries. I feel uncomfortable reading it.

I go back and look through more files. There are details of financial schemes and bank transfers from people, including my neighbours. To fill the holes, he's taking money from them that he can't repay.

My brain is moving at a speed I no longer thought possible in a scramble to connect the dots. Mr Braithwaite's a conman, taking people's money in the same way that nature's robbing me of my memory. Slowly, penny by penny, bit by bit. Attacking the vulnerable, like this disease. Conmen prey on the elderly too, play tricks with their minds, cause embarrassment, create fear and take away dignity, security and self-respect. From now on I'm going to call my disease Braithwaite. Diseases shouldn't be called after the doctor who discovered them but after an evil person they represent. Doctors should say, 'I'm sorry but it's a case of Stalin', or you'd say, 'My Mussolini is playing up today.' Braithwaite is an illness and that's what mine shall be called.

If I cannot defeat this disease, then I can at least defeat him.

I find a little image of what I guess is a printer. I click on it. Nothing happens. Then a whirring noise makes me jump and paper is sucked into the printer and spat back out again. I hope this doesn't take long. That urge to leave is now screaming at me, but it's beneath a frisson of excitement, that race against time to crack the Enigma codes.

I print out Barbara's will, then snatch the sheets of paper. Jab the off button. The computer screen goes black. I have a mountain of evidence. I have to get the police here to seize everything and question him. I put it all inside Barbara's file, where I notice a folded-up letter. I shut the drawer, lock the filing cabinet and place the key under the little mat. Then unfold the single piece of paper.

A noise makes me stop. From the front of the house. I listen carefully. The unmistakable sound of a key in a lock.

My time is up.

CHAPTER 37

I grab my stick and leave the room as the front door bangs shut. There's no way out. Never did a heart beat so fast.

Stay with me, Albert.

We enter the lounge simultaneously. Braithwaite lifts his head. Stops dead. Those thick eyebrows hoist high. My brain and body freeze.

'What the hell are you doing in my house?' Surprise twists into anger.

I'm silent. Braithwaite's usual smartness isn't quite there: a smattering of stubble, heavy bags under bloodshot eyes, his hair missing its normal slickness, and creases in his white shirt. He studies me as a geologist might do a stone.

'Do you know where you are, Margaret?'

Perhaps I could use my illness to my advantage; act all confused and pretend I'm lost and have somehow wandered in accidentally. It would at least buy me some time.

Braithwaite's eyes settle on the folder and letter I'm clutching in one hand, my other gripping the stick. An icy stare. 'What have you got there?' The tone accusing. 'Are they mine?'

His miscasting of himself as the victim unlocks my brain as

easily as that key in the door, my tongue untying. 'They're not yours. They belong to my friend.'

'What are you up to?' Braithwaite looks towards the front door. 'It was locked. How did you get in?'

'I have a spare key.' My instinct to tell the truth might not be an asset in this situation.

'Should have changed the locks.' He shakes his head. 'But I didn't expect neighbours sneaking in.' He glowers at me. 'So why have you?'

'Because I know what you are.' I shake the papers. 'And I have the proof in my hand.'

'That's just paperwork.' A calm bemusement possesses him now. 'It means nothing.'

'It connects everything.'

'What exactly do you think you know, Margaret?' Braithwaite takes a step towards me, he's just feet away.

'You're in financial trouble and have been tricking people to take their money.'

'My, you have been busy.' He flaps a hand as if dismissing a servant. 'This confused state you do. Is it all just an act?'

'Yours is the act. Pretending to be respectable while deceiving people.' I lay all my cards on the table as if it's bridge night. I'm looking past him, though, and through the front window, hoping to see someone going by. Blast. I can't see any further than his blooming garden. 'I know you killed Barbara.'

Eight weeks ago today. Eight long, bewildering weeks.

Braithwaite looks as if he wants to crack that geologist's stone right open. 'You know nothing of the sort.' His pallid face reddens, his fingers curling inwards. 'Breaking in here, taking things, making false accusations.'

'I know it was you.'

'You're just a stupid old woman whose husband must have been a saint to put up with you for so long.'

I won't let him poison our relationship. Yes, you were a saint, not like this sinner. 'My Albert did have the patience of a saint, but he also knew how much I loved him and appreciated everything I did for him.' A smile stretches across Braithwaite's face. 'Your charm has vanished. I can see what you're capable of.'

'Who's going to believe a senile pensioner?'

I glance at the letter that's now flattened against the folder. Barbara's handwriting, nearly as scrawling as mine. *I'm so sorry, but please leave me alone*, it reads, *I want to live out my final years in peace and keep my past behind me.*

I feel the ground beneath me shift and the light in the room seems different, hazier. Barbara is responding to that letter she gave me. It must have been from Braithwaite. Each word falls into place until the meaning is clear.

'You're Barbara's son!'

Braithwaite watches me take everything in. He has lived next door for all these months and I hadn't an inkling of who he really is. He moved so close to her without even a hint.

'How could you? To your own mother?'

Adrenaline surges through me, keeping me alert. I have to find a way out of here while I'm thinking clearly. What would the great detectives do? I have to take control. I rest my stick against my leg, putting my free hand in my cardigan pocket to clutch something smooth. It's my turn to question him.

'Poor Barbara. What possessed you?'

Braithwaite sits on the leather sofa, running a hand through his thinning hair. 'Stop saying her damned name.'

That's it. I need to get inside his head and under his skin. 'Why would you do such a thing?'

'I didn't mean to,' he snaps.

No emotional control under that icy exterior. I've found a way in. I've cracked his code. 'You knew what you were doing.'

He slams the armrest. 'That's not how it was.'

I try not to flinch. 'You killed her for money.'

'You don't know the half of it.' Braithwaite looks away from me. 'It was her fault.'

'You're blaming the victim?'

'I had everything once.' He looks me in the eye, his voice weary. 'Then things slipped away from me. I worked damn hard, focused everything on my career. The wife left, the divorce was expensive.'

A self-pitying whine. He's not a true man like yourself, Albert, who would stay loyal and dependable no matter what life threw at you. People don't take responsibility for their own actions these days.

'The business began to struggle and I had little money left to invest. I'd already lost my dream house. I just needed a bit more time to stabilise the business then make it profitable again but the banks wouldn't give me that.'

Always wanting more than God has given them, some people.

'The business was about to go into administration. I'd have nothing left. I found out who my mother was. Moved here, hoping we could get to know each other a little first. Started persuading people to invest, telling them I had schemes giving a good rate of return.'

'You stole their money.'

'I didn't steal it. If I can turn things round they'll get it back.'

These financiers and their greed. The effect it has on people. 'It's fraud.'

Braithwaite shrugs. 'I needed more, so I turned to my mother.' He almost spits out the words. 'But I was her dirty secret.'

That affair, Albert! Barbara fell pregnant.

'She gave me up for adoption without anyone knowing.'

With her religious beliefs and upbringing, Barbara wouldn't have wanted an abortion. But there's no way Don would have brought up another man's child. Barbara wouldn't have felt able to walk away from her marriage and would have felt ashamed at her indiscretion. Don would have controlled the situation, kept it hushed up, made her give the child away.

'She had plenty and could have helped me. I went to see her with my best suit on, wanting to impress. I told her who I was and she wanted nothing to do with me.'

It must have been such a shock for Barbara.

'I wrote to her but she just wrote back, cutting me off. I went round again, to tell her how I felt. She could see I was angry but let me in so that the neighbours wouldn't hear. Maybe she thought she could calm me. But she didn't really listen. You'd think your own mother would want to help. I thought she'd be desperate to make things up to me.'

Braithwaite stares at the flat-screen television.

'It could have been a fresh start for both of us. That money was rightly mine anyway – she'd never given me anything growing up so she owed me.' He clutches his shirt at the chest, screwing the material into a tight ball in his fist. 'All the anger and pain.' His face growing redder, his knuckles white. 'This rage. I grabbed her. Shook her. She screamed. I put my hand over her mouth to shut her up and we struggled to the floor.'

His gaze is fixed on the black screen.

'I put my hands around her throat. Closed my eyes. Just squeezed. And squeezed. Until my anger was gone. When I opened my eyes, she was a ragdoll on the floor.'

My stick is propping me up, queasiness engulfing me.

'Couldn't believe it. Didn't know what to do. So I drove off to some financial meeting in the city and acted as if nothing was wrong. At least that gave me a chance to say I wasn't around that evening, so suspicion didn't fall on me.'

Braithwaite puts his head in his hands and sniffs. Not a hint of compassion for Barbara.

'I was curious, though, to find out more about you and your family. *My family*.'

My blood freezes. 'What do you mean?'

Braithwaite snorts. 'You haven't worked out who my father is?'

And suddenly I see it. A tall man with rounded shoulders. The shape of his nose and those green eyes with that same look of venom. I think of that photograph again, Barbara and him standing so close.

'Harry!' I gasp.

CHAPTER 38

My world has shifted on its axis again. I had no idea Harry had been involved with Barbara. Did he know she was pregnant? Did that add to the reason why he fled? It would have been around the time I told Barbara about my trouble with Harry. No wonder she couldn't tell me. No wonder she stayed with Don rather than try to follow Harry.

I let the stick take my weight. My body so heavy, my head just air. 'Why didn't you tell me?'

Braithwaite shrugs. 'Shirley made it clear that talking about Harry was off-limits.'

His words roam my mind. 'How have you tried to find out things about me and my family?'

'The only way was to have a look around without you knowing. I took your purse and copied your keys, then put them back in that box of photographs, figuring you'd have nothing better to do than reminisce over old snaps so you'd soon find it.'

Another chill slides through me. 'Was that you who came into my house that night?'

'Thought you'd be fast asleep and I could have a good look around. Didn't have much chance. I was barely home when

Shirley rang and invited me straight back! You'd changed the locks the next time I called.'

'And you were tapping me up, you were after my money. Did you take anything?'

'Maybe you owe me too, Aunty Margaret.' He sneers. 'I thought you'd have a nest egg. Newly widowed, frugal lifestyle. Must be some money stored somewhere. But I wasn't after a few quid from an old woman's purse.'

Something else occurs to me. 'My brooch!'

Braithwaite lets out a hollow laugh. 'Stupid mistake. I dropped it while rummaging through your purse to get the keys. It fell on the car floor and in my rush I couldn't find it. Presume you did though.'

'You were happy to let people think I was making it up that my purse had been taken.' I squeeze the stick's handle. 'You used my illness to your advantage. You're just a common thief.'

His face changes, something dawning. 'You made your way into Barbara's house too, didn't you.'

'I don't understand.'

'You must get used to that feeling.'

I see Harry's superior and arrogant manner, but I can't detect any of Barbara's kindness. It takes me a moment to make the connection: that strange figure when I stumbled into Barbara's.

'I went round again last week,' he says. 'Had a copy of her keys too. I wanted to get the letter I'd written to her in case the police found it, but it wasn't there, she might have got rid. And to find her will, was wondering about challenging it, if your grandson went down for her murder. I found it. Thought about ripping it up. Then that I could just change it, so I took it to scan. Hadn't expected you to walk in.'

'It was you. It was you all along.' I've been seeing him everywhere.

'Don't know which of us was more alarmed.' His stare is cold and hard. 'Could have got rid of you there and then. That would have left the police with a puzzle: another body in the exact same spot just weeks apart.'

I picture Barbara lying there, the life choked out of her. I look to the door. With him seated, would I be able to get past him and reach it? I can barely move, never mind run. 'Whatever pain she caused you could never justify what you did.'

'You wouldn't understand. It's all right for you. You've lived your life. You're seeing your time out in comfort.'

I glare at him. 'You're a killer and a thief whose crimes have caught up with him.'

He gives the same hollow laugh. 'You won't remember any of this. You're just a forgetful old bag who'll shuffle off none the wiser.'

I'm not taking any criticism from this piece of work. All I have to fight him with are words. 'I've forgotten more things than you'll ever know. And I've outwitted much cleverer enemies than you.'

Your character shows through when you're in conflict and under pressure. His true colours are emerging like the paint beneath torn-away wallpaper. I rest my stick against me and pull James's mobile out of my cardigan pocket, waving it in the air. 'I have all I need here. I've recorded everything you've just said.' I hold the folders in the air too. 'I have your confession in one hand and documentary evidence in the other.'

A flash of anger in his eyes.

'There are moments, Braithwaite, when I know exactly what I'm doing.'

A burst of song emits from the object in my left hand. I almost throw it at him in shock. Somehow the damn thing is ringing. I grip it tight.

Braithwaite springs from the sofa, blocking my path, a bitter smile playing on his lips. 'Then I'll just have to take those off you.' He steps towards me. 'Why couldn't you just leave it alone?'

I throw the phone so that it slides under the sofa, out of his reach. If nothing else, it might stall him.

He looks at me as if I'm dirt on his shoe, then lurches forward. I step back. Stumble. Balance gone, I fall. My stick hits the floor with a dull thud. I land with a sharp crack, pain searing through me. I cry out, clutching the top of my leg. It feels as if my hip is jagged shards.

That image of Barbara, prone and helpless.

Braithwaite blocks out the light. 'Didn't even need to touch you.'

The pain is so intense it's all I can do not to vomit.

'Could just leave you here.' He crouches over me with the expression of a chess master pondering their next move. 'With my key in your possession. Maybe I should go away for a few days. See what I find when I get back.'

A noise. Braithwaite swivels round. The door flies open.

'Get away from her.' James's voice loud and clear.

Braithwaite moves towards him.

As long as I have breath left in my body, I won't let that bastard hurt my grandson.

I ignore the pain, swallow the bile. It's all in the mind. Rolling onto my side, I bite so hard on my lip that I taste blood. I grab the bottom of the stick. Swing it, the curved end hooking Braithwaite's leg as he charges at James.

Braithwaite trips. Yelps. Crashes face first.

James takes advantage. Drops onto Braithwaite's back, restraining him. Braithwaite writhes like a worm.

Agony pulses from my leg to the rest of my body. Cold sweat clings to my forehead.

'You all right, Gran?'

'Just don't let him go.' My voice is distant, as if someone else spoke the words.

Braithwaite squirms. James rams his weight against him. 'Can't hold him forever.'

I can't move. The pain is pinning me down. I have nothing left.

Braithwaite's shoving back, kicking out.

'Where's my phone?' yells James.

I can see it under the sofa. I can't reach it.

Braithwaite grunts, uses his arms to push himself upwards. James clutches him as if he's a bucking bronco.

The stick is still in my clammy fingers. I swing the handle out again. A fresh swell of torture, another surge of nausea. I fish under the sofa until the hook hits and I can reel in my catch.

I pull the mobile to me. The shiny screen is blank. 'James,' I groan, 'I can't even turn it on.'

Braithwaite's head rises. 'You said you were using it to record.'

'I made that up.' I take a great gulp of air. 'Hoped you'd just give yourself up.'

'You've nothing on me.' He struggles again. 'Get off.'

James drives him back down. 'Pass me the phone, Gran.'

With one final effort I hurl the mobile towards James. It arcs in the air. He catches it one-handed. With a few swift movements he brings it to life.

James's garbled words to the operator, a murderer attacking his gran, demanding police, an ambulance, fade in and out like a radio reception, full of static and crackle. Weak, woozy, I lie still, the floor hard, sweat dripping.

'Talk to me, James.' I need something to focus on. 'Where were you?'

'I followed this loser around, trying to make sense of it. When he came back, I went to yours.' I concentrate on his voice, so full of life and energy. 'Didn't think you'd be round here too. When I couldn't find you or my mobile, I phoned it but you didn't answer. I got a bad feeling. I was looking outside. Heard voices from in here.'

The white ceiling hazy. The Artex swirls the one thing Braithwaite didn't decorate over. He's saying nothing. Maybe he's given up, resigned to his fate, outsmarted by a forgetful old lady and a brash kid.

My ears are ringing. No, there's sirens. Urgent. Louder. Blaring. The ceiling grows darker, the sirens recede.

The pain fades.

CHAPTER 39

Hospitals are no place for old people. They're rife with disease. I could catch all manner of superbugs here that would finish me off – I've been reading all about it in the newspaper. I've just a few clues left to get in the crossword, it's taken me hours. It's no good, the answers won't come. I put it to one side.

I shuffle in the bed. Propped up, with my leg fixed rigid, it's impossible to get comfortable. At least the ward is clean, with crisp, white sheets and a shine to the floor. It's as clinical and perfunctory as every other health building: plain and with a whiff of disinfectant, machines that beep and whirr and a few basic chairs for visitors. The nurses rush around more than Shirley. They're pleasant enough, just don't seem to have time to stop still. I've had to tell a few to take a moment of calm.

Sometimes, I need them to reassure me. It's disorientating waking up in this strange room surrounded by beds and strangers, and my familiar furniture, patterned wallpaper and floral curtains replaced with this alien view. I've cried out on a few occasions. It takes a while to make sense of the situation. The soreness from my shattered hip can actually be a useful reminder.

The doctor says I need a hip replacement. I'm on all manner of painkillers while I wait for an operation. I fear I may be here some time. It's not easy being cooped up. I long to stand on my own two feet again, to do what I want, when I want, without people fussing over me. I miss my home. It's strange that despite having all these people around me it feels lonelier here. I wouldn't be so adrift back home. I can sense your presence there.

I've been trying to get to know my new neighbours. Mrs Thompson, in the next bed, is recovering from a heart attack, like you had, dear. Her family say the paramedics arrived just in time and had to cut through her blouse with a huge pair of scissors to get the defibrillators on her. All sounds very undignified. She's not said a great deal, I think it's been too unsettling for her.

Mrs Anderson, opposite, is in much better spirits after a mild stroke. She's the luckier of us, looking forward to going home shortly where she lives with relatives who'll be able to help her find her feet again.

I can hear our family now, their voices and footsteps bounding the corridor. I think there are restrictions on the number of visitors at any one time but that doesn't seem to stop them.

The double doors swing open. James leads the way ahead of his parents. He's been super confident since our crime-solving; I do hope it's not going to his head. With me stuck in here, I'm not around to keep an eye on him and provide some guidance.

'How you doing, Gran?' James perches on the side of my bed, his slick hair trimmed a touch and tucked behind his ears. An improvement, of sorts. 'They looking after you all right?'

'Mustn't grumble. Just need them to fix this blasted hip so that I can go home.'

'You're looking much better than when you were on Braithwaite's floor.' He gazes into the distance. 'Thought you were a goner when you passed out.'

Shirley's clutching a big bouquet of flowers and immediately sets about clearing away a dying old bunch.

'Just make sure you get plenty of rest.' She spreads out the colourful new additions in the vase before positioning it on a little chest of drawers next to my bed. 'After all you've been through you need to recuperate.'

Shirley steps back to admire her handiwork. 'There. That brightens the place up.'

She turns her attention to smoothing out my sheets and moves me around to plump up the pillows. 'How's your memory, Mum? Once you're out of here we'll have to take you for more tests so that they can get you some medication.'

'My Braithwaite has been fine.'

Their faces crease with confusion. Matthew stares at me as if I've finally lost my marbles.

'It's what I'm calling my illness from now on,' I explain. 'I'm naming it after the person it most reminds me of.'

'Great idea, Gran.' James laughs. 'It'll soon trend on Twitter.'

Shirley shakes her head. James looks around the room, taking in all the medical equipment and my fellow patients. They're all asleep. I doubt our chatter will even stir them.

'Still no date for your op, Margaret?' Matthew hovers behind his wife.

'No, still waiting.'

A moment of awkwardness lingers as they seem unsure what

to say, but there's plenty I want to find out from them. It's been a few days since the police carted Braithwaite off. James said later they looked astonished to find an old lady lying prone on the floor with a middle-aged man trapped beneath a teenage boy. As soon as Braithwaite was in handcuffs, James was at my side, making sure the paramedics were taking good care of me. He said Braithwaite was silent, seemed shell-shocked. Perhaps he'd finally realised what he'd done.

'So what's happened to Braithwaite?' I ask James. 'Have they locked him up for good?'

'The detectives gave us the latest this morning.' His voice is hushed, despite the gentle snores around us, and he moves closer, as if delivering state secrets. 'They've got all the financial documents showing how he's transferred money from people's accounts into his business. That button the police found is the one missing from his suit. I've given a statement about what he was about to do to you, when I got into his house just in time. They've charged him with murder, attempted murder and fraud. He's admitted everything. They say he'll plead guilty.'

'It'll save us from going through a trial,' adds Shirley. 'I was worried that might be too much for you.'

Oh, I don't know, I would have loved my day in court. It would have been a new experience. Still, I'm glad he's confessed. He needs to repent for what he's done.

'He'll get life for murder,' says James. 'The police reckon it'll be twenty years, minimum.'

'They should lock him up and throw away the key.' Shirley shudders. 'To think, his own mother.' She's changed her tune about Braithwaite.

I lean over to James. 'We got there in the end, eh.'

'I still can't believe you went into his house and put yourself in danger.' Shirley tuts. 'What were you thinking?'

'Without us he'd still be on the loose,' I tell her. Shirley opens her mouth, hesitates. Matthew gives her shoulder a gentle squeeze.

'The fact that you're both still with us and he's been caught is the main thing, I suppose,' she says, eventually. 'To think that man was living next door to you. And part of our family. And none of us knew.'

The thought of Harry makes me shift position.

James sees my reaction. 'I searched the internet for any trace of Uncle Harry.' He pulls his phone from his pocket. 'You were right, he fled to Russia. I found a Russian newspaper article about a car accident in the nineties in St Petersburg and used Google to translate. It involved a Harry Spencer. Same age. His photo. Not much detail.' He shows me the screen. 'He's dead, Gran. He can't hurt you, or anyone else, any more.'

A stillness. I can't see it through the blur of tears. James reads it out. The gist finds its way into my comprehension. An English expat killed in a collision. Wasn't wearing a seatbelt.

Harry died alone.

A volcanic eruption of emotions. Grief's gut punch, bubbling hot in the darkness. Yet a ripple of relief as it cools that I'm free from his shadow.

I burst into tears and let them flow.

James holds me, my sobs soaking into his T-shirt. Shirley's arms wrap around me too, and I feel Matthew's hand on my shoulder. When I can cry no more, they pull away.

I say a quiet prayer.

James has something else in his hand. He gives me Harry's

letter. One last look at my brother's elegant handwriting and then I tear it into pieces, each rip feeling more liberating than the last. It's of no use to me now. I wonder how well the words are committed to memory.

Relief is the overwhelming force. My tears are drying. I have answers.

'You OK, Gran?'

I give James a weak smile.

'What about your own trouble with the law?' I ask him.

'Solicitor says if I plead guilty to theft, I'll get community service. Then I can put it behind me.'

'Good,' I say. 'They should take into account what you did to help too.'

'The police were impressed with how we'd managed to solve it before them.' James looks pleased as punch. You must be so proud of him too, Albert, at how he's helped me since you've been gone. I've decided on his career: he'll actually make the perfect detective.

'I'm proud of you both,' says Shirley. 'Though if you ever do anything like that again you'll be for it.'

'We make a good team you and me, Gran. We should go into business together as a crime-fighting duo like Batgran and Robin.'

I don't think I'd suit a cape. 'I fear my crime-fighting days are behind me. I might just have to take an advisory role.'

'What did I just say? You two can forget about getting yourselves into any more trouble. Don't be getting your gran all excited, James. Now, Mum, you just concentrate on getting better and building up your strength.'

'Yeah, I need you back home,' adds James. 'I can't be without you and Granddad.'

A sadness in his young face, a palpable sense of loss.

'You'll never be without either of us. Your granddad is always with you.' I tap James's forehead. 'In here.' I lower my hand and hold it over his chest. 'And in here. That's where I find him.'

The room seems to pause, a moment of peace in the stillness. Then the noise resumes, the murmurs of sleep, the humming of machines.

'One more thing.' I pick up my purse from the table.

'Bit late for more clues, Gran.'

I unclasp the purse, pull out a tenner and push it into James's hand.

'No,' I reply. 'Go and get yourself a new belt. Those jeans are almost around your ankles.'

Laughter reverberates between us. I soak it up as I look at my family, trying to sear their images into my brain so it will never ever forget them. Even when they annoy me, everything about them is so familiar and reassuring. I know their pasts, their mannerisms, even sometimes what they're going to do next. I've marvelled as Shirley's grown from the sweet baby we created into a mother herself. I know everything she's been through, every tribulation and triumph. Surely, it's not possible that I could forget all of that, that I could look at her and see a stranger staring back.

And I can't help but be worried for them, as I know they'll be the ones left having to look after me, having to deal with everything. I don't want them to be saddened for me or upset if I forget people or places or events. All those memories I've lost or will lose, I experienced them, I lived them, I enjoyed them. All those individuals I had the pleasure of meeting and getting to know. You can't take that away from me, no one can remove my past or wipe away my history. I've led a remarkable life and I'm lucky to have experienced what I have and to have a loving and supportive family, lifelong friends and such an incredible career. And to have had you by my side for so long, Albert – to love and to cherish – and to still feel you near.

'We'd better be going, Mum, and leave you to get some sleep. We'll be back tomorrow to see how you're doing. Anything we can bring? Magazines or books? Maybe some crosswords?'

'I've everything I need, thank you.'

Shirley bends over to kiss my cheek. I take her hand and give it a gentle squeeze.

'Thank you for everything you've done for me,' I say, quietly. 'I do appreciate it.'

She doesn't say anything. Just smiles. And that's enough. More than enough. Because it's a long time since I've seen her smile that genuinely.

My family wave goodbye, the boys blowing extravagant air kisses as they go, and I'm alone once again with just the hum of the machines for company.

I pick up the newspaper and stare at the crossword clues and, would you believe it, the answers come to me. I grab a black biro and fill in the blanks with a spidery hand. Gazing at the box of words and black squares, I take in the satisfaction of its completeness. Then fold up the newspaper and put it on the chest of drawers beneath the flowers.

I shuffle again. It's not just my hip that hurts. When the painkillers start to wear off, the rest of me aches as well. The doctors seem optimistic, but you never know how things will go.

I close my eyes. You're there in front of me, Albert, arms

open wide, ready to take my hand, to whisk me off my feet for another waltz.

I don't think it'll be long before I'm really with you again.

I'll see you soon, my love.

ACKNOWLEDGEMENTS

Like many a book, this novel was long to come to fruition. I'd like to thank everyone who contributed along the way: all those who organised and held the workshops, writing groups and story competitions I took part in which sparked creativity, and provided motivation, feedback and confidence.

The original inspiration for *The Margaret Code* was my late grandmother who bore a cruel illness stoically. My childhood memories of our time together pepper these pages with warmth; all the freshly-battered fish and chips and baked bread, the entertaining games of marbles and tiddlywinks, the fun trips to the park. These are reminiscences of a different time. This book is dedicated to grandmothers everywhere!

Thank you to Sam Copeland for seeing the potential and giving my writing journey the much-needed impetus, and all at Rogers, Coleridge and White for your help and support. And to Rosanna Forte for your brilliant editing and all the expertise and advice that brought *The Margaret Code* to completion, and your colleagues at Sphere for their sterling work, assistance and enthusiasm.

I'm also grateful to Sophie Parkes and all at Mossley Writers for your feedback, camaraderie and encouragement.

I am indebted to many factual articles and books about the history of Bletchley Park, particularly *The Secrets of Station X* by Michael Smith, which aided my research for Margaret's career.

And to my family: Mum – the book is finally here and available to buy in bookshops! – Claire and Tim; Natalie, Michael and Benjamin; Abbie, Sam and Harry. To my partner Sîan for reading the early drafts, putting up with all the writing, and your love and support. And to Lee Thornley for your goodwill and encouragement.